T0195994

The Girl with the Kitten Tattoo

The Cat Lady Mystery Series by Linda Reilly

The Girl with the Kitten Tattoo

A Cat Lady Mystery

Linda Reilly

LYRICAL UNDERGROUND
Kensington Publishing Corp.
www.kensingtonbooks.com

LYRICAL UNDERGROUND BOOKS are published by

Kensington Publishing Corp.
119 West 40th Street
New York, NY 10018

All Kensington titles, imprints, and distributed lines are available at special quantity discounts for bulk purchases for sales promotion, premiums, fund-raising, educational, or institutional use.

Special book excerpts or customized printings can also be created to fit specific needs. For details, write or phone the office of the Kensington Sales Manager: Kensington Publishing Corp., 119 West 40th Street, New York, NY 10018. Attn. Sales Department. Phone: 1-800-221-2647.

Lyrical Underground and Lyrical Underground logo Reg. US Pat. & TM Off.

First Electronic Edition: May 2020
ISBN-13: 978-1-5161-0986-9 (ebook)
ISBN-10: 1-5161-0986-4 (ebook)

First Print Edition: May 2020
ISBN-13: 978-1-5161-0988-3
ISBN-10: 1-5161-0988-0

Printed in the United States of America

This book is dedicated to rescue pets everywhere,
and to the caring moms and dads who give them loving homes.

Acknowledgments

I'd like to thank my own personal cast of characters for their contributions to this book. My wonderful editor, Elizabeth May, gave me sound advice and inspiration. We did some great brainstorming together! The marketing team at Kensington, as always, did an outstanding job with promotion. A huge thank-you to my fellow Cozy Mystery Crew authors for their friendship and encouragement. A tip of the hat goes to readers Christina Radcliff, Joy Hejl, and Mandy Golze for naming Amber, Sienna, and Panda. All great names, by the way! Finally, I want to thank my husband and my mom for putting up with my absence from their lives when I'm in deep writing mode. I love you both to the ends of the earth.

Cast of Feline Characters

Twinkles: An aging, orange-striped tiger cat with big gold eyes; his favorite place to snooze is atop Aunt Fran's bed.

Munster: This easygoing, orange-striped male, the unofficial greeter of all human visitors and a perpetual lap cat, goes with the flow no matter which felines are currently living at the shelter.

Dolce: Long-haired, solid black, and as sweet as a box of cream-filled hearts, he's found his favorite spot curled up in Aunt Fran's lap.

Panda: This chubby, black-and-white boy with long white whiskers is fast becoming Mr. Popularity. Now the problem is…is there enough of him to go around?

Sienna: This petite tortie is a feline lovebug, but she's also FIV positive. Will she find the *fur*ever home she deserves, in spite of her diagnosis?

Amber: Shy and reserved, she spends most of her time in Lara's room perched on the cat tree. Lara knows there's a lovable kitty inside, if only she'd come out of her shell.

Holly & Noella: A pair of beautiful gold-and-white sisters, these sweethearts were transferred to the shelter after their foster mom developed health problems. To everyone's delight, they've been able to entice the elderly Twinkles into playing with their catnip mouse!

Blue: This fluffy Ragdoll cat that only Lara can see has an uncanny knack for pointing out clues that help her solve crimes. But Blue might not be the only guardian cat that watches over someone…

Chapter 1

"Okay, so get this," Sherry Bowker said breathlessly. "I'm picturing red and white heart-shaped balloons hanging from the ceiling," She waved her arms at strategic spots on the dropped ceiling of the coffee shop. "And cream-colored linen tablecloths on each table, with wrought-iron candle holders and cranberry glass holders in the center. We'll use the counter for the food—oh God, wait till you see the spread Mom has planned! And—" She propped her hands on her hips and glared at Lara. "What are you grinning at, artist lady? Come on, I need your input here. You're the one with the creative flair, not me."

Lara Caphart couldn't help herself. Giggling, she went over and gave her bestie a fierce hug. "Sher, I'm sorry—but I'm not laughing at you. I'm just thrilled at seeing you so excited. If you only knew how happy I am for you and David."

Several months earlier, Sherry had gotten engaged to the man of her dreams, David Gregson. She'd met him a year and a half earlier, when he dropped into Bowker's Coffee Stop one morning for breakfast. They'd both felt an instant attraction, but Sherry, who'd never been lucky in love, had tiptoed cautiously into the relationship. Fortunately, David was as patient as he was kind. One year after they met, he proposed.

"Sher," Lara said. "It's your wedding, not mine." The words almost snagged in her throat. "If you want giant purple hearts with pink polka dots dangling from the ceiling, then I'll paint them for you."

Sherry made a face. "That sounds awful. Come on, you know what looks good. Help me out here, will ya?"

Lara looked around the coffee shop, a place that was like a second home to her. Since her move back to Whisker Jog, New Hampshire, over two years before, she'd come in here nearly every morning. Fresh-brewed coffee, one of Daisy Bowker's yummy muffins, and a daily chat with Sherry was her favorite way to jump-start any day.

"Okay, then. Let's get serious. The big heart-shaped balloons? Um, not a fan. We'll save those for your tenth-anniversary celebration, okay?"

Sherry nodded. "Agreed."

"I'd opt instead to put your cake on a square table in the far corner, with a cluster of *miniature* red and white balloons at each of the two back corners. On the far wall"—she pointed toward the rear of the coffee shop—"we can make a swag of red and white roses, interwoven with creamy lace."

Tears filled Sherry's eyes. "Oh God, Lara. This is really happening. It's only three weeks away. Am I ready for it?"

"Of course you are," Lara soothed. "You're having a case of nerves, that's all. It's totally understandable. Be honest. When you look at David, what do you feel?"

"I feel like I just hit the jackpot."

Lara grinned. "Then remember that when you're walking down the aisle, okay?"

"Aisle?" Daisy Bowker bleated as she came through the swinging door from the kitchen. She slipped an arm around her daughter's shoulder. "I guess we can make an aisle, if we set up the tables just right."

Too late, Lara realized her poor choice of words. She'd meant "walking down the aisle" in a figurative sense, not an actual one. To the dismay of David's mother, Loretta Gregson, Sherry and David both agreed on tying the knot in the very place they'd met—the coffee shop. Loretta, a traditionalist, felt it would be unseemly for them to get married in any place other than a proper church. Several times she'd made vague noises about not attending, but David felt sure it was only that—noise. His mom would never miss his wedding, he assured Sherry. "Let her huff and puff if she wants to," he'd told his bride-to-be, "but she won't blow our wedding plans down."

It made Lara admire David even more.

"Hey, I've gotta run," Lara said, shrugging on her winter jacket. "Cats to feed, litter to scoop, and all that."

"How's Sienna doing?" Daisy asked.

Lara and her aunt Fran ran the High Cliff Shelter for Cats out of her aunt's Folk Victorian home. Most recently they took in a sweet girl who was FIV positive. Their vet, Amy Glindell, assured them that the petite tortoiseshell cutie could lead a happy life without their fearing she could infect other cats. Having that knowledge was a huge relief, but educating potential adopters was a whole other matter.

"Actually, she's doing great. We're hopeful that she'll be adopted in spite of her diagnosis. She's one of the most lovable cats we've ever had."

"Glad to hear that," Daisy said. She frowned at Lara's open collar. "Bundle up your jacket, Lara. It's dropped about ten degrees since you got here."

The quintessential mom, Lara thought, snapping her top button in place. "Yes, ma'am."

"Sher, I forgot to ask you," Lara said. "Did you decide on the wedding favors? Last I knew, you chose the foil-wrapped chocolate hearts in those cute lacy boxes."

"I chose them, but I'm not wild about them. The little boxes are great—I love those. They're, what do you call it, die-cut? Delicate, with lacy heart cutouts." She wrinkled her nose. "It's the chocolate hearts I'm not wild about. Too boring, you know?"

Lara agreed, but kept that to herself. "I'll try to come up with something a little more fun."

"That would be awesome," Sherry said, digging a ring of keys out of her pocket. "I'll let you out."

Lara hugged them both, then followed Sherry to the door. A face popped into view just as Sherry stuck the key in the lock. An attractive brunette with stunning blue eyes waved at her through the coffee shop's glass door. Clad in an aquamarine wool coat and a knitted hat, she had a button nose that was red from the cold.

Sherry unlocked the door and smiled at the woman. "I'm sorry, but we close at four," she said.

"I know. I saw your sign," the woman acknowledged, rubbing her mittened hands together. "I'm only looking for directions. I'm trying to find a local attorney's office. Gideon Halley? Do you know him?"

Lara swallowed. Gideon. *Her* Gideon.

"I do," Lara said. "I can point you in the right direction. Do you have an appointment with him?" Not that it was any of her business.

The young woman wrinkled her nose. "Um, not exactly. I'm—well, I kind of want to surprise him." She gave Lara a wide-eyed look that was intended to mean something. What, Lara wasn't sure.

"Are you driving or walking?" Lara asked her.

"Driving. That's my car right there." She dipped her head toward a cherry-red Honda parked in front of the coffee shop.

Lara heard the door lock behind her. She peeked around the cardboard cupid taped to the glass door and waved goodbye to Sherry.

"Okay, then," she said, turning back to the woman. "After you back out, head that way." She pointed toward the traffic signal. "After you go through the light, go one more block. His office is in an older home on the right, painted dark green. You'll see his sign on the front lawn. Can't miss it."

"Thanks! You're a lifesaver. I can't wait to see him again. Is there parking?"

"Yes, there's parking on the side. Is he…an old friend?" Lara asked, her attempt at sounding casual coming out like a squeak.

A blush tinted the young woman's creamy cheeks. "I guess you could call him that. We dated for a while, but it's been a few years since I've seen him." She shrugged. "Anyway, I'm hoping he can help me. I've got, like, a legal problem. Thanks again for the directions!"

A few years? Lara and Gideon had been a couple for close to two years.

Lara stood there, shivering under a pitifully weak January sun. She watched the young woman jerk her Honda out of her parking space and head toward Gideon's.

A weird feeling tugged at her insides, forming a tiny knot. She knew exactly what it was.

Jealousy.

* * * *

It was approaching dusk by the time Lara got home. The sky was pewter, blotted with clouds.

"You look half frozen," Aunt Fran said, closing the door behind Lara. "Want some tea? We can try one of those gourmet brands Jerry gave me for Christmas." Jerry Whitley was Whisker Jog's chief of police. He and Aunt Fran were good friends—*very* good friends.

"Tea sounds good," Lara said. She shed her jacket and scarf and hung them in the hall closet. Sitting on Lara's usual chair in the kitchen was their newest arrival—Sienna. A darling tortoiseshell with a white chest and forepaws, she loved to be held and cuddled.

Sienna's initial diagnosis of "FIV positive" worried Lara at first. She knew that the condition could not be transmitted to humans, but what about other cats? After doing some online research and talking to their vet, Lara felt confident that Sienna would be a safe addition to the shelter. Finding her the perfect home might be more of a challenge, but as long as she remained at High Cliff she would be cared for and loved.

"Hey there, are you in my seat again?" Lara lifted the cat and held her close, smiling at the loud purr coming from such a small kitty.

Lara sat with Sienna snuggled in her lap. Aunt Fran held up two mugs. "Cranberry or organic peppermint?"

"Peppermint," Lara said.

Aunt Fran prepared their mugs and set them down on the table, then sat down opposite her niece. "I can tell by your expression something's bothering you."

"Good gravy," Lara said with a groan, "am I that transparent?" She took a sip of her peppermint tea, which smelled and tasted heavenly.

"Only to those who know you as well as I do. Nothing's gone awry with the wedding plans, I hope."

"No, it's not that." Lara absently rubbed the handle of her mug. "Aunt Fran, before I moved back here, do you remember if Gideon was dating anyone?"

"Dating? As in, did he have a girlfriend?"

"Yes, exactly."

Aunt Fran looked away, thinking. "I can't answer that question with any certainty, Lara. Before you got here, I hadn't been getting around very well, as you know. I was even having my groceries delivered."

"I remember," Lara said quietly.

How could she ever forget how frail her aunt had looked on that fateful October day over two years before? Lara had rented a car in Boston and driven to her aunt's home. They hadn't seen each other in sixteen years, and Lara didn't have a clue what to expect. All she knew was what she'd learned from Sherry—that her aunt was failing and in dire need of help.

It wasn't until Lara made the decision to move in with her that Aunt Fran got the surgeries she needed. Two knee replacements later, her aunt was walking like a woman ten years younger, and completely pain-free.

"You must be asking that for a reason," Aunt Fran said, concern evident in her voice.

Lara sighed. "A woman stopped by the coffee shop today as I was leaving, asking for directions. She was looking for Gideon's office." She sipped her peppermint tea, her mind filled with visions of Gideon with another woman—a very attractive woman, at that.

"And?"

"I asked her if Gideon was an old friend, and she said they'd dated for a while, but that she hadn't seen him in a few years. She wanted to surprise him." The words tasted sour in her throat.

Aunt Fran patted the black, long-haired cat who'd crawled into her lap and settled there like a furry pillow. Dolce was one of her three original cats, Munster and Twinkles being the other two. "Lara, surely you didn't think Gideon had never *dated*, as you put it, before you moved back here.

The main thing is, he loves you now and you love him. That's the only thing that should matter."

"I know," she said with a groan. "I know you're right, but now that I've seen this woman, I can't stop picturing them together."

"I take it she was pretty, for lack of a better descriptor."

"Quite attractive," Lara acknowledged.

"I'm sure Gideon will tell you all about it when you talk to him later. Any plans for this evening?"

On Fridays, Gideon and Lara often ate dinner out, and occasionally saw a movie. The weather tonight was not only frigid, but also the roads were supposed to be icing over. Driving anywhere would be dicey.

"If we do, we won't go far. Probably just to the Irish Stew. How about you?"

Aunt Fran smiled. More and more, she reminded Lara of the actress Audrey Hepburn in her later years. "Jerry and I both decided we had plenty of things to catch up on at home, so we're going it alone tonight."

Lara raised her eyebrows. "I noticed that you've been using your new laptop quite a bit these days. Projects for school?"

Aunt Fran's deteriorating knees had initially forced her to give up her teaching job, but when the school year started last fall, she returned as a substitute teacher.

"A few," her aunt said, a rosy blush tinting her cheeks. "I love subbing the classes with younger kids. I talk to them about ways to show respect for animals, and they really get excited by the discussion. Many of them ask about ways they can help."

"Anything else you're doing on your laptop?" Lara teased. "I caught you a few times putting it away when I walked into the room."

For a long moment, her aunt was silent. "I suppose there's no harm in telling you. I'm…well, I'm trying my hand at writing a book."

"A book?" Lara's eyes widened. "Aunt Fran, I think that's great. What kind of book?"

"It's a novel, about a young woman torn apart by the sudden loss of her husband. I know I never bring it up, Lara, but those few months I was married to Brian were probably the best ones of my life. His death shook me to the core. I didn't know if I'd ever recover."

Sometimes Lara forgot about her aunt's brief marriage. Aunt Fran never talked about Brian Clarkson, and she didn't display any photos of him, not even in her bedroom.

They'd eloped when Aunt Fran was a junior at UNH, working toward her teaching degree. Brian had already earned his master's and was teaching middle school in a town near the campus. He'd been killed by a snowplow while helping a stranded motorist, shattering Aunt Fran's short-lived joy.

"I never really dealt with the grief after Brian's death," her aunt went on. "My no-nonsense mother had never approved of our getting married while I was still in school, and I had no one to mourn with me. Not properly, anyway. I suppressed my grief so that I could finish getting my degree."

Lara blinked back tears. "How is it coming along? The novel, I mean."

"Actually, it's coming along decently. I've signed up for an online writing class, too." Aunt Fran smiled. "I know I've got a long way to go before I let anyone read a word of it," she added. "But the sheer act of putting words on paper, so to speak, has helped me tremendously."

"I hope you'll let me read it someday."

"No worries there. You're the first person I'll show it to, but only after it's polished." Aunt Fran's smile faded, and her expression grew pensive. "I've felt for a long time now, Lara, that everything happens for a reason. Writing this novel has helped me to see that."

Clutching Sienna to her chest, Lara went over and hugged her aunt. When she looked across the Formica table, she saw that a fluffy Ragdoll cat had claimed her seat. Her turquoise eyes half-closed, Blue rested her furry chin on the table.

"I think someone else agrees with you," Lara said, nodding toward her chair.

"Blue?" Aunt Fran said with a smile.

Again, Lara nodded.

Aunt Fran, Gideon, and their shelter assistant, Kayla, were the only ones who knew about Lara's spiritual guardian—the cat only Lara could see. Once a living, breathing feline, she'd passed on the day Lara was born—nearly thirty years earlier.

As a child, Lara had been only vaguely aware of a blue-eyed cat who materialized whenever she felt sad or troubled. But as Lara grew older, she decided that the kitty she'd named Blue had simply been an imaginary friend. Since Lara's return to Whisker Jog, Blue had been there when she needed her most, intervening when Lara's life was at risk.

She thought about her aunt's statement. *Everything happens for a reason.*

Did it apply to Gideon's former girlfriend showing up, unannounced, on his doorstep?

Lara didn't know, but she intended to find out.

Chapter 2

"That shepherd's pie was unreal," Gideon said, after swallowing his last bite. He dabbed his napkin to his lips. "Did you like yours, honey?"

"It was delicious," Lara agreed. "Best version of that dish I've ever had."

The classic "cottage pie," as it was known, had been prepared using beef tenderloin, prosciutto, and pearl onions, and topped with a port wine sauce. The chef at the Irish Stew had outdone herself. The new entrée outshone even her legendary beef stew. In spite of that, Lara hadn't really tasted it much. Her mind was stuck on Gideon's visitor. She couldn't get her out of her head.

"You seem quiet," Gideon said. He reached over and took Lara's free hand. "You okay?"

Lara smiled and squeezed his hand. "I'm fine. A little distracted, I guess."

"Is it because of Megan?" he asked, shifting on his chair.

Lara thought for a moment. "I guess it just took me by surprise, Gideon. You've never talked about old girlfriends before, except to say you had a few brief relationships that fizzled."

"As did you," Gideon pointed out.

It was during the ride to the Irish Stew that Lara had questioned Gideon about the mystery woman. He'd explained who Megan was, and how they met. His relationship with her had never gone past the friendship stage. A few lunches and dinners together had pretty much been the extent of it. While Gideon's tone had sounded casual, Lara sensed that he'd felt uneasy talking about it.

"I know." Lara shrugged. "Your relationship with Megan just seems so…recent, I guess. It seems weird that you never mentioned it."

Gideon folded his napkin on the table. "Lara, I've never lied to you before, and I'm sure as heck not going to start now. I met Megan Haskell at the Registry of Deeds in Concord, well over a year before you came back to Whisker Jog. I was working on a nightmare of a title search, so I had to spend several days there. She worked as a paralegal for a Concord law firm and was doing research for a civil litigation case. We chatted a little every day, and then one day decided to have lunch at the Chinese restaurant across the street."

Lara swallowed. Did she really want to hear this?

"We lived about an hour away from each other, so any dates we had were few. My schedule didn't exactly leave me a lot of time to trek back and forth to Concord. After a few months, we sort of, you know, just drifted away from each other. It wasn't even a breakup because there was nothing to break up from. It turned out that we didn't have that much in common."

Lara got it. She really did. But why hadn't Gideon ever mentioned Megan before? Even in passing, her name had never come up.

"So now she lives in Bakewell, because she got laid off from the law firm."

Gideon blew out a quiet breath. "That's right. She has an aunt and uncle there, so she moved in with them—just until she can afford her own place."

Bakewell was only a few towns away from Whisker Jog. A bit too close for comfort, in Lara's opinion. She wondered when Megan had moved there.

"And now she wants you to represent her?"

"She does. For obvious reasons, I can't discuss her issue."

Lara tied her knitted scarf around her neck. "So, are you?" she said, a bit more sharply than she intended.

"Am I what? Going to represent her?"

Their server came by just then to collect their empty plates. "You guys want coffee?" she asked.

"None for me," Lara said.

Gideon frowned, and Lara knew what he was thinking. They always had coffee after dinner.

"Just the bill," Gideon said. "Thanks."

After the server strode off, he said to Lara, "To answer your question, I'm not sure yet. I'm thinking of referring it out. I know a few people who'd be more than qualified to handle it."

Lara tugged on her jacket and looked over at Gideon, a sight that always made her heartbeat quicken. They'd been seeing each other for almost two years now. Their relationship had become so comfortable that somehow, it'd gotten stalled.

There was a time when Lara thought Gideon wanted to become engaged. Although she knew she loved him, she'd also known then that she wasn't ready. The shelter had just gotten off to a start, and Aunt Fran was still depending on her to keep it running. Lara also had her art projects—she was a watercolor artist by profession—and had clients to answer to.

Excuses, excuses, she chided herself. None of that would have prevented her from getting married. It was the permanency of marriage itself that had held her back. She hadn't been sure she was ready to take that final step.

Gideon had clearly sensed her hesitation. Since then, he was careful never to utter the "m" word—marriage. But enough time had passed now. He should know.

She was ready to make that commitment.

"You're staying at my place tonight, right?" Gideon asked her, once they were inside his car. He flicked on the ignition to warm up the engine.

Normally, Friday nights at Gideon's were a given. It was their private time, the one night a week they could count on being together. A night Lara looked forward to all week.

"Maybe I'd better go home tonight," Lara said, regretting the words even as she said them.

He reached over and tucked a strand of her copper-colored hair into her collar. "Are you sure? Orca and Pearl will miss you. They haven't seen you since last week."

Lara smiled at him in the darkness. He'd adopted the sibling cats from the shelter the prior summer, and the two kitties adored him. "I know. I'll miss them, too. But maybe it's better if I head home tonight. It's been a long day."

Without another word, Gideon drove her home. She'd upset him, she knew, but she hadn't been able to stop herself. What was that saying? Cutting off her nose to spite her face?

In her heart, Lara knew she was overreacting. She was punishing the man she loved for reasons she couldn't explain, even to herself. But she couldn't help wondering why he'd never mentioned Megan before now. In fact, if Lara hadn't told him that she'd directed the woman to his office, would he have brought her up at all?

That was the question, in her mind.

Then again, did she really want to know the answer?

Chapter 3

The wind howled like a zombie on Saturday morning, bringing along temperatures that struggled to climb into the teens. It was a perfect morning to stay inside and work on one of her art projects.

Saturday was an adoption day, so first she needed to be sure that the "meet-and-greet" room, formerly Aunt Fran's back porch, was spiffed up and ready for potential visitors. After a light breakfast, she brushed all the cats, then set a cat-themed runner over the table in the meet-and-greet room. She dusted and vacuumed, eliminating as much cat hair as possible. Finally, she wiped down the windows with glass cleaner until they sparkled.

While she had the vacuum out, she ran it over the floor in the reading room they'd tacked on to the shelter the summer before. Every Sunday, the shelter held "read to a cat" day, during which they hosted kids who wanted to read books to cats. The reading room was a library of sorts. Along with shelves packed with children's books, it had comfy cushions and chairs designed for kids and their folks. Five children had already made appointments for tomorrow, one a little boy who came every week with his grandmother.

"You've been very quiet this morning," Aunt Fran said to Lara when they were putting together an early lunch. "Would you like to talk about it?"

Lara shook her head. "Not really. It's something I have to work out on my own." She slathered peanut butter on a slice of wheat bread, then caught her aunt staring at her. Lara went over and kissed her on the cheek. "Stop worrying. It's no biggie."

"If you say so," Aunt Fran said. "But remember, I'm here if you want to chat."

"I think I'll eat in my studio," Lara said. "I want to do some preliminary sketches for the painting I'm doing for Amy's new house."

Amy Glindell, their veterinarian, had contracted with Lara to paint a watercolor of her three dogs—all gorgeous Australian shepherds. Lara had toyed with a few ideas but wanted to work up some pencil sketches and run them by Amy first. Hopefully the task would take her mind off Gideon, at least for a little while.

She'd thought of heading down to the coffee shop that morning and pouring her heart out to Sherry. Ultimately, she'd decided against it. Sherry was caught up in the throes of planning for her wedding. Lara didn't want to make her feel bad about her issue with Gideon so close to the big day.

Every ten minutes or so, Lara caught herself checking her phone. The absence of the telltale ping of an incoming text should have been enough, but she checked anyway.

Nothing from Gideon. Which wasn't like him.

Of course, she hadn't texted him either. Was it going to be a standoff?

Eventually, she set down her sketching pencils and went out to the kitchen. Munster, their lovable orange-and-white-striped boy, launched himself at her legs, wrapping his furry form around her ankles. Lara lifted him and kissed his whiskers, then propped him on her shoulder. "You're getting cat hair on my favorite leggings," she told him. "Which I know you don't care a fig about."

Aunt Fran was sitting at the kitchen table, tapping away at her laptop. Dolce snoozed in her lap. She closed out the document she was working on and pushed the laptop aside. "Make any progress?" she asked.

"Not much." Lara sat down and plunked Munster in her lap. "How about you?"

"It's coming along at the speed of honey flowing on the North Pole." Her aunt smiled. "That's okay, though. I'm enjoying the process." Her kind smile morphed into a look of concern. "Maybe you'd feel better if you confided in someone."

"Hint, hint, right?" Lara said. "Aunt Fran, you're about as subtle as a cattle prod."

"Whatever works." She winked at her niece.

Lara relented. She gave her aunt a recap of her conversation with Gideon the evening before. She wasn't sure what troubled her the most—the idea that Gideon might decide to represent Megan, or the fact that he hadn't called or texted her since he'd dropped her off the night before.

"So, you're currently at an impasse," Aunt Fran said.

"I guess you could call it that." Lara tickled Munster between his ears.

"Which means someone has to make the first move."

Lara made a face. "That's what I figured you'd say. But I'm—" Her cell rang in her pocket. "Excuse me a sec," she said to her aunt, then hurried to answer her phone. She sagged when she saw the caller. "Hi, Sher."

"That...that *woman* was just here," Sherry bellowed.

"Woman? What woman? You mean Megan?"

"Megan? Who the heck is Megan? I'm talking about Loretta, my future mother-in-law. Lara, are you okay? You sound like you're on a different planet today."

I am. Planet Feel-Sorry-for-Myself, Lara thought wryly. "Never mind. Tell me about Loretta."

Sherry launched into a rant about Loretta's visit to the coffee shop. In her sly way, Loretta had produced snapshots supplied by their local florist showing how the pews of St. Lucy's church could be decorated for the ceremony.

"Oh no," Lara said. "What did you tell her?"

"It was all I could do not to tell her where she could stuff those pictures," Sherry hissed. "I calmly explained that while those photos were lovely, our ceremony was going to be held here at the coffee shop, where David and I first met. Like I haven't already told her that fourteen times."

"Oh boy."

"Yeah, you said it. Luckily, Mom came out of the kitchen in time to rescue me. She gushed over Loretta's new wool coat, then sweetly explained our plans for decorating the coffee shop. Loretta didn't know what to say, so she shoved the pictures back in her purse and left. Oh, Lara, this isn't going away. What are we going to do?"

"All I can say is, in the wise words of the Beatles—let it be. David and you are in total agreement, and that's what counts."

"I know. You're right," Sherry said glumly. "But I feel so bad for him, I know his mom's been trying to work her guilt trips on him."

"Think of it this way," Lara suggested. "Three weeks from today, you and David will be husband and wife. All her grumblings over a church wedding will be water over the falls, right?"

"I guess so," Sherry said. "By the way, you didn't come by this morning after you left Gideon's. What gives?"

After a long pause, Lara said, "Um, I didn't stay at Gideon's last night. We were both out of sorts, so he drove me home after dinner."

Sherry was quiet for a moment, then, "Is everything okay?"

"Everything's fine. No worries. I've got a ton of projects to work on today, plus it's an adoption day. It was all for the best."

"If you say so," Sherry said, sounding unconvinced.

After they disconnected, Lara set down her phone on the table and said to her aunt, "I'd better hang out in the meet-and-greet room in case we get some early visitors."

As if on cue, a hefty-sized black-and-white kitty with long white whiskers strutted into the kitchen. He issued a loud *meow*, then reached up and rested his forepaws on Lara's leg. Munster yawned in his face but didn't budge from Lara's lap.

"Well, Panda, you're just in time." Lara rubbed the cat's head. "If you didn't come down for adoption day, I was going to come looking for you."

Panda purred, but then decided to check out the food bowls resting along one wall of the kitchen.

"I've got to bring Sienna and Amber down, too," Lara said.

"Or you could wait to see if we get any visitors," Aunt Fran suggested. "Last Saturday only one family showed up."

"I know. That was disappointing. But it snowed that day, and the roads were bad. It's freezing out today, but at least the roads are clear."

Her cell rang again. When she saw the caller, she snatched it up in an instant. "Gideon? Hi, I was—"

"Lara, sorry to interrupt, but I have some news."

Lara swallowed. "Sounds serious."

"It is. Megan's been taken in for questioning by the police. Her ex-boss was found dead this morning in a snowbank, right beneath the second-story balcony of his home. Apparently, she showed up at his home last night—his wife was throwing a birthday party for him—and Megan created a scene in front of a few dozen witnesses." His voice sounded taut with frustration.

For a moment, Lara was speechless. Then, "Gideon, that's awful. But why would the police want to question her? It must've been an accident, right? Maybe he drank too much and fell off his balcony."

"Didn't sound that way. The police are talking possible foul play. Anyway, I just found out about it a few minutes ago. Megan hasn't been charged with anything—yet. I'm heading over to Bakewell now to see what I can find out."

Lara felt her limbs go numb. For a woman he supposedly had nothing in common with, he was sure rushing to her aid awfully fast.

"I understand," she said, trying to keep her voice from quaking. "Call me when you know more, okay?"

"Will do," he said, then, "Love you."

"Love you, too." She disconnected and dropped her cell on the table.

"Something's wrong, isn't it?" Aunt Fran said. "You're as white as a sheet."

"That was Gideon," Lara said. "That woman who went to see him yesterday—Megan? Well, get this. She was taken in by the police for questioning this morning. Her boss, I mean her *ex*-boss, was found dead outside in the snow, right under the balcony of his home."

"Oh…my," Aunt Fran said. "Do they think someone pushed him off?"

"Gideon wasn't sure." Lara took in a long breath, forcing back the lump forming in her throat. "He's going over to the police station now to see what he can find out."

Aunt Fran looked away, her expression grim. Lara knew exactly what her aunt was thinking because she was thinking the same thing.

Another murder in our midst.

Chapter 4

Only one person showed up for adoptions on Saturday afternoon. A woman looking for a pet for her grandson's birthday thought she could pop in, pick up a kitten like it was a stuffed toy, and drive it over to him in a giant gift bag. She'd even purchased a colorful bag and brought it into the shelter with her.

First, Lara had calmly explained to her that it wasn't kitten season. While kittens were sometimes born during the winter, it was far more common for female cats to give birth anywhere from March through late fall. Lara next lectured her—tactfully, she thought—as to why a kitten shouldn't be treated simply as a toy to be added to a child's collection.

The woman left looking a bit overwhelmed, but she agreed to read over the brochure Lara gave her about their "read to a cat" Sundays.

It was late Saturday evening before Lara heard back from Gideon. He'd apparently spent several hours at the police station in Bakewell. After that he'd driven Megan to her aunt and uncle's home to be sure she got home safely.

"So," Lara said, when he finally called, "they didn't detain her overnight?"

Gideon sighed into the phone. "Thankfully, no. There's no direct evidence tying her to her ex-boss's death. Only a lot of witnesses reporting that Megan crashed the party and accused him of all sorts of things."

Lara quietly digested this information. "Do they know yet how he died?"

"No. That's turned into a bit of a puzzler. At first it looked like he might have had a heart attack, but a few other things didn't add up. He'd also vomited—sorry to be graphic—and they're suspecting it might have been some kind of poison. Problem is, they haven't identified the source. No one else at the party even got sick."

"Poison?" The thought made Lara clutch her stomach. "How awful. The poor man."

"I agree. If that's how he died, it was not a pleasant way to go. One big problem, though: There was so much food and drink at Chancer's birthday party last night that the poison could've been in almost anything. The crime scene people have literally removed the entire contents of his fridge, along with everything left over from the party, including the trash bags."

"Does he have a wife? A family?" Lara asked.

"He has a wife, Karen. No kids. Here's the thing—until they figure out how the poison was administered, they can't even begin to narrow down the suspects."

Lara's head spun. "How is Megan taking all this?" She tried to keep her voice neutral, but she knew a touch of snark had crept into her tone.

"Um…not good. By the time I got to the police station, she was nearly hysterical. A female officer helped calm her down with some chamomile tea and yogurt."

"Sounds like a kind woman."

"She is. In fact, all the officers involved were exceptionally respectful with her. Oh, guess who's taking the lead in the investigation for the state police? Your old pal, Conrad Cutler."

Lieutenant Conrad Cutler. Lara's insides churned with the memory. He'd been a tough interrogator the summer before, after the local health inspector was murdered. Once the culprit was in custody, however, his attitude toward Lara had changed. He'd transformed into an *almost* decent guy. Almost.

"If that's the case, then I feel bad for Megan," Lara said. *Unless she killed Chancer.*

"I know Cutler's tough, Lara, but he's fair."

Lara asked the question to which she dreaded the answer. "How do things stand now?"

"Right now, things are in limbo with Megan. In spite of her stunt at the party last night and her bad blood with the victim, there's nothing yet that ties her directly to the murder. Unfortunately, this is only the beginning."

Only the beginning.

"I assume she'll be getting a lawyer," Lara said. "Are you going to work with whoever represents her?"

"Absolutely not. She's already contacted someone at her old firm in Concord—a crackerjack criminal lawyer. I'm out of it entirely."

Lara breathed out a quiet sigh of relief. "If Chancer really was poisoned, I hope they land on his killer soon."

After a long pause Gideon said, "I do, too."

Something in Gideon's tone set off an alarm. Did he think Megan might be guilty? Did he know more about her than he was letting on?

"Lara, I miss you. I hated that you didn't stay at my place last night."

"I did, too," she admitted.

"Orca and Pearl kept watching the door," he said. "They have an uncanny sense of timing, you know. They know when it's Friday. I'm sure they expected you to walk in any minute."

"I missed them, too," Lara said, smiling.

"Is it okay if I show up tomorrow for 'read to a cat' day? I can help make hot cocoa, or whatever you're serving the kids."

Lara laughed. It felt good. "You sure can. And don't worry. I'll put you to work."

After they said good night, a huge wave of relief washed over Lara. She didn't want things to be weird between them. She wanted things to be the way they were before.

At least for now.

Deep inside, though, she had a sick feeling. Something told her that this mess with Megan wasn't over.

Gideon said he was out of it entirely, but was he? If Megan was arrested, what if she tried to suck him back in? What if she begged him to help her?

Knowing Gideon, he wouldn't be able to refuse.

Chapter 5

"Read to a Cat Sunday" was busier than ever.

Five children had scheduled half-hour sessions with cats, three with Munster and two with Panda. Munster wore a blue collar to show that he wasn't available for adoption.

Panda, the shelter's most recent resident, was an enigma. When he'd first come into the shelter, Amy had estimated him to be about three years old. He'd been found hanging around the parking area of a local auto body shop. The woman who'd been doing their bookkeeping had been feeding him, but as winter approached, she knew the cat shouldn't stay outside any longer. High Cliff was asked if they had room to take him in, and Lara and Fran happily said yes.

Their weekly visitor, Nathan, arrived with his grandmother right at one thirty. The little boy, who adored cats, lived with his folks and two sisters in a small apartment. His parents were against taking in a cat, for financial as well as space reasons. It warmed Lara's heart to see Nathan curled up on a beanbag chair with Panda plopped in his lap and a book in his hands. Lara noticed that Nathan's reading skills had improved over the past few months. Reading to Panda gave him the confidence to read aloud that he didn't have in school.

"Long afternoon," Lara said, smiling over Gideon's elbow. He was standing at the sink, sweater sleeves rolled up, rinsing out cocoa cups and snack dishes. The sight tugged at Lara.

"Yeah, but a fun one. It's a great way to wind down after a stressful week."

Lara nodded. She didn't want to give voice to the source of the stress.

"That Nathan," Gideon went on, rising off his hands. "He's so cute, isn't he? He'd take Panda home in a minute if he could."

"I know." Lara handed him a clean dish towel. "When the day comes that Panda gets adopted, he's going to be so disappointed. He can still read to a cat, but he's really bonded with Panda."

They made cocoa for themselves, then sat at the kitchen table. Aunt Fran was in the large parlor watching an old movie. Lara suspected she'd made herself scarce to give Lara and Gideon a chance to chat alone.

Gideon took a sip of his marshmallow-topped cocoa, then reached his hand over and touched Lara's. "Lara, are we okay? I mean, *really* okay?"

Lara swallowed. She wrapped her fingers around his. "We are," she said softly. "But...this thing, with Megan. It's not going to go away if she's arrested for murder."

"I'm out of it, Lara. I made that clear to her."

"I know you did."

The question Lara really wanted to ask stuck like a blob of glue in her throat. *Does Megan want to start seeing you again?*

Immediately, she chided herself. She had complete faith in Gideon, and they loved each other. Megan's sudden reappearance in his life didn't change that.

"How much do you know about the man who was murdered?" Lara asked.

Gideon blew out a long sigh. "Megan told me some, but I checked him out online myself. I learned a lot just from reading his Facebook and Twitter posts. To say that the man was an egotistical braggart is putting it mildly. I don't like to speak ill of someone whose life was cut short, but from what I read online, Chancer was his own biggest fan."

"What about his family?"

"Chancer's married—*was* married—to a woman named Karen. She takes up very little space on his social media pages, but she has her own Facebook page. She has a small business of her own. She makes gourmet jams and jellies and sells them to a local shop.

"Karen's dad is a fellow named Gary Becker. He's a Realtor, has his own agency in Bakewell. From what I gleaned, the police are talking to him as well. Becker supposedly despised Chancer. He'd been trying for years to get his daughter to divorce him."

"Interesting," Lara said. "Do you think Chancer was abusive?"

"Reading between the lines—the police were being careful—I gathered that he was mostly a philanderer. And he didn't try too hard to hide it. The main thing I learned, and this is a general observation, is that Chancer had few friends and a slew of enemies. The man was not well-liked."

"Which means the suspect pool should be rather large," Lara commented. "Gid, what's your gut feeling about this? I mean, is it possible Megan is guilty?"

He sat back, his face unreadable. "I'm not sure how to answer that. People can surprise you. I've learned that the hard way."

As have I, Lara thought grimly. But Gideon was holding back something. Lara felt sure of it.

"My gut feeling? Megan doesn't have it in her to commit premeditated murder. If Chancer was poisoned, and that hasn't been confirmed, most likely it was planned in advance." He reached over and squeezed Lara's hand. "I am so grateful that you're not involved in this, Lara. I don't think my heart could withstand your getting tangled up in another murder investigation."

She laughed. "I'm with you there. I've had enough murder to last me through nine lives."

But even as she said it, she had a bad feeling. Any icy shiver trickled down her spine, making her rub her arms against a sudden chill.

She wondered if it had anything to do with the blue-eyed Ragdoll cat staring at her from across the table. The cat no one else could see.

* * * *

After Gideon left, Lara went into the large parlor. She gave her aunt a brief account of everything Gideon had told her.

"Oh my, what a mess," Aunt Fran said. "If Megan is actually innocent, then I feel very bad for her."

"Yeah, *if* she's innocent," Lara repeated.

Panda strutted into the room and gazed up at Lara. In the next instant he was curled up in her lap, purring a steady drumroll.

"You're a lovebug, you know that?" Lara said, looking over at her aunt. "So, how's the book coming?"

Aunt Fran smiled. "Slowly but surely, as they say. I'm thinking of joining an online critique group, but I'll need to ratchet up my courage a bit first."

"Well, I'll be glad to offer my opinion any time, when you're ready to share. No pressure, though."

"Thanks, I appreciate that." Aunt Fran reached for the remote. "It's nearly six. Do we dare turn on the news?"

"May as well," Lara said, though a big part of her dreaded it.

As she'd expected, the news was all about the murder. A female reporter wearing a padded maroon coat and a matching hat stood on a sidewalk holding a microphone. She looked a bit frozen. The camera then panned to the home behind her—a lovely white colonial with black shutters, its wide balcony supported by four broad columns. A layer of snow coated the roof.

Yellow crime scene tape stretched across the yard in front of the house, wrapping around to the back.

Her expression grim, the usually perky reporter spoke soberly of the untimely death of local attorney Wayne Chancer. With each earnest word, her breath came out in puffs. "Wayne Chancer was well known to the community, and his loss will be deeply felt. At this time, the police have not made any arrests. They *are*, however, questioning a number of people, including a former employee."

A former employee.

Megan, no doubt.

A photo of Chancer flashed on the screen. Big and burly, with a handsome face and a practiced grin, he wore the expression of a man who thought he owned the world.

Lara was grateful when the news switched to the local weather report. The reporter hadn't mentioned how Chancer had died, so presumably the police weren't able to confirm it yet. Either that or they didn't want to reveal it.

Gideon had mentioned poison. Lara shuddered. What a horrible way to die. Taking in any poison had to be terribly painful. She'd read of people swallowing things like cyanide or strychnine. The results had not been pretty.

"I think I'll go check on Sienna and Amber," Lara said. "Neither of them has come downstairs much today."

"It might be because it's warmer up there. Go ahead. I'm going to read for a while."

Lara kissed her aunt's cheek and headed up to her bedroom. Munster and Sienna were snoozing on her chenille bedspread, Munster's chubby orange-and-white form curled protectively around his lovable new bud.

Amber was on the cat tree. Her huge gold eyes followed Lara as she approached her and tickled her under the chin. Amber rarely purred, but Lara hoped that would change.

"Hey, sweetie, how're you doing up there? Are you getting a bird's-eye view of everything?"

Amber blinked and closed her eyes.

Half an hour later, Lara tried to do the same, but sleep eluded her until the middle of the night. By morning, her eyelids felt glued together.

Her cell ringing at 6:47 AM jolted them apart.

She fumbled for the phone. "Sherry?" she grumbled. "What's wrong? Why are you calling so early?"

"Oh, Lara," Sherry blubbered. "I think David and I are going to have to elope!"

Chapter 6

"Thank God Jill's working today," Sherry sobbed into a flimsy napkin. "No way I can keep my act together today. *No way.*"

They sat on stools, huddled in a corner of the coffee shop's kitchen. Daisy stood at the stove, flipping pancakes and cracking eggs.

"You've only got three more weeks," Daisy reminded her daughter. "Less, actually. After that, you're golden. You and David will be married and on your honeymoon."

"Mom, don't you get it?" Sherry threw up her arms. "Loretta's trying to spoil the most important day of our lives! If she's this interfering before the wedding, just think what she'll be like after the wedding."

Daisy exchanged glances with Lara.

"Is she flipping out over the justice of the peace?" Lara asked. "Or over the wedding in general being in the coffee shop?"

"She's furious about the JP," Daisy explained. "Who, by the way, is a lovely woman, and who's going to perform a beautiful, tasteful ceremony."

Lara thought for a moment. "Would Loretta be happier if a pastor performed the ceremony?"

"Probably," Sherry said. "But since David and I aren't really churchgoers, that's out of the question. I haven't been to Saint Lucy's in like, *years.*"

"Have you spoken to Pastor Folger?"

"No. I don't even know him that well. I've met him a few times, but…" She shrugged and let her words trail off.

Wheels turned in Lara's head. Would Pastor Folger be willing to perform a ceremony in the coffee shop in tandem with the JP? Did she dare suggest it?

It killed her to see Sherry going through such angst this close to her wedding day. While Lara agreed that Loretta was being unreasonable, she also knew that David's mom was going to be a permanent part of their lives.

Something had to give.

Daisy left the kitchen carrying three dishes of eggs, pancakes, and bacon. The aroma drifting behind her was delectable.

"Lara, go and have your coffee," Sherry said glumly. "I'll get over this. I have to, right?"

Lara gave her friend a sideways hug. "Maybe we can work something out. Call me later, okay?"

Sherry nodded, then, "Wait! What's happening with that crazy murder? I saw it on the news last night. Isn't Gideon's old flame involved?"

Lara wasn't sure Megan had exactly been a *flame*, or to what extent she'd ignited Gideon's passion. "I don't know very much at this point, but I'll keep you informed, okay?" She pushed into the coffee shop through the swinging door before Sherry could ask any more questions.

By the time she got back to Aunt Fran's, her nose felt as if it had frozen onto her face. She peeled off her boots, scarf, hat, and gloves, then rubbed her chilled hands.

"I made a whole pot of tea," her aunt said. "The old-fashioned way, in a teapot. I figured between the two of us, we could use a whole pot."

"You're a lifesaver," Lara said. She fetched cups and plates and set them on the table next to a platter of warm cinnamon rolls. "Did you just make these?"

"I did. I thought we deserved a treat today. They're from a package, but they're still delicious."

"Oh man, you said it."

Tired as Lara was, she was beginning to perk up. Today was not an adoption day, so she hoped to work on some of her art projects in between her cat duties.

Panda and Munster joined them, each one choosing a lap. Dolce looked stricken when he saw that Panda had plopped onto Aunt Fran's lap. In the next instant, Panda leaped off and started toward the food bowls. Dolce quickly claimed his rightful place.

"I miss Kayla," Lara said, licking frosting off her finger. "When did she say her exams end?" She allowed Munster a tiny taste, and he licked his lips in response.

"By the end of the week," Aunt Fran said. "She's like part of our family, now. I really notice when she's not around."

Kayla Ramirez had come into their lives shortly after Aunt Fran's home had been transformed into a cat shelter. A vet tech student, she was smart and capable and wonderful with cats. She lived with her grandmother in nearby Tuftonboro, and helped out at the shelter several days a week.

They were cleaning up the breakfast dishes when the front doorbell rang. "Are you expecting anyone?" Lara asked her aunt. Only strangers went to the front door. Their friends always came in through the kitchen door.

"No, and it's awfully early."

Lara dried her hands on a towel and went to answer the door. A gasp caught in her throat.

Standing on the doorstep was Megan Haskell.

AKA...Gideon's ex-girlfriend.

Chapter 7

"My gosh, you look frozen!" Lara said, ushering her inside.

"I-I am. The heater in my car is on the blink."

Lara took her coat and gloves and set them down near the heat register. What was the woman doing here? Come to think of it, how did she even know where Lara lived?

"I-I'm sorry to drop in on you like this, Lara, but I really need to talk to you." Megan tucked her slender hands under her armpits. "After I talked to Gideon the other night, I checked you out online. I read about how you caught killers."

Figures, Lara thought. The internet had made privacy a thing of the past.

"Megan, I didn't really catch killers. It wasn't like that."

It was also impossible to explain. Especially when a cat no one else could see had helped lead Lara to the murderers.

"Well, from what I read it sure sounded that way." Megan tilted her head like a curious puppy. "It's like, I don't know, you have this *knack* for hunting them down. Anyway, that's why I wanted to talk to you. You probably heard that I've gotten myself into, well, kind of a mess."

Lara was far from thrilled that Gideon's ex-girlfriend had tracked her down. Her first instinct was to let Megan warm up for a bit and then send her on her way. The poor woman really did look cold, though—and on the verge of tears.

Even if it was tempting, Lara couldn't be heartless. "Megan, can I get you something warm? Tea, or hot chocolate?" With any luck, Megan would refuse.

"Oh, gosh, a hot chocolate sounds great."

Of course it does.

"I don't suppose you have any whipped cream?" Megan asked.

Lara nodded, then went into the kitchen and pulled a hot chocolate mix from the cupboard. She put on the kettle and waited, her mind burning with suspicion. Why was Megan really here? Was she cooking up some sort of scheme to gain Gideon's sympathy?

Aunt Fran looked questioningly at her.

"It's Megan, Gideon's old…friend," Lara said quietly. She stirred boiling water into the cocoa and squirted a mound of cream on it. "Come on in and I'll introduce you."

"I'll be there in a few. I just want to tidy up the sink."

When Lara returned to the large parlor, she nearly stopped short. Megan was sitting on one end of the sofa, Panda nestled on her lap. She was talking to the cat in a quiet, singsong voice. Lara set the mug of cocoa and a napkin on the table next to Megan.

"Thank you," Megan said. With one hand she reached for the mug, and the sleeve of her sweater rose a bit. Lara's heartbeat spiked. Just below Megan's sleeve, on the inside of her wrist, was a tattoo that appeared to be a black-and-white kitten.

"Megan, is that a kitten on the inside of your wrist?" Lara asked her.

Nodding, Megan took a careful sip of her cocoa and then set down the mug. She pulled up her sleeve to display the entire image. "That's exactly what it is. And you know what's totally weird? It looks a lot like this cat, doesn't it?" She smiled and pointed to the feline hunkered in her lap.

Almost exactly, Lara thought. She peered more closely at the tattoo. The lines were crisp and clean, expertly done. The markings were so much like Panda's, Lara had trouble believing he hadn't been the model for the tattoo. "How long have you had it?"

Megan's smile faded. She took in a sharp breath. "Since the day I turned eighteen."

At that moment, Aunt Fran came into the parlor and greeted Megan. "Hello, I'm Fran Clarkson, Lara's aunt."

"Oh, um…hi, I'm Megan Haskell. I'd get up but—" She smiled down at the feline taking up prime real estate on her wool slacks.

The two made small talk for a minute, then Aunt Fran excused herself with "a bundle of errands" awaiting her.

Megan took another sip of her cocoa, then set down her mug. "Lara, I don't know how much Gideon told you about my…situation." She paused.

"If you mean why you went to see him on Friday, essentially nothing," Lara said, sitting in the chair opposite the sofa. "I'm sure you know all about client confidentiality. As far as anything else—"

"Wait a minute," Megan cut in. "Did Gideon tell you I was a client?"

Lara realized she'd have to choose her words more carefully. "No, I didn't mean that. I only meant that he respects any private communication between him and a *potential* client."

Megan hung her head. "Oh. I guess I'd hoped—"

You'd hoped you could start seeing him again? Lara almost blurted.

"I know Gideon's not a criminal lawyer," Megan said. "But before this…nightmare with my ex-boss, I was hoping he'd help me sue him for wrongful termination. But I guess that's water over the dam now, isn't it?"

"By nightmare, I assume you mean his death?" Lara said quietly.

"Yes. His murder, actually. At least that's what the police are saying."

Megan said the word in such a casual manner, it made Lara wonder about her mental state.

"I did a stupid, *stupid* thing Friday night," Megan said bitterly. "Gideon warned me not to, but I couldn't stop myself. Sometimes"—she swallowed—"sometimes my temper gets the better of me."

"Megan, before you go any further, you should talk to whoever your lawyer is. There's nothing I can do to help you."

Megan's face fell. A tear leaked from one blue eye. "I'm sorry. I probably shouldn't have bothered you. It's just that…well, Gideon spoke so highly of you. He said you were kind and intelligent and creative, and…well, he said you were the best thing that ever happened to him."

Lara's heart rate sped up a notch. Was Megan pulling her chain, or was she genuine?

"Did Gideon actually say that?"

Megan nodded. "At his office on Friday. I told him why I was there, all about my case. He said he'd think about it, but that he'd probably refer it out."

"I'm sure he had his reasons," Lara said.

Why is this happening to me? How did Gideon's old girlfriend end up here, pouring out her troubles to me?

A sudden movement from behind the sofa made Lara jump. A cream-colored Ragdoll cat with azure blue eyes landed silently next to Megan, just to the left of her shoulder. Blue inched closer to Megan and then looked over at Lara, her gaze firm and steady.

Lara rubbed her eyes and then opened them again. Blue was still there.

What are you trying to tell me? Do you want me to help Megan?

Lara had never connected telepathically with Blue, but the cat often gave off vibes. On occasion the vibes were negative, meaning that something was amiss. But in the past, whenever Blue had graced Lara with that serene gaze, it meant she was fully at ease, and that Lara could relax. So far, Blue's instincts had never been wrong.

"If only I'd listened to Gideon," Megan said bleakly, "I probably wouldn't be in this mess. He told me it would be a bad idea to crash Wayne's party, but I couldn't stop myself. I wanted to embarrass him in front of all his guests. Not just for how he treated me. For how he treated other people, too. Lara, Wayne Chancer was not a nice man."

"Again, Megan, I'm so sorry for your troubles. But you need a lawyer, not a watercolor artist. There's nothing I can do to help you."

She smiled at that. "Gideon told me you were an artist. I saw the painting you did for his office. It's beautiful."

"Thank you."

The watercolor she was referring to was one of Lara's favorites. The scene showed a young Gideon with his dad, poring over a legal document. She'd painted it from an old photo of Gideon's, and had presented it to him the Christmas before last. He treasured it as much as she'd hoped he would.

"You rescue cats too, don't you?" Megan added.

"On occasion," Lara said carefully. "Most of the cats who find their way here are brought in by other people who've rescued them."

Where was Megan headed with her questions? Lara wondered.

Megan ran one finger along Panda's back, and for a long moment was silent.

Lara felt trapped. Megan had barely touched her cocoa, so she couldn't throw her out. Not yet, anyway. Blue had already vanished, her spiritual energy expended.

Tears began to flow down Megan's cheeks. "I don't really have anyone else I can ask for help," she said in a tiny voice. "My aunt and uncle are sweet, but I don't like burdening them with all this. My folks don't live close by, plus my dad thinks I cause all my own problems."

Lara sagged. "Megan, what kind of help are you looking for? You've already retained a lawyer, haven't you?"

"I have," she replied. "What I really need is a friend."

* * * *

The truth struck Lara like a blow to the stomach.

She wants to be rescued.

Lara listened quietly while Megan launched into her story.

"Early last summer, I got laid off from the law firm in Concord I was working for. My living expenses were getting too high anyway, so I asked my aunt and uncle in Bakewell if I could bunk with them for a while. They're so wonderful—they said they'd love to have me, for as long as I wanted to stay."

"They must be kind people."

"They are," Megan confirmed. "I thought I hit the jackpot when I found a job right away. Wayne was a personal injury lawyer, and I'd done some of that at my old firm. But I found out pretty quickly Wayne was super aggressive, you know? He'd sue anyone, for anything."

"Did that bother you?" Lara asked.

She shrugged. "Not at first it didn't. Most of the people or places he sued deserved it. Besides, it was usually the insurance companies that had to pay, you know?" She frowned and looked away.

Lara waited. Megan seemed to be struggling.

"But then this one place"—she twisted her hands over Panda's sleeping form—"those poor people. I felt so bad for them."

Munster came down the stairs just then, his ears perked at the sight of a newcomer. Normally he was the first cat in the household to check out a stranger, but lately he'd been spending more time with Sienna.

"Oh, isn't that a pretty cat!" Megan said. She patted the sofa, and Munster accepted the invitation. He padded over to her, then jumped up and leaned his plump form against her arm. Panda gave him the evil eye and snuggled farther into Megan's lap.

"I think they're competing for my attention," Megan said, grinning. The idea seemed to please her.

Lara smiled. "You were telling me about some people."

Megan instantly sobered. "Yes. The Tanaka family. Such a sweet couple. They owned a small restaurant called the Japanese Garden. One day a guy who was eating lunch there found a bloody Band-Aid in his miso soup. Or claims he did," she added with a twist of her lips.

"Yikes."

"He created a scene, right there in the restaurant. Even tossed his cookies on the carpet. This happened last summer, right after I started working for Wayne. At first I thought it was an interesting case, but it turned sour for me very quickly."

"I assume the man hired your ex-boss to sue the restaurant for him?"

"Oh, did he ever. Wayne was practically salivating at the chance to sue them. He sent me to interview some of the witnesses—I was actually pretty good at that. I found out one thing, and it was crucial to the case. When this all happened, Mrs. Tanaka *did* have a cut on her left pinkie finger. She was honest about it, even admitted that she'd put a Band-Aid on it. But…she also said she wore plastic gloves all the time, so there was no way that Band-Aid could have gotten into the soup."

"So, it was one person's word against the other?"

Megan nodded. "Pretty much. A private lab did tests on the Band-Aid. Secretly, I was cheering for the Tanakas. Unfortunately, the results weren't conclusive. The blood sample had been compromised by the soup, among other things."

Lara was impressed with how concisely Megan spoke. When it came to her job, she appeared to know her stuff. In other ways, she was childlike.

"Long story short, the client sued for medical costs, loss of wages, and pain and suffering. The Tanakas agreed to settle, and the client ended up with a pretty decent payout."

Of which Wayne Chancer would have snagged one-third, Lara mused.

"It didn't make anyone rich, but for Wayne it was a victory. The Tanakas should have gotten their own lawyer," Megan went on, "but they were very old-fashioned. They felt the system would work in favor of the truth." She shook her head, and a strand of brunette hair fell forward. "They ended up paying the settlement out of their own pockets. After that, most of the locals stopped eating at the restaurant. Between the loss of business and the humiliation, it was too much for them. They ended up closing shop."

What a sad story, Lara thought. If the Tanakas' fate was an example of how Wayne Chancer operated, he must have made plenty of enemies.

"Lara, Wayne had it in for those poor people," Megan said suddenly. "They didn't stand a chance." She took a small sip of her hot chocolate, her hand shaking slightly.

"But why? What did they ever do to him?"

Her slender jaw hardened. "They, personally, didn't do anything. It was all about their daughter, Tina. Wayne had a *thing* for her, if you get my drift. Tina's about my age, beautiful as all get-out. Classy, quiet, smart. She worked in the restaurant, but she juggles a few other jobs, too. I know she works at a bridal shop in Bakewell. Anyway, Wayne was always ogling her, trying to flirt with her. When she ignored him, he started sending her creepy texts."

"How did you know about the texts?" Lara asked.

Megan slid her fingers through Panda's fur. "He used to leave his cell phone on his desk whenever he went to the, you know, *john*," she said, blushing. "Look, I'm embarrassed to admit I did this, but there were days when he acted real testy, like he was mad at something. I was afraid it was *me* he was mad at, that I'd screwed something up, so I peeked at his phone. That's when I discovered he'd been text-stalking Tina."

Lara felt ill. *What a lowlife.* "Did Tina respond?"

"At first, she told him to stop bothering her, but that only made him escalate. Finally, she texted something like 'does the term restraining order mean anything to you?' It infuriated him. The Band-Aid incident happened shortly after that. Lara, I'm almost sure it was a setup. I think that Band-Aid was planted."

If Megan was telling the truth, then Wayne Chancer was truly the lowest of the low, in Lara's mind. It also meant that Tina Tanaka had good reason to loathe the man. Even so, it might have had nothing to do with his death.

"There's still something I don't understand," Lara said. "After those creepy texts your ex-boss sent to Tina, wasn't it a conflict of interest for him to represent the plaintiff in the tainted soup matter? Seems like any judge with his head on straight would've removed him from the case."

"Maybe, but the Tanakas never told anyone about those awful texts. Even though Tina was the victim, I think they were afraid of what people might say about her. Like I said before, they're super old-fashioned, and very protective. That's why I wish they'd gotten their own attorney."

"Have the police spoken to Tina?" Lara asked. "I mean, they must have looked at Wayne's cell phone, right?"

"I'm not sure. So far, my attorney hasn't shared that with me. Plus, if Wayne did set up the Tanakas, it's possible he deleted the texts first."

Lara knew the authorities had ways to retrieve deleted texts, but they had to have reason to suspect something first. With so many potential culprits, Lara couldn't help wondering why the police were so focused on Megan. Or were they? Was it possible that Megan had exaggerated her situation in order to gain sympathy from Gideon?

The thought had no sooner left her mind when Megan said, in a wobbly voice, "Lara, after I crashed Wayne's birthday party and screamed all sorts of accusations at him, I said a *really* dumb thing. I told him he'd better watch what he ate and drank because nearly every guest in that room had reason to want him dead."

Chapter 8

"Talk about being your own worst enemy," Aunt Fran said, absently petting the long-haired black cat curled in her lap.

"I know. For someone who's clearly quite bright, she did a very dumb thing." It made Lara wonder what else Megan might have done to harm her own case.

"I don't see that you can do much to help her." Aunt Fran gave her a wry smile. "This is one murder you can leave to the police. Thank heaven for that," she added.

Lara nodded, but she couldn't stop thinking about Blue. Why had her spirit cat landed almost on Megan's shoulder? And why had the Ragdoll given Lara that enigmatic look, as if to say, *You need to think about why I'm here.*

Lara went into the storage room and pulled out a large container of kitty litter.

"Now, back to Sherry's problem," Aunt Fran said when she returned. "Are you going to speak to Pastor Folger?"

"I think so," Lara said. "Sherry's no shrinking violet, but I think she feels weird approaching him because she doesn't really go to church."

It was one of the many things on Lara's agenda for the day, *if* the pastor was available, that was.

A car door slammed in the parking area near the shelter entrance.

Lara grinned. "Yay. That must be Kayla."

A minute later, Kayla knocked on the kitchen door, then let herself in. She'd gotten so comfortable with Lara and her aunt that she didn't need to wait for them to answer.

"God, it's freakin' cold out there," she grumbled. "My glasses are even fogged up."

Lara hugged her. "Take off your things. Want some tea?"

"I'd love some," Kayla said. She draped her puffy jacket and accessories over a chair. "I've missed you guys! Exams were like, brutal, but I think I did pretty well. Time will tell, right?"

"I'm sure you aced them," Aunt Fran said with conviction. "So, you're on vacation from school this week?"

"Glory, yes," Kayla exclaimed. "I can spend as much time as I want here. Well, as long as you want me around."

At the sound of Kayla's voice, Panda strutted into the kitchen.

"Hey, there's my buddy," Kayla said, scooping the black-and-white feline into her arms. "Ooh, I've missed you. I think your whiskers are even longer than they were last week!" She tucked Panda's head under her chin and sat down, setting the cat in her lap. "Quick cup of tea, then we'll get to work, right?"

"Right," Lara agreed. "Let's change the litter boxes first and then go on to the grooming. After that I want to see if we can work up something for the local paper. I've been thinking about writing an editorial urging people not to abandon cats in dumb places, especially in this freezing weather."

"Amen to that," Kayla said.

A thought tickled Lara's brain. The one thing she hadn't yet bought for Sherry's wedding were the shoes to match her teal-blue maid-of-honor dress. Because she wore a narrow size, she had better luck finding shoes online than she did in the stores.

Ivory would be perfect, especially if she could find a pair of low heels in satin. She'd tried finding something online that appealed to her, but hadn't landed on anything she liked enough to risk buying them without trying them on.

Hmmm. Hadn't Megan said that Tina Tanaka worked at a bridal shop in Bakewell?

Keeping that little tidbit to herself, she chatted with Kayla for a bit over a cup of tea, and then they got to work.

"So, how're things in the dating world?" Lara said while they were changing the litter boxes upstairs.

Kayla had recently met someone who'd transferred to one of her classes. According to Kayla, he loved cats as much as she did. They'd had a few "coffee" dates, but so far that was it.

Kayla's face brightened. She pushed her glasses farther up her nose. "Um, hard to say, but I think it's progressing. I'm not counting my chickens…

yet," she added. "But at least he has his head on straight, which is more than you-know-who did."

The summer before, Kayla had started dating a man who'd come out of a dysfunctional marriage. While he'd been sweet and respectful toward Kayla, his pain over losing his ex was still too raw. They'd parted on good terms, but Lara knew Kayla had been hurt.

"What about you?" Kayla asked, deftly switching gears. She mimicked tilting her ear toward downtown Whisker Jog. "Are those wedding bells I hear tinkling from the coffee shop?"

Lara chuckled, but a piece of her heart ached. It seemed she and Gideon were even further than ever from making that final commitment.

"Those are Sherry and David's wedding bells," Lara said firmly, trying to sound casual. "And I, for one, can't wait to see them tie the knot."

"Yeah, me too. I'm so psyched that Sherry invited me to the wedding. Hey, did you ever find shoes to go with your dress? I've been out of the loop for almost a week."

Lara tied up a trash bag and set it down in a corner of the upstairs hallway. "No, but someone told me there's a bridal shop in Bakewell. I'm thinking of taking a drive over there to see what I can find."

"Bakewell." Kayla pulled her cell out of her jeans pocket and tapped at it. "Oh my God. That's where I heard about Bakewell recently. Some guy was found dead in the snow at his house a few nights ago. The cops are saying it was *not* an accident." She looked at Lara. "Did you know about it?"

Lara winced. "Unfortunately, yes. One of the people the police are looking closely at just happens to be an old girlfriend of Gideon's."

Kayla's eyes widened. "I hope you're kidding."

"I wish I were." Lara sighed. "She came to see me, a little while ago."

"Who came to see you?" Kayla squeaked. "Gideon's old girlfriend?"

Lara nodded. "Let's take the trash out. I'll tell you about it while we brush the cats."

They took they trash bags downstairs. Lara ran outside and dumped them in the outside barrel.

Aunt Fran was at the kitchen table, her laptop open in front of her. She looked deep in thought, and merely waved at them as they trotted back upstairs.

In Lara's bedroom, they each took a cat and began brushing. Sienna looked blissful, but Amber, as always, was a bit skittish. Once Kayla began cooing to her and softly running the brush over her fur, Amber closed her eyes and submitted to the grooming.

Lara told Kayla everything. She began with Megan stopping at the coffee shop for directions on Friday, right through her visit to Lara that morning.

Kayla looked stunned. "What did Gideon say about all this?"

"He doesn't know about Megan's visit here this morning." *And I'm on the fence about sharing.* "He told me yesterday that he's washed his hands of any involvement with her. He helped her out on Saturday when she was in a pinch, but she's already hired a criminal lawyer to represent her so he's out of it." *Completely, I hope.*

"You're not seriously thinking of helping her, are you?" Kayla said. She tickled Amber under the chin.

Lara gazed down at Sienna. "Kayla, I honestly don't know what to do. When Megan was here this morning, Panda jumped right into her lap on the sofa. But then...I looked over and saw Blue nestled up against her shoulder. Blue was staring at me, like she was trying to get some point across. I know that sounds crazy, but—"

"Not to me, it doesn't."

Other than Aunt Fran and Gideon, Kayla was the only person in whom Lara had confided about her spirit cat. In fact, she'd been the first one to learn about her.

Kayla removed Amber's hair from the rubber brush and looked at Lara. "I know you wanted to work on that editorial today, but I'll be back tomorrow so we can work on it then. I think you and I should take a ride to Bakewell this afternoon and look for those shoes."

Lara smiled. "Maybe to a certain bridal shop?"

Chapter 9

Bakewell turned out to be about a forty-minute drive from Aunt Fran's. The town center was longer than Whisker Jog's, and, Lara had to admit, a bit more picturesque.

Despite the cold, and the dreary feel of winter, the sidewalks looked meticulously maintained.

Lara pulled the Saturn into the parking lot of an eatery dubbed Joey's Diner. Housed in an old-fashioned railroad car, it looked both quaint and inviting. Since it was mid-afternoon, only a few cars dotted the lot.

"Are you hungry all of a sudden?" Kayla smiled over at Lara.

"Not really. I just wanted to park somewhere to get the lay of the land, so to speak. Did you figure out the name of the bridal shop?"

Kayla tapped at her cell phone. "I had it a minute ago. Yup. Here it is. Valeria's Bridal Salon. Forty-two Main." She pointed at the windshield. "Should be in the next block, according to Google Maps."

"Good ol' Google," Lara said, grinning. She pulled out of the diner's parking lot and headed up the street. Luckily, the bridal shop had its own parking area behind the pastel-painted building.

"Wait a minute," Lara said, passing by the bridal place. "Does that sign up ahead say the Peach Crate—Gourmet Delights?"

Kayla squinted through the windshield toward the right side of the street. "Um…yeah, it does, but you just went past the bridal shop. What's so important about the Peach Crate?"

"Gideon said that Chancer's wife sold her jams and jellies at a gourmet shop in Bakewell. How much you want to bet…?" She raised her eyebrows at Kayla.

"Now I know why you catch so many killers," Kayla said dryly. "You think of things that never would've crossed my mind."

"I don't *really* catch killers," Lara insisted. "But I'll take that as a compliment."

Lara lucked out by finding a diagonal parking spot directly in front of the shop. She angled the Saturn into the space and killed the engine.

"So, what are we trying to find out?" Kayla said.

"I'm not sure, so let's play it by ear. Maybe we can subtly work Karen Chancer's name into the conversation with whoever's working there."

"Roger." Kayla gave her a two-fingered salute.

A bell tinkled over the door when they stepped inside the shop. A heavenly scent immediately drifted over them—a combo of vanilla and peach, Lara thought.

Wooden shelves stacked with all sorts of goodies were placed strategically throughout the store. Terrified she might accidentally break something, Lara pulled her elbows close to her ribs as they strolled among the shelves. At the back of the store, an elderly woman stood behind a counter that was designed to look like a wooden peach crate. It had to have been handmade, and by someone quite clever with a hammer and nails.

"Good afternoon," the woman called to them. "Please let me know if there's anything I can help you with. Everything in here is homemade in New Hampshire."

With that opening, Lara went over to her. A heart-shaped crystal bowl filled with chocolate candies wrapped in red foil rested on the counter. Resisting them, Lara said, "This is a darling shop you have here. So, everything is made in New Hampshire?"

The woman, slim and petite with a helmet of dove-gray hair, nodded vigorously. "Yes they are, and I'm so proud of that. My vendors are all top-notch chefs and bakers. Their goods are vetted before they're allowed to display here."

A sharp businesswoman, Lara thought.

"Also," the woman said, pulling her green cardigan closer around her chest, "the pottery on that shelf along the wall is locally made. I'm Felicia Tristany, by the way. I own the shop." Her pink-tinted smile was kind and genuine.

Lara and Kayla introduced themselves, but Lara was careful to disclose only her given name.

"Are you here for anything in particular?" Felicia asked.

"No, but I can never resist homemade goodies. When I spotted your sign, I just had to come in." She could almost feel Kayla rolling her eyes behind her.

Felicia nodded. "Well, you've come to the right place. Take your time and look around."

And look around they did.

One entire shelf was devoted to homemade shortbread cookies of every shape and design. Lara snagged a wire basket from the front of the store and placed two packages of almond-flavored shortbread inside. They'd be perfect for adoption days, especially since the shelter occasionally ran out of Daisy's adorable cat-shaped cookies.

Kayla strolled the aisles, wide-eyed. Lara knew she had a wicked sweet tooth, so she was probably deciding how to treat herself without overspending.

"Kayla, I'm treating to whatever we buy today."

"No! You don't have to—"

"I insist," Lara said quietly. "I'm grateful that you came here with me. I didn't really want to do it alone."

Kayla gave in and plucked a stack of cellophane-wrapped, raspberry-filled cookies from one of the shelves.

Lara sidled over to a shelf where jams and jellies were displayed. One brand in particular caught her eye—Karen's Fruit Spreads. She lifted a jar labeled *Karen's Peachy Fine Spread*. It was a mason jar covered with a swatch of orange-checkered cloth and tied with a length of twine. Lara read the label: *Made with love by Karen Chancer. All comments welcome.* Below that, a link to a Web site was shown. Lara placed the jar into her basket and glanced over the other flavors.

Kayla came up behind her. "Oh, ugh," she said, a bit too loudly. She pointed at a jar containing an olive-green spread. "Who would want to eat avocado jam?"

"Lots of people, probably," Lara said, worried that Felicia might've heard her. "Avocado is very healthy, you know."

Kayla wrinkled her nose. "I'll pass." She reached for a jar of cherry fruit spread. "Gram will love this. She goes nuts for anything with cherries."

Gideon also loved cherry-flavored anything. Lara grabbed a jar for herself.

Felicia came up behind them. "I see you've found Karen Chancer's products." She shook her head sadly. "Poor woman. You may have heard about it on the news. Her husband—"

"Was murdered!" Kayla blurted. "Yeah, I watched it last night. The cops still don't know what killed him, though, right?"

Lara appreciated Kayla's zeal, but wished she'd tone it down a bit.

"That's right," Felicia said. "In my opinion, he probably had a plain old heart attack. But for some reason the police seem to suspect foul play. Wayne was a…big man. Husky, with a large belly. While I certainly didn't know him very well, I suspect he indulged in foods that weren't exactly the healthiest."

"Well, we all do that at times," Lara said. "How well do you know Mrs. Chancer?"

Felicia smiled. "Actually, I know her quite well. She's a lovely lady, the total opposite of her—" Felicia pursed her lips. "Never mind. I don't want to speak ill of the dead. I was raised better than that."

"I understand," Lara said somberly. "This must be a tough time for Mrs. Chancer. Does she have family close by?"

"Only her dad," Felicia said. "She was an only child. Her mom died some time ago. Her dad's a local Realtor—Gary Becker. Maybe you've heard of him?"

Lara shook her head. "I've never bought or sold property, so…no."

"Anyway, he's always been so protective of his daughter. It's well known that he disliked Karen's husband intensely. I'm surprised the police haven't homed in on him."

"Maybe, like you said, they figured out that Mr. Chancer simply had a heart attack."

"Let's hope so," Felicia said. "For everyone's sake." She deftly switched topics. "Are you familiar with fruit bits?"

"No, not at all. What are they?"

With a sly smile, Felicia crooked her finger, indicating that they should follow her. She went over to another section and lifted a small glass jar off the shelf. "This one, for example, has peach bits. They're made from fruit puree, and they hold their shape during baking. They're ideal for muffins, scones, and the like." She waved a hand over the shelf. "As you can see, they come in several flavors. One for every palate." She winked at Lara. "These are also made by Karen," she added. "She is such a talented young woman."

"I can see that." Lara smiled. "And you—you're a great salesperson, you know that?"

Felicia shrugged. "It's what I do," she said. "My living depends on it." A shadow crossed her face, a sudden display of emotion. It disappeared as quickly as it came. "I won't bother you girls anymore. Spend as much time here as you like. I'm not one of those people who gets antsy if customers browse for too long."

"Thank you." Lara glanced at her watch. It was already three thirty, and they hadn't even gone to the bridal shop yet. Time to get a move on.

"We'd better get going," Lara said quietly to Kayla, who'd just stuck a bag of something colorful into her basket.

They went up to the checkout counter, and Lara's eyes popped open in surprise. Felicia was holding a tiny white dog in her arms. The pup appeared to be a poodle mix of some sort. "Oh my, where did he come from?"

"She," Felicia said proudly. "This is my Lily, my darling Lily." Her eyes moistened. "She's fourteen and still going strong, although she does have health issues."

"Aww," Kayla said.

"Is it okay if we pet her?" Lara asked.

"Oh, she'll love you forever if you do that."

Lara and Kayla took turns petting the dog, then Felicia gently set her down on the floor. "She has a comfy bed under there. I never come to work without her. She's getting on in years, and I don't like leaving her alone."

Felicia rang up their purchases and invited them to visit again. Lara paid with her debit card.

"Take my card," Felicia said, handing each of them a pink business card. "Some of our vendors do custom orders. You never know when you might need something special. And I do hope you'll check out the shop's Facebook page. I confess to being somewhat of a Facebook junkie." She winked at Lara. "Keeps me out of trouble, and I love connecting with people," she added with a musical laugh.

"I'll definitely check it out," Lara assured her.

With a final wave at Felicia, they left the shop. The bell above the door jingled as they exited.

"That was interesting," Kayla said as they hurried toward the car. "One more suspect to add to your list."

Lara paused on the sidewalk and gawked at her. "What do you mean—to add to my list? And who's the so-called suspect?"

They hopped inside the car, and Lara started the engine. "Come on, Lara. Aren't you keeping track of people who might have killed Chancer?" Kayla pulled over her seat belt.

Lara looked away. Was she? Was this another one of her quests to find a killer?

"No," Lara said crisply. "I'm not keeping track, and I'm not making a list. Again, who's the so-called suspect?"

Kayla looked at Lara, her eyes glittering. "Gary Becker. Karen's Chancer's father."

Lara squirmed in her seat and snapped her seat belt into place. The problem was that Kayla knew her all too well. "We have no reason to believe that Karen's dad killed Chancer. Come on, let's visit the bridal shop before it closes. I'd like to make it home before it gets too dark."

Chapter 10

On the way to the bridal salon, Lara spotted a large black car in her rearview mirror. Was it following a bit too close, or was that just her imagination? A lot of drivers tailgated, especially in local traffic. But this driver looked familiar, and not in a good way. It was the profile she recognized more than anything, but his sunglasses made it impossible to make out any of his features.

It was going to drive her crazy until she figured out who it was.

When she turned into the parking lot behind the salon, the mystery car didn't follow.

Thank heaven.

Valeria's Bridal Salon was the kind of shop that made Lara feel as if she had to speak in a whisper.

Beyond the marble entryway, three shallow steps led to a sea of plush, dark red carpeting. A crystal chandelier hung in the center of the shop, its conical design giving it the look of an elegant beehive. A polished wooden table in the center of the room boasted a huge Oriental vase bearing an arrangement of gorgeous white lilies. Adjacent to the table, on either side, were two pink-toned love seats. They sat at an angle, presumably to give the area the feel of a cozy parlor.

Along both sides of the shop, wedding gowns hung on long wooden racks. Lara glanced at Kayla, whose eyes were the size of dinner plates.

"Look at these dresses," Kayla said, bouncing her gaze all around. "Oh man, I sure hope I'll be shopping here someday."

Lara smiled. "Don't worry, you will be. Just don't be in a hurry, okay?"

Kayla made a face.

A young woman emerged from the back of the shop, her radiant smile displaying a set of snowy-white teeth. She'd appeared so suddenly that Lara wondered if she'd been observing her and Kayla from some hidden vantage point.

"Good afternoon. I'm Tina," the young woman said, her straight black hair brushing the tops of her slender shoulders. She wore a plain white blouse over a black pencil skirt. She couldn't have been more than a size two.

She must be Tina Tanaka, Lara thought.

Careful to give out only her first name, Lara introduced herself. Kayla followed suit.

"Welcome to Valeria's," Tina continued, with a surreptitious glance at her watch. "So, which one of you is the lucky bride?"

"I'm the lucky maid of honor," Lara said. "The wedding's in less than three weeks. I have a teal dress, but I haven't found any shoes I like yet. Do you carry shoes?"

"We do, but only a limited number. It's not that we don't want to carry them, but space is at a premium here. But—we can order anything you like if we don't have it in stock. Do you have a picture of the dress?"

Fortunately, Lara did. She pulled out her cell and went to her photos. "This is me wearing it."

Tina stared at the photo, which showed Lara in her stocking feet modeling the dress. "That's quite beautiful," she said, beaming at Lara. "I can see how it complements your red hair, and I love the lacy shoulder. With that length dress, I'd suggest a high heel in a soft shade of ivory."

"That's exactly what I was thinking, but maybe a lower heel. Is ivory okay for a February wedding?"

"It most certainly is," Tina assured her. "What size are you?"

"A seven narrow usually fits me to a T."

Tina held up a finger. "Give me a few moments. We don't have a lot in narrow sizes, but again, if there's something you like that's not your size, we can always order them for you."

Tina scurried out through a rear door, returning a few minutes later with a stack of boxes. She directed Lara over to a chair near the rear of the shop. Kayla watched eagerly as Lara tried on numerous pairs.

The first three pairs Lara tried on were not what she was looking for. The heels were either way too high or the shoes were adorned with too many doodads. The last pair made Lara's breath catch in her throat.

The shoes were peep-toe, made from ivory silk. The outer side of each shoe was a creamy sculptured lace that caressed the top of the foot and wrapped around to the back. The inner side of the shoe was plain. Lara was thrilled that the shoes had only a three-inch heel. Definitely better than the stilts she'd tried on earlier.

"Oh, I love these," Lara groaned, walking in a small circle. "Unfortunately, they're too wide. I can feel them slipping off."

"I was afraid of that. We have very few narrow sizes." Tina smiled at her. "I'd be pleased to order them in your size, if you'd like. Shipping only takes a few days if I put a rush on it." She quoted the price.

Lara swallowed and said, "That's fine. It's for my best friend's wedding, so I'm not going to skimp."

Kayla clapped. "I'm so glad you picked those, Lara. They're going to look fabulous on you."

Tina wrote up the order and accepted Lara's credit card. "I'll only be a moment," she said, leaving the room.

Uh-oh. Using her credit card meant that Tina would see her full name. Unfortunately, it couldn't be helped. Lara never carried much cash with her. And she desperately wanted those shoes.

Not that Lara was famous, but she'd been in the news a few times for having stumbled into the path of killers. Hopefully, her name wouldn't ring a bell with Tina.

"I'm psyched that you found those shoes," Kayla said. "Are you going to ask about you-know-who?"

Lara bit her lip. "I'm not sure. Only if I can think of a way to do it tactfully."

Tina seemed to be taking a while ringing up Lara's order. She finally returned holding a slip of paper and a pen. Her former smile had faded to a flat line. "Sign here and I'll put the order right through," she said. "I'll need your phone number so I can call you when the shoes are in." She returned the credit card to Lara. "By the way, your name looked familiar to me, so I just Googled you. This is about Wayne Chancer, isn't it? Did you come here to spy on me?"

Uh-oh. *Nailed.*

Should she tell the truth or make up a fib? Lara juggled her choices. She decided to try an end run and avoid the question altogether.

"Actually, it was a friend who told me about this salon. I think you know her. Megan Haskell?"

Tina's jaw went taut. "And you just *happened* to run into her, and you just *happened* to need a pair of shoes for your friend's wedding."

"Sort of. I definitely needed the shoes. My friend Sherry is getting married on Valentine's Day, which is coming up fast."

"Valentine's Day. So cliché." Tina rolled her eyes.

Lara bristled. The cordial persona Tina had displayed earlier seemed to have fallen off the edge of the earth. "It was the date my friend chose. Personally, I think it's quite romantic."

"Whatever." Tina shoved the shoes Lara had tried on into their proper boxes and made a stack. "I need to put these away. The store closes in fifteen minutes. Valeria will call you when your shoes are ready to pick up."

"Tina, I didn't mean to upset you." Lara rose from her chair, hoping she could smooth things over. "It's only that Megan is very worried. The police questioned her, and she's terrified they think she's somehow involved in his death."

"Which is dumb, because they don't even know how Chancer died," Tina sniped. "I'll tell you this. There's no way Megan was involved. The girl can talk, *ad nauseum*, but she doesn't bite. I suppose she told you about him stalking me."

Tina said it with such vehemence that Lara was taken aback. "I—um…"

"Let me tell you one last thing. If you thought you were going to trick me into confessing that I killed Chancer, then you sorely underestimated me."

Lara felt chastised, and embarrassed. "I'm sorry if I offended you, Tina. It wasn't my intention."

Stone-faced, Tina stared at Lara, the boxes balanced in her arms.

Lara was going to add that she really did come to the store to look for shoes, but decided it might be overkill. At this stage, nothing was going to erase the fury in Tina's expression. She quickly left the store, Kayla on her heels.

"Shoot," Kayla said. "That could've gone better."

They scurried toward the parking lot and hopped into the Saturn. The sky had darkened. Traffic had picked up considerably, presumably from people leaving work. Lara stuck the key in the ignition.

"Lara, your hand is shaking," Kayla said. "Are you all right?"

Nodding, Lara forced back tears. She had to see to drive. "Tina was right. I did go there to spy on her. What right did I have? I'm just…so mad at myself. I'm an idiot."

Kayla reached over and squeezed Lara's shoulder. "You're not an idiot, so stop beating yourself up."

Lara started the car and backed out of the parking space. Traffic on the main road had picked up, for which she was grateful. It kept her focused on something other than the mess she'd made of things with Tina Tanaka.

It was ridiculous to think that she could help Megan. It was the job of the police to figure out how Chancer died, not hers. She'd helped in the past, yes—but that was by sheer happenstance.

The hard truth was that she'd been blinded by her faith in Blue, who'd cozied up to Megan as if they were best buds. Maybe Blue had only been trying to comfort Megan. Maybe she wasn't trying to signal that Lara needed to help her.

God, what a fiasco.

They made it back to Whisker Jog a little after dark. Kayla left right away, since she knew her grandmother would be worried about her.

Aunt Fran knew immediately that something was wrong, but she didn't ask any questions. They put together a light supper of tomato soup and grilled cheddar sandwiches—a meal Lara normally devoured. When she shoved aside almost half her sandwich, Aunt Fran spoke up.

"Lara, it's obvious something is very wrong. Is it anything I can help with?"

Lara shook her head. "Probably not. But I'll tell you about it anyway."

She launched into her story of their trip to Bakewell. Aunt Fran listened without commenting, only nodding her head here and there.

"Why don't you give yourself a break?" Aunt Fran said, after Lara was through. "You're being way too hard on yourself, in my opinion."

Lara rose from her chair and kissed her aunt on the cheek. "Thanks for always being here for me, Aunt Fran. I can't imagine what I'd do without you."

Chapter 11

That evening, Lara was restless. She couldn't keep her mind on any one thing. Her attempt to work on Amy Glindell's watercolor project sank like a rock to the bottom of her heart.

She hadn't heard from Gideon since early that morning. Normally he texted throughout the day, even if it was just a *"Hello! Love you!"* Today he'd been oddly silent, almost as if he knew what she'd been up to. But how could he?

She'd already decided that she would tell him everything. If their relationship wasn't completely open and honest, it didn't have a chance of lasting.

Aunt Fran had made her feel a little better. She'd pointed out that Lara had only been trying to help, not to harm anyone. But the look on Tina Tanaka's face when they left the bridal salon wouldn't leave Lara's head. She felt sure she'd ruined the young woman's day. She wished she could hop into a time machine and take back the entire mess.

Realizing she wasn't going to accomplish much this evening, she remembered that she wanted to check out Felicia Tristany's Facebook page. On her tablet, she Googled the name of the gourmet food shop, and the page popped up instantly.

Lara couldn't help smiling. The profile photo for the shop wasn't a pic of the shop itself—it was a close-up of Felicia's treasured dog, Lily. Lily's collar, made from pale green fabric, was adorned with images of ripe peaches. The banner along the top was a snapshot of one of the rows of goodies inside the shop. Karen's Fruit Spreads were prominent in the photo. Lara wondered if Felicia had recently changed the banner to honor her friend in her time of sorrow.

Lara gave the page a "like" and then scrolled down, perusing the posts. Accolades from customers were abundant on the page. Nearly all the reviews of the shop's products were positive, if not glowing. Especially popular were Karen Chancer's fruit bits, along with the specialty teas created by Felicia herself. Felicia apparently offered her patrons "custom-made" teas for special occasions, such as a coconut-pineapple blend for a Hawaiian-style tea party, or a pumpkin spice–flavored tea for an autumn occasion.

Impressed with Felicia's business chops as well as her creativity, Lara wondered if she had a personal page. A quick Facebook search pulled up nothing, so Lara decided to Google her. Only one name came up—a Felicia Tristany from Canfield, Ohio, who'd died four years earlier.

Lara sighed and powered off her tablet. After ensuring that all the cats were set for the night with fresh water and clean litter, she wished her aunt a good night and crawled into bed with three cats—Munster, Sienna, and Panda—and a book.

Ha. Wouldn't that make a great movie title? *Three Cats and a Book.*

Panda had nestled up close to her, his long white whiskers brushing her neck as he purred like a smooth-running motor. Lara read until her eyes started to droop, then set aside her book and shut off the light. She was just drifting off when her cell rang, jolting her wide awake. Gideon's smiling face appeared on her screen.

"Hi, stranger," she said, her voice coming out a little shaky.

After a moment of silence, Gideon said, "Stranger, indeed. Lara, were you in Bakewell today?"

Lara's heart jumped in her chest. "Good evening to you, too," she said curtly. "Yes, I was in Bakewell. How did you know?"

"Oh, maybe because a certain state police investigator saw you parked in front of a gourmet food shop. And later saw you pull in behind a bridal shop."

Lara suddenly got it.

Lieutenant Conrad Cutler.

The black car. It was an unmarked state police car.

Had he been following her? The thought made a ball of ire rise in her chest.

Bad enough if Cutler followed her—he had to report it to Gideon?

"First of all," Lara said, trying to keep her tone even, "Kayla went with me to Bakewell to look for a pair of shoes for the wedding. Which, in fact, I found—although they had to be ordered in my size."

Gideon huffed into the phone. "Lara, I am really trying to understand this, but frankly, I'm not having much luck. Are you poking around in another murder?"

"'Poking around'?" Lara said tightly. "No, I'm not *poking around*. It's just—" She clutched Panda for moral support. "Megan came to see me this morning. She was in a bad way. She asked if I would help her."

"Oh my God. And you agreed? After everything you've been through?"

"No, I didn't agree. Not...exactly. I told her she needed to deal with her attorney." Lara sighed. "The problem is, I felt sorry for her. After talking to her, I realized that she's very intelligent, but she's also immature. I think she lacks impulse control, which is what got her into trouble in the first place."

For a long time, Gideon was silent. Lara was afraid he'd disconnected.

"Lara," he finally said, "I am so frustrated right now that I can barely talk. Three days ago, you were upset that I'd never told you about Megan. Now you're helping her? Have you forgotten what you went through last summer? And before that, at Christmas—"

"No, Gideon. I haven't forgotten. I'm sorry if this has upset you, but something about Megan made me scared for her. Yes, I went to Bakewell today to be nosy, to 'poke around,' as you put it. But I really did need shoes for the wedding, and I found the perfect pair." *And I have to go back there to pick them up.*

Gideon's tone seemed to deflate. "Anything else?"

"I talked to a few local store owners. That was it." She pulled in a calming breath. "Well, not *quite* it. The woman who assisted me at the bridal salon—her name was Tina Tanaka—Googled me when she saw the name on my credit card."

"Oh boy."

"Actually, Megan knows Tina. Megan told me this morning that Tina had bad blood with Chancer." She related the story of Chancer text-stalking Tina. "After Tina checked me out, I guess she decided I'd gone there to spy on her. She was not happy, to put it mildly."

"No, I don't imagine she was. But I can't help thinking what a coincidence it was that you just *happened* to bump into Tina Tanaka while you were looking for shoes."

Lara choked back a lump. "Gideon, I don't think we should continue this discussion on the phone. Do you have time tomorrow when we can talk in person?"

"Lara, I always have time for you." His voice was gentle. "You should know that by now."

I'm not sure what I know anymore.

"Then pick a time. Any time. I'll be there," she said.

"Okay then, early," he said. "Is eight okay?"

"Perfect," Lara said, though she didn't think anything would ever be perfect again.

The timing of all this couldn't be any worse. Sherry's wedding was in less than three weeks. If Sherry suspected that Lara and Gideon were having troubles, she'd worry herself into a knot. Lara couldn't let that happen.

"See you tomorrow, then. Love you." Gideon hung up.

"I love you, too," she murmured to a disconnected phone.

Sensing her dismay, Panda crawled closer to Lara. Lara buried her face in the cat's neck. "Oh, Panda, why can't people be as easy to get along with as cats?"

Panda responded with a sharp *meow*.

"Yeah, that's what I thought. You don't have a clue either."

Munster and Sienna had bailed on her. They were curled up in the corner cat bed, happy in their own kitty world. Amber was on the cat tree near the window in Lara's room, gazing out into the night. Dolce and Twinkles were no doubt hunkered down in bed with Aunt Fran.

In the world of cats, all was peaceful at High Cliff.

If only things were as tranquil in the world of humans.

If only she could sleep like a cat.

Chapter 12

The next morning, at Gideon's office, Lara was greeted by the part-time assistant he'd hired seven months earlier.

"Good morning, Lara." Marina Martin's deep brown eyes twinkled from a kindly, wrinkled face. "Another frigid day, isn't it?" She rubbed her hands together as if to ward off the chill.

"It sure is," Lara agreed, pasting on a smile. "How are you doing, Marina?"

"Oh, I'm doing, for an old lady." She smiled and whisked her cell phone off her desk. "The latest pic," she said, her plump chest swelling with pride.

Lara stared at the photo of a chubby little boy with a head full of dark curls. "Oh gosh, that's little Dwight, isn't it? He's adorable. What is he, six months now?"

"Seven," Marina said. "Going on eighteen, if you know what I mean."

Lara laughed. How lucky Marina's grandkids were to have her to dote on them. She was a wonderful woman. She'd also been a godsend to Gideon.

The summer before, Gideon had taken on added responsibilities when he accepted the job as the town's attorney. A mother of two and grandmother of five, Marina had retired from her days as a legal secretary and hadn't worked in years. When she went into the town hall to renew her dog's license, she saw Gideon's ad for a part-time assistant posted on the bulletin board. She applied, and Gideon saw right away that she was a gem. He'd hired her on the spot.

"Gideon's waiting for you." Marina winked at Lara, as if to assure her that everything would work out. "I'll be in the back room doing some filing."

Lara knew most of Gideon's filing was done electronically. Marina was pulling a disappearing act so they could chat without her overhearing.

In Gideon's office, a cup of freshly poured coffee and a cinnamon-chip muffin awaited her on the front of his desk. A yellow legal pad acted as place mat. A folded napkin sat beside the cup.

"Hi." Instead of wrapping her in a huge hug, as he normally would, he kissed her lightly on the cheek. "Have a seat."

Lara slung her tote over the chair facing his, then sat and slid her jacket off her arms. She smiled. "Thanks for the coffee." He'd already added the cream and sugar. It was the exactly the way she liked it. Lara took a long sip. It tasted heavenly.

"I heard you come in, so I got it ready."

Instead of sitting in his usual chair, he came around and perched on the edge of his desk facing her. He looked tired, as if he'd slept poorly. His eyelids drooped, and he had two tiny cuts where he'd nicked himself shaving.

"Lara, I apologize for sounding like such a bully last night. It was uncalled for. I was totally out of line."

A huge breath of relief escaped Lara. She hadn't expected their conversation to start off this way. She hoped it was a sign that they were getting past this hiccup in their relationship.

"I understand why you were worried," she said. "I know that I've had… *encounters* in the past that put me in some danger."

"Some danger? Come on, Lara. It was more than 'some,' and you know it."

She nodded. "All right. I admit that. But something about Megan got to me. She seems, I don't know, friendless, I guess."

Gideon fixed her with a look. "Maybe there's a reason for that."

"What do you mean?"

Gideon closed his eyes and tilted his head toward the ceiling. Then he looked back at Lara. "Lara, Megan has a hair-trigger temper. I only got a taste of it once, but once was enough. That's why I don't feel one hundred percent sure about her innocence. Ninety-nine percent, yes. But not a hundred."

"But before this, you told me you didn't think Megan had it in her to commit premeditated murder. Now it sounds like you're hedging."

"I know, but I've had time to mull it over. I'll tell you a story, something that happened on our last and final date. I don't like speaking ill of Megan, but this is serious stuff. If Wayne Chancer was, in fact, murdered—and it's beginning to look that way—you could be putting yourself in danger if you keep asking questions."

That reminded Lara of something else that was bugging her. "By the way, how did you happen to run into Conrad Cutler? Or did he call you specifically to tattle on me?"

Gideon sighed. "Yes, he called me. You can call it tattling if you want, but the man has a great deal of respect for you. He remembers what happened last summer. He doesn't want to see a repeat of that nightmare."

Lara's hands curled into fists. "And I do? Oh yes, poor little me. I'm only a woman, so I guess I can't keep track of things like someone trying to kill me."

Gideon paled, and for a moment Lara felt a twinge of guilt. She knew it wasn't his fault that Cutler was old-school in his thinking.

"I know he can be overbearing," Gideon said, "but he's an excellent investigator—one of the best. Remember, in his job he's seen the worst of the worst—things neither of us can begin to imagine. It tends to make him overprotective."

At that, Lara felt bad. She knew cops saw terrible things on a regular basis. It had to be depressing sometimes.

"All right, I'm going to let it go," she said, unclenching her fists. She tore off a piece of her muffin and popped it into her mouth. It gave her a moment to think. After she swallowed, she said, "I guess I don't understand why you're suddenly so chummy with him."

Gideon shrugged. "I think he's just keeping me in the loop because of my past dealings with Megan."

Dealings? Lara hated to think what that word meant.

"Why don't you tell me the story about Megan?" she prompted.

He nodded. "This one day—maybe three, almost four years ago?—we were eating at a pizza place in Concord. Cute little place, nothing fancy. It was around the time I started to realize that Megan and I had very little in common. I knew I didn't want to see her again. I just didn't know how to tell her."

Lara knew from experience how that felt. Usually, though, she'd been on the receiving end.

"In the scheme of things, what happened was minor, but it told me a lot about her. It was enough that I knew I had to end things before it went any further." Gideon crossed his feet at the ankles and shifted on his desk. "An elderly woman sitting at the table next to us happened to get up just as we were leaving. The woman was holding a plate of half-eaten spaghetti. I guess she was going to toss it out—either that or ask for a take-out box. Anyway, Megan didn't see her, and when she got up, the woman's greasy spaghetti sauce ended up all over the sleeve of her blouse." He stared off at the wall, as if reliving the scene in his mind.

"I gather Megan got upset?"

"Upset? She went ballistic. Started shrieking at the woman and making wild gestures. Told her it was a such-and-such blouse—some designer I can't remember—and that she'd paid over two hundred dollars for it."

Lara didn't own any designer blouses. If she did, she definitely wouldn't wear one to a pizza parlor, where it would almost certainly end up spotted with cheese and pepperoni.

Gideon went on. "Megan threatened the woman, told her she worked for lawyers and she was going to sue her butt off. Everyone in the place was staring at her."

Lara was horrified. "I can't even imagine what you were thinking. What did that poor woman do?"

He linked his fingers over his knees. "That was the thing that got to me. The woman started to cry. She kept apologizing and pulling cash out of her purse. She tried to give it to Megan so she could have the blouse cleaned, but Megan slapped the money away. At that point I got angry. I insisted that the woman put her money away, and I sent her on her way—as gently as I could."

Lara sat back and mulled over the story. She hadn't seen any signs of Megan's temper during her visit the day before. Then again, Megan had been on her best behavior for sure. Was the woman a master manipulator?

She thought about the way Megan had enjoyed the cats' attention, how they'd cuddled up to her and made her feel welcome. Blue had nestled close to Megan's shoulder as if she was trying to comfort her. Lara couldn't reconcile it with the story Gideon had just related.

Then again, they were cats, not psychologists or mind readers. Sometimes she had to remind herself to keep it in perspective.

And technically, Blue wasn't a cat. Not a flesh-and-blood one. She was the spirit of a cat who'd passed long ago.

"That day, at the pizza place," Lara said, "is that when you ended things with Megan?"

"Yes, though I waited until I drove her back to her apartment. It didn't seem fair to tell her in the car." He shook his head. "By the time I walked her inside, she'd done a complete one-eighty. She started to sob. She was totally repentant for the way she'd behaved. She told me she was going to find out who that woman was and send her a huge bouquet of flowers."

"Maybe she really was sorry," Lara said.

Gideon threw up his arms. "I'm sure she was. I never doubted that. It was her meltdown that was so unexpected."

Lara stared into her coffee cup. "She told me that you warned her against crashing Chancer's party, but that she didn't listen. She said it was the dumbest thing she'd ever done."

"She told you that?"

"Yup."

"I guess that's another example, then," Gideon reflected. "Bursting into Chancer's home and losing her cool at the party. It's part of the same pattern."

Not quite, Lara thought.

When Megan lost her temper in the pizza parlor, she hadn't planned it in advance. But crashing Chancer's birthday party? Flinging accusations at him in front of a roomful of guests?

That was premeditated.

Lara was so confused. She didn't know what to think.

Gideon reached for her hand and wrapped it in his own. "Lara, I don't want any of this to come between us. Not Cutler, and not Megan. They're outsiders. They don't have anything to do with us. They shouldn't even be in our orbit."

It was a strange way to put it, but Lara agreed.

"Why don't we reboot," he said, gently squeezing her hand. "Let's go back to the way things were before Megan showed up in town on Friday. I'll tell Cutler I don't want to be kept in the loop. You can forget you ever met Megan. Bottom line, she's not our problem, Lara."

Lara wished it were that easy. She needed him to understand why that wasn't possible.

"Gideon, remember the time you told me about a title search you did? You said you searched back in time further than you had to because something about the starting deed bothered you?"

"Yes, it was the Fitzgibbons search. I could have started the search with the nineteen sixty-two quitclaim into the daughter. Something about it bothered me, though, so I went back further. When I did, I discovered a huge gap. There were two missing heirs."

"Exactly. And remember I asked you why you couldn't just ignore the gap and pretend you started the search with that deed in 'sixty-two?"

He chuckled. "I guess so. Where are you going with this?"

"Because of how you answered me. You said you couldn't ignore it because you were already *tainted with knowledge*. That's the term you used. You said it was a legal phrase. It meant that you couldn't 'unknow' what you now knew."

Gideon slowly shook his head. "My God, Lara, you're comparing apples and oranges. Once I knew about the two missing heirs, I was ethically bound not to ignore them. I don't see how that relates to your asking questions of total strangers because you think someone got away with murder."

Lara's heart sank. "Then I can't explain it any better."

Should she tell him about Blue? How the cat that no one else could see had cozied up to Megan as if she were trying to get a point across to Lara?

"Honey," Gideon said in a low voice, "is there a cat involved in this latest quest of yours? Does this have something to do with Blue?"

Latest quest. He made it sound like she was on a treasure hunt. But it was his patronizing tone she didn't appreciate.

Still, she should have known he'd figure it out. Gideon knew her all too well.

"It does, in a way. Yesterday, when Megan was sitting on our sofa, Munster and Panda were all over her, and it was obvious she loved the attention. But then Blue suddenly jumped up, almost onto her shoulder. It took me by surprise. I couldn't figure out why."

"Maybe you're reading too much into it," he offered.

"Maybe." Again, that tone. It was so unlike Gideon.

For the first time, Lara wondered if Gideon truly believed in Blue's existence. Was it possible he'd been humoring her all this time?

"Listen," she said abruptly, "you have work to do, and I'm taking up your time." She rose from her seat and took her last swallow of coffee.

Gideon grabbed her napkin and wrapped up the remains of her muffin, slipping it into her tote. "Let's talk again later, okay? I'm not sure we really resolved anything."

Lara's smile was flat. She couldn't keep the tightness from her voice. "We'll see. I've got a ton of projects lined up for today, plus this is an adoption day."

"How's Sienna doing?"

"Really good. Munster adores her. I'm hopeful that the right mom or dad or family will come along for her."

"They will. Don't worry."

They parted with a light embrace, not their usual polar bear hug.

Tears stung Lara's eyes as she headed outside to her car. She forced them back. She didn't want Sherry to know that anything was wrong.

Not that she could fool her bestie. Sherry could spot a dried tear across a crowded coffee shop from twenty paces.

Countdown to wedding day: seventeen days.

Which reminded Lara—she wanted to have a chat with Pastor Folger. It was one more thing she could do to help Sherry—if it worked out as she hoped.

She suddenly changed her mind about going to the coffee shop. She was glad, now, that she'd driven to Gideon's instead of hoofing it in the cold. This was the perfect time to stop over at Saint Lucy's and have a chat with Pastor Folger. With any luck, she'd catch the pastor at the tail end of his eight-thirty service.

As she drove toward the church, her mind spun like a top from her conversation with Gideon. One thing Gideon had been right about—they hadn't really resolved anything. Were they at an impasse? A point of no return?

Once again, she couldn't help wondering, in the pit of her heart, if Gideon fully believed in her spirit cat. Aunt Fran and Kayla did, without reservation—Lara was sure of that.

Gideon had always professed his belief in Blue, but now Lara had her doubts.

Her thoughts switched to Megan—the person who'd started all this drama. Gideon's tale of Megan losing her cool with that poor older woman was disturbing, for sure. While Lara was no shrink, she couldn't help wondering if Megan suffered from some form of anxiety disorder.

She pulled into the parking lot of Saint Lucy's, close to the front entrance to the white-steepled church. On weekdays, only a few faithful attended the morning service. Lara locked the car, then hurried up the granite steps and into the vestibule. From there she entered the church and slipped into a pew at the rear.

Her timing was perfect. Pastor Folger had just given the final blessing and concluded the service. He took his prayer book from the podium and strode up the center aisle. Along the way, he stopped to greet a few parishioners. Lara couldn't help smiling. He had a kindly way with people that she'd always admired.

The pastor's pale blue eyes widened when he spotted Lara. "Lara, what a nice surprise. You don't usually attend on weekdays."

"I know. I didn't really attend today, either," she confessed. "Pastor, do you have a few minutes to spare for a chat? I probably should have called first, but—"

"No need, Lara." He looked at his watch. "I don't have an appointment until eleven, so right now I'm free as a bird. Why don't you come into my office, but you'll have to forgive the mess. I'm afraid I haven't tidied it up in a while."

"No problem."

She followed him past the confessional and through a doorway at the rear of the church. After a short walk down a lighted corridor, he opened the door to what Lara could only describe as sheer chaos.

Mess was an understatement. Lara couldn't imagine how the pastor functioned in the rubble that was his desk. Papers sat in piles along three sides. A stack of books, mostly with religious themes, teetered in one corner. Lara was afraid that if she breathed too hard they'd topple over. Amazingly, there was a free chair adjacent to the one in front of the desk.

"Please, Lara, sit. Can I get you a cup of coffee? A parishioner donated one of those newfangled machines with the pods. I'm finally getting the hang of it," he added with a chuckle.

She smiled. "No thanks. I won't take up too much of your time, but I do have a question."

He sat in his chair and faced her with a smile. "Fire away."

"I'm sure you're familiar with the Bowkers. They own the coffee shop in town."

He nodded. "I surely am. Daisy Bowker makes the best cranberry muffins in New Hampshire."

Lara grinned. "I agree. Anyway, Sherry Bowker, who's my best friend, is getting married on Valentine's Day. It's a Friday, so they're having the ceremony in the evening…in the coffee shop."

Another nod.

Lara squirmed on her chair. "They want to get married in the place where they first met, which is why they chose the coffee shop. They've arranged for a justice of the peace to perform the ceremony."

The pastor located a pencil under one of the smaller stacks of papers. He picked it up and twirled it.

"The thing is," Lara went on, "the groom's mom is less than thrilled with the venue, if you know what I mean."

Pastor Folger nodded sagely. "She wants them to get married in church."

"Exactly. Which is not going to happen. So, my thought was, do pastors ever perform ceremonies outside of the church?"

He thought a moment. "Some do, yes. But I thought you said they already had a justice of the peace lined up?"

"They do, but here's what I was thinking. If the JP is okay with it, would you be willing to co-officiate the ceremony?"

The pastor swiveled in his chair and tilted his gaze toward the ceiling. "I would have to think about this, Lara. It is possible, yes, but may I ask you a question now?"

"Of course." *Oh God.*

"Why is it that you're speaking on behalf of Sherry and her fiancé? Is there some reason they don't want to ask me directly?"

Lara sighed. "I think Sherry's worried because she doesn't attend church services. She's afraid you'll refuse them on that alone."

He sat back in his chair and rested his elbows on the arms. "In my humble opinion, Lara, faith lies within the individuals." He tapped his heart. "The church is a vehicle for observing that faith, but it's not the only one. Why don't you have Sherry call me and set up an appointment? If she's willing to do that, we may well be able to work something out."

Yes!

"Thank you so much, Pastor. I'll do that. She'll be working all day, but I'll stop in and see her after the coffee shop closes. I'm really grateful for your offer."

He glanced around his desk and began peeking under piles. "I have business cards somewhere...never mind, I'll write down my number."

While he searched for a slip of paper, Lara reached into her tote and pulled out her cell phone. "How about I text it to myself. That way I won't lose it."

"Ah, the perfect solution."

Lara took his number and thanked him profusely. It was probably overkill, but she was so relieved that one thing went right today, she felt like dancing a jig.

She couldn't wait to tell Sherry.

She texted her friend, and they agreed to meet at the coffee shop right before closing time.

Chapter 13

Kayla showed up shortly after lunch. Aunt Fran immediately put on the teakettle.

"Sorry, I meant to get here earlier," Kayla said. "I got yakking on the phone in my car and lost track of time." She blushed a bright pink.

"Chatting with someone special?" Lara teased.

"Sort of. It's the guy I told you about. From my class?" Kayla peeled off her coat, gloves, and scarf just in time to have Panda nearly leap into her arms.

Smiling at them, Aunt Fran poured boiling water into a mug and dropped in a tea bag. "Ah, yes, but I don't think you told us his name."

Kayla shrugged and pushed at her glasses. "I didn't want to jinx anything. I still don't, so I might wait until I know him a little better. The whole thing might tank, you know?"

After a short tea break, they spent the next hour tidying up the meet-and-greet room for adoption hours and grooming the cats, in the event anyone showed up. Tuesdays were usually slow, but anything was possible.

"While we wait, let's work on that editorial," Lara suggested. She needed to push Gideon out of her thoughts. Temporarily, at least. She fetched her tablet, and she and Kayla spread out on the table in the meet-and-greet room.

"I read last week about two cats who were dumped in a landfill," Kayla began, her expression darkening. "They survived, but only because someone heard them crying and rushed in to rescue them."

"I know which case you mean," Lara said. "I saw it on the news. There was a no-kill shelter only a few miles away from there, too. If they'd waited till morning, they could have brought the cats there."

Kayla's eyes blazed with anger. "Why are people so horrible? Sometimes it makes me sick."

"I know what you're saying, but luckily, most people know better. It's the few who don't that I hope to reach. That's why I want to get this editorial in the paper. If it helps to save even one cat or dog, it'll be worth it."

They worked together on the piece for a while, Panda in Kayla's lap and Munster in Lara's. Shortly after two, a pair of faces peeked through the glass pane—a woman and a little girl. The woman smiled and rang the doorbell.

Kayla gently set Panda on the floor and raced over to let them in. "Hello," she greeted. "My name is Kayla. Welcome to the High Cliff Shelter for Cats. Come on in and have a seat."

"Thank you," the woman said, tucking her gloves inside the pockets of her puffy pink jacket. "I'm Phoebe, and this is my daughter, Pia." She gazed down at a girl of about seven. The child had the same big brown eyes and dark curls as her mom. "Can you say hello, Pia?"

Pia nodded at the floor. "Hello," she said shyly.

Lara introduced herself and offered to take their jackets. Pia stuffed her little red mittens into her jacket pockets.

"Nah, we'll keep them on," Phoebe said. "It's such a pain taking them on and off. Hey, look, I'll tell you why we're here. My daughter's in the second grade, and recently the school invited someone from one of the local humane societies to speak to the class. The speaker explained what they did, and why it was so important to spay and neuter your pets. The problem is"—she squeezed her daughter's shoulders—"Pia got very, very upset when the woman brought up, you know, *euthanizing*." She whispered the last word.

Lara's heart wrenched. No wonder the child looked so forlorn.

She invited them both to sit, urging them to have a glass of juice or cocoa. Pia decided on a glass of milk, while her mom opted for apple juice.

A smile emerged from the little girl when she saw Panda gazing up at her. "Mommy, can I hold that cat?"

"Let's ask first," Phoebe said, raising her eyebrows at Lara.

"Of course you can," Lara said. "Panda is very friendly. Plus, he has some of the longest whiskers I've ever seen!"

Lara lifted the black-and-white cat and set him gently on Pia's lap. Pia giggled when Panda's motor revved up. She wrapped her little hands around Panda's chunky form. "Look, Mommy, he's purring!"

"He sure is," Phoebe said, winking at her daughter. She turned to the women. "Anyway, I thought that if Pia saw how a shelter actually worked, she'd feel a lot better about it." She bounced her gaze around the meet-and-greet room. It landed on the corkboard that showed scads of photos of the shelter's successful adoptions. "I have to say, I think I chose the right one. I don't see any cages, though. Is the shelter part of the house?"

"The shelter *is* the house," Kayla piped in. "The cats have free range and get only the best of care. This is the room where we greet visitors and introduce them to cats that are available for adoption."

Lara smiled. She loved it when Kayla rattled off her spiel about the shelter. Kayla was immensely proud of the care she gave to the cats. The shelter was firmly embedded in her heart and soul.

Phoebe winked at Lara as if to say, *You'd better answer this right.* "So, what happens if a cat doesn't get adopted right away?"

"Most cats don't get adopted immediately," Lara explained. "Sometimes it takes a while for a kitty to find their forever home. That's because we always make sure we send them to the *perfect* home. But while they wait, they stay here with us as part of the household, where they're loved and cared for. No matter how long it takes."

Pia, who'd clearly been absorbing everything Lara said, looked over at her. "Even if it takes a year?" she asked softly.

Lara nodded. "Even if it takes more than a year."

Pia pulled Panda closer. "Mommy?" She tugged at the sleeve of her mother's jacket. "Can we come back and get this cat after we move?"

Phoebe's face softened. "I'm not sure, honey. We'll have to run it by Daddy first." To Lara and Kayla she said, "We're moving to a larger house next month. Maybe after we get settled, we'll come back. You... have other cats, right?"

Lara knew exactly what she was thinking. By the time they were ready to adopt, Panda might be gone.

"We do, and we always will."

Lara thought about trekking upstairs to fetch Amber and Sienna, but then changed her mind. Once Phoebe and Pia were ready to adopt, she'd be sure they got acquainted with all of the cats ready for placement.

Before they left, Kayla gave them a brochure about their "read to a cat" Sundays, as well as some other helpful printouts. One was the sheet identifying plants and other substances that were poisonous to cats. Lara had sketched the illustrations herself.

With Phoebe's permission, Kayla also presented Pia with a cat-shaped sugar cookie, frosted in black and white to resemble Panda. The little girl left with a happy smile.

"Poor little kid," Kayla said after they left. "I remember myself at that age. I was so sensitive to anything that had to do with animals. I swear, I cried myself to sleep half the time thinking about everything."

Lara understood exactly what she meant. "It's a fine line, isn't it? We want to teach kids to be kind and caring, but we don't want to make them feel sad about the way others behave. Not until they're old enough to understand it, anyway. There's no easy answer, I guess."

Kayla stared at her. "Do you ever think about having kids? I mean, not now, but someday?"

Lara waved a hand at her. "Get real. You know I'm not ready for that."

Except that I'm going to be thirty in a month, and I'm not even close to starting a family.

"Yeah, but someday, right? I mean, you've got the perfect temperament for being a mom. You're smart, you're patient, you're creative. Me, I think I'm gonna stick with cats. Easier all around that way."

Lara laughed. "Don't be surprised if you change your mind one day."

Kayla shrugged. "What will be will be."

They went back to working on the editorial, but Lara's thoughts went off on a sidetrack. The printout about household poisons stuck in her mind.

She'd done her homework before putting it together. So many everyday plants, both indoor and out, were deadly—not only to cats but to humans. The same went for household products, such as detergent and mothballs.

Was it one of those poisons that killed Wayne Chancer? Had the medical examiner figured out exactly what killed him?

Chancer had been dead for over three days now. As far as Lara knew, the crime lab was still conducting tests on everything they'd collected at his home. If they'd made any progress, it hadn't been reported. Maybe the police were keeping mum until they had something definite to announce.

"Oh! Lara, I completely forgot to show you something," Kayla said. "Give me a sec. I have to run out to my car." She dashed outside without putting on her coat. A minute later, she returned holding a cellophane bag filled with what appeared to be colorful snacks. Lara recognized them—they were the ones Kayla had bought the day before at the Peach Crate.

Kayla grinned. "These are so cool. Wait till you see them." She handed the bag to Lara.

"They look like fortune cookies," Lara said, intrigued. She removed the twist tie and peeked into the bag.

"Take one out," Kayla urged. "They're made from fruit."

Lara removed a bright red fortune cookie, which was twice the size of a typical one. She sniffed it. "Mmm, smells like strawberry. It looks like they're made from those fruity rolled-up snacks kids eat."

"They are. Open it—there's a message inside each one."

Lara opened the cookie and pulled out a fortune typed on pink paper. "Kindness never goes out of style," she read. "Hey, I like that."

"Taste it. They're good."

Lara bit into the cookie. It was delicious. "Wow. It's tasty," she said, after she swallowed. "I can see why kids would love these."

"I thought they'd be fun to give to my nieces and nephews on Valentine's Day," Kayla said. "But that's not all. Look at this." She reached for the bag and turned it over, then pointed to the label.

Lara examined the label, and her jaw dropped. "Well, isn't this interesting? Custom fortune cookies created with you in mind by Tina Tanaka," she read aloud. "It gives a Web site address and a Facebook page."

"I thought you'd find that interesting," Kayla said, her eyes lighting up. "Tina Tanaka seems to have a nice little business going for herself."

Lara nodded, thinking. She pulled her tablet over and went to the Web site listed on the label. Almost immediately, a beautifully designed site came up. "Oh my, look at this. Tina makes custom fortune cookies for all sorts of occasions—including weddings."

Sherry had been looking for something creative to give out as wedding favors. These might be just the ticket!

"Are you thinking of Sherry?" Kayla asked.

Lara smiled. "I sure am. She was complaining that the foil-wrapped chocolate hearts she was planning to use were too boring. We might have just stumbled on the perfect favors for those darling little boxes she bought. I'm so glad you landed on these in the gourmet shop."

"'Course there *is* a slight problem," Kayla pointed out. "You're not exactly Tina Tanaka's favorite person right now."

"True, but I don't have to be, do I? Sherry can get in touch with her directly—if she's interested." Lara grinned. "And I just bet she will be."

Still intrigued by Tina's Web site, Lara checked out the other drop-down links. Traditional fortune cookies could be special-ordered in nearly any color in the rainbow. The available colors, and flavors, were as varied as the ones in Lara's watercolor palette.

An entire section was devoted to weddings. Lara especially liked the fortune cookies whose bottom edges had been dipped in a vanilla glaze and then coated in pearly white sprinkles. Knowing Sherry, though, the ones with the sparkly red sugar coating would be more to her taste. They'd be perfect for a Valentine's Day wedding.

"You can either create your own messages or have them done by Tina," Lara noted. "I'm seeing Sherry right after the coffee shop closes, so I'll show her this Web site. It says most orders can be shipped within a week, so she has plenty of time, if she's interested."

Kayla was quiet for a moment. Then she said, "I didn't like it when Tina said that stuff about getting married on Valentine's Day being cliché. What did you think about that?"

"I think she was just being snarky," Lara said, "because she thought I was spying on her. I still feel awful about how that all went down yesterday."

Kayla smiled down at Panda, who had strolled over and was gazing up at her. She reached down and lifted the cat into her lap. "Yeah, but Lara, what if she *did* kill Wayne Chancer?"

Lara sat back in her chair and shoved her tablet aside. "Then the police will figure it out and she'll be arrested for his murder. That's all I have to say about that."

Chapter 14

"Hey, what's cookin'?" Sherry said, setting a mug of hot cocoa in front of Lara. A glob of tiny marshmallows floated on top. "You sounded kind of excited on the phone."

They'd snagged a table at the back section of the now-closed coffee shop, where they could relax and have a long chat. Sherry set out a plate of cookies. Lara snagged a frosted heart pierced with an arrow and bit off the tip.

"I have some news, and I think it's good," Lara said. She told Sherry about her conversation with Pastor Folger, ending by giving her his contact number.

Sherry's face lit up like a string of Christmas bulbs. "Oh my God, you're like, a miracle worker. He actually said he'd consider doing the ceremony with our JP?"

Lara smiled. "He did. He also wanted to know why you didn't ask him yourself, but I explained that you were nervous about approaching him."

"This is like, such wonderful news." Sherry entered the phone number into her cell phone. "What time do you think I should call him? Would six be too early? Is eight too late? I mean, do you know when he eats dinner? I wouldn't want to interrupt him."

Lara laughed slightly. "I don't either, but don't stress yourself out, okay? He's a very nice man, and he'll be expecting your call. I'm guessing he'll want you and David to meet with him in person, so be prepared to set up an appointment."

"We can do that," Sherry said. Her eyes glistened. "Lara, thank you for going to the pastor for us. I don't know why I was so chicken. If this works out, we might even be able to please Loretta for a change."

It bothered Lara that her friend had to work so hard to please her soon-to-be mother-in-law. "*She* should be pleased at the idea of having *you* for a daughter-in-law."

"Yeah, well, don't count on that happening any time soon."

"Hey, I have something else to show you," Lara said. "Something very, very fun." She pulled her tablet out of her tote and opened to Tina Tanaka's fortune cookie Web site. "Kayla stumbled on these when we were at that gourmet shop in Bakewell yesterday. Aren't they sweet? I thought—"

"Wait a minute. You were in Bakewell yesterday?"

"Yup. Kayla and I took a ride. There's a bridal shop there, and I found a stunning pair of shoes to go with my dress. Wait till you see them—your eyes will pop out."

"Did you bring them?"

"No, the bridal shop had to order them. I should be able to pick them up in a few days. Anyway, look at these, Sher. What do you think?" She passed the tablet across the table and watched her friend's eyes widen.

Sherry almost leaped off her chair. "Oh my gosh, these would make the most wonderful wedding favors!"

"Exactly what I thought."

Sherry tapped and swiped her way through the site. "Look at all the choices. Wait till David sees these. He's going to go nuts!" She grabbed Lara's arm. "You're the best, you know it?"

"Yeah, I know. There is one tiny little thing," Lara cautioned. "Don't let on to Tina Tanaka that I recommended her to you." She explained what happened at the bridal shop the day before.

"Wow. You must've really ticked her off." Sherry slid Lara's tablet over to her. "Um, Lara, you're not going around asking questions about the murder, are you?" Sherry asked, her tone tinged with suspicion.

Lara chewed her lip. So far, the only people she'd talked with who knew Chancer were Felicia Tristany and Tina Tanaka. Of the two, only Tina was a possible suspect.

"Not...exactly," Lara said.

Sherry pointed a finger at her. "I can tell just by the way you said that, Miss Girl Detective, that you're already getting way too nosy for your own good. Now, I want you to stop it. I'm getting married in less than three weeks, and you're going to be standing beside me with a bouquet of red carnations and baby's breath, and you're not going to get into trouble before then. Got it?"

Lara laughed, but the part about getting into trouble made her squirm. "Got it. I promise. But I think you're blowing things a bit out of proportion."

"Out of proportion! Oh my God, have you forgotten your track record?" Sherry sat back and gave Lara a hard look. "Listen, Lara, asking questions can be dangerous. Especially if you ask them of the wrong people. If you haven't figured that out yet, then you have a very short memory."

What could Lara say? How could she explain that a cat no one else could see had led her to solving murders? As close as she was to Sherry, she'd never confided in her about Blue. That day would come, but she wasn't ready. Not yet.

"All right, I hear everything you're saying. But nothing bad is going to happen, okay?"

Sherry gave a crisp nod. "It better not. Because if I hear you've been playing Nancy Drew again, I'll come over to that shelter and strangle you myself."

* * * *

Neither Lara nor Aunt Fran was in the mood to prepare a meal that evening. They heated a can of chicken vegetable soup, warmed some whole wheat rolls, and shared it over a pot of orange spice tea.

"You've been a bit secretive lately," Aunt Fran said when they were through eating. "Anything going on that I should know about?"

Lara shrugged and looked away. Her aunt knew her too well not to know when something was up.

"For starters, Gideon's annoyed with me for listening to Megan. Who, by the way, I haven't heard from at all today. She showed up yesterday in a whirlwind of drama, and now she's pulled a disappearing act."

"I'd say that's good news," Aunt Fran offered. "I'm sorry to say this, Lara, but I don't think the young woman is very stable. You mentioned that she lives with a kindly aunt and uncle. Let them take over and help her."

"I know, and I agree with everything you're saying," Lara said.

Then what's bugging me?

Even Blue hadn't shown herself since Megan's visit.

Lara couldn't explain her feelings, not even to herself. Something about Wayne Chancer's death was drawing her to Bakewell. That was the only way she could describe it.

She remembered her promise to Sherry. *Nothing bad is going to happen.*

"I'll have to go back to pick up the shoes I ordered," Lara said. "But after that, I'm done. Bakewell will just be a dot in my rearview mirror."

Aunt Fran smiled. "Good."

Lara cleared the dishes while Aunt Fran sat at the table with Dolce and glanced at the paper.

After Lara dried her hands, she peeked at her cell phone. She'd texted Gideon a few times during the day, but he hadn't texted back. Nor had he called.

Was this the beginning of the end? The thought made her heart sink like a stone to the pit of her stomach.

"I think I'll work on Amy's painting for a while," Lara said, trying to sound cheery. "Not really the painting, but the sketches."

Her aunt looked up. "How's it coming?"

"Slowly. Amy's not in a rush, but I'd like to make some progress this week."

Lara hated to admit it, but so far she'd only managed to complete a few preliminary sketches. And she hadn't even been thrilled with those.

She went into her studio and closed the door. The photo Amy had given her was on her worktable. It was a picture of Amy's sprawling farmhouse, taken in the dead of winter—Amy's favorite season. The sky was a vivid blue and the sun a pale yellow. The snow looked fresh and clean. Adjacent to the farmhouse was an open pasture—an area where dairy cows once grazed. Amy had asked Lara to paint her three gorgeous dogs running across the field through newly fallen snow.

Lara studied the pic again. This time, she focused on some of the farmhouse details. Although the Australian shepherds would be the focus of the painting, she knew that small details could make a watercolor pop with realism.

Painted white with black shutters, the farmhouse boasted a towering chimney on one side and a wraparound porch along the front and opposite side. The landscaping was minimal. Along the front of the house, patches of shriveled leaves were all that remained of the flowers that had bloomed there in the spring and summer.

Lara grabbed her sketch pad and her colored pencils. She wanted to put together three or four different rough sketches for Amy to have a look at. If the veterinarian favored one, Lara would run with it.

By seven thirty, she'd completed only one sketch and part of a second. She hadn't been able to concentrate. Her mind had been roaming in all directions.

Over the last hour and a half, she'd checked her phone at least a dozen times. Still no word from Gideon. It wasn't like him. He'd seemed okay when she left his office that morning. Had something else happened during the day?

It was close to eight when her cell rang. She slumped when she saw the screen. Instead of Gideon, it was a number she didn't recognize.

"Is this the High Cliff Shelter?" a woman's voice asked. "I called the regular number, but it said to call this one."

"It is," Lara said, thinking the voice sounded familiar. "This is the emergency number." The message Lara recorded on the shelter's answering machine gave her private number in the event of a cat emergency. "What can I help you with?"

"This isn't an emergency or anything. This is Tina Tanaka. I'm sure you remember me."

Lara bolted straight up in her chair. "Tina. Yes, of course I remember you."

"First off, I'm sorry I called the shelter's number. I left your private number at Valeria's, but with the salon locked I didn't have access to it."

"That's okay. What can I do for you, Tina?"

"I…look, I checked you out online," Tina said, sounding contrite. "I mean, *really* checked you out this time. I'm sorry I came on so strong yesterday. I thought you were accusing me of murder."

"It was the furthest thing from my mind," Lara fibbed. "I really love those shoes I bought at Valeria's."

"They should be in by Friday. I'll give you a call as soon as we get them. Hey, I probably have a lot of nerve asking this, but would you be able to meet me tomorrow morning? For a quick cup of coffee?"

Uh-oh. Killer alert.

"That might be possible, but can I ask why?"

"It's hard to explain. I promise, I won't take up much of your time. I just…want to ask you something."

Lara knew she'd be crazy to say yes. Hadn't she promised Sherry nothing would happen to her?

"Okay, sure. Did you have a place in mind?" *A nice public place?*

"There's a diner in downtown Bakewell. They tend to empty out after the breakfast crunch is over. Is ten thirty okay? I don't have to be at the bridal shop till noon."

Relief flooded her. Nothing bad could happen to her in the diner, right?

"I know exactly where that is," Lara said. "See you at ten thirty tomorrow."

After she disconnected, a blade of worry stabbed at her. What was she doing?

Tina hadn't said why she wanted to talk to Lara. Maybe it had nothing to do with Chancer's murder. Maybe Lara was reading way too much into the phone call. Maybe Tina wanted to adopt a cat from the shelter.

Maybe, maybe, maybe...

Tina had definitely sounded cryptic on the phone. Lara couldn't imagine what the young woman wanted to chat with her about—unless she had an idea who killed Chancer. If that was the case, Lara would refer her directly to the police.

Lara straightened her work space and began putting away her sketches. Her cell rang, and she jumped. This time, Gideon's smiling image appeared.

"Hey, I've been trying to reach you," she said, a telltale tremor in her voice.

"Lara, I got a call from Megan today."

Shocked at the lack of a greeting, and by his gruffness, she said, "You did?"

"I did. She called to sing your praises, and to tell me how wonderful you were to want to help her. I'm...I don't know. I'm blown away, I guess. I don't know what to say anymore."

Lara felt a surge of emotions well up in her chest. Anger. Disappointment. Heartbreak.

She had to pull herself together. "It's interesting that she called you, Gideon, because I haven't heard a word from her all day."

"That's because she thinks you're hot on the case. She's living in a fantasy world, Lara. In her mind, you're going to find the killer and absolve her from all wrongdoing."

"I never meant to give her that impression. I told her that she needed to talk to her lawyer, not to me."

Gideon huffed into the phone. "Well, whatever you said, she thinks you're out there hunting down suspects so she can be in the clear."

Lara closed her eyes, trying to remember exactly how she left things with Megan. She recalled trying to sound vague, so that Megan wouldn't count on her for too much.

"Best I can remember, I told her I'd keep my eyes and ears open." Lara was pretty sure that was how she'd worded it.

"Well, in her mind you're running with the ball all the way to the finish line. She must have found out that you were in Bakewell yesterday."

If that was the case, Lara wondered who'd told her. Had Tina Tanaka been the squealer? Maybe that's why Tina wanted to meet her at the diner on Wednesday—to talk about Megan.

Right now, the chill coming through the line from Gideon was hurtful, and unacceptable. Lara boosted her courage. "Gideon, right now I'm feeling so much anger coming from you that I don't want to stay on the phone any longer." Her voice rattled slightly. "I'm…I'm sorry, but I'm going to say good night."

She disconnected before he could respond—something she'd never done before. Tears leaked from her eyes, but she swiped them back.

A new resolve took hold of her. Whether or not she helped Megan, it would be her decision and hers alone.

She was gathering up the last of her sketches when the photo of Amy's farmhouse suddenly flew to the floor. Lara reached to pick it up, only to find a certain Ragdoll cat holding it down with one cocoa-colored paw.

Heart thumping, Lara held her breath. "What is it you want me to see?" she whispered to her spirit cat.

Instead of meeting Lara's gaze, Blue stared down at the picture. Then the cat moved slightly backward, and Lara lifted the photo off the floor.

She studied it, trying to see if she missed something she should've seen earlier. She examined every detail until her eyes nearly crossed.

Nothing came to her.

As she always did after a Blue sighting, she questioned whether or not she was losing her mind. The possibility that her spirit cat was no more than a hallucination was always there, taunting her.

What troubled her most was that Sherry's wedding was creeping closer every day. If she and Gideon weren't together, it would kill Sherry. Sherry would feel so bad. It would create a cloud over her wedding.

Lara couldn't let that happen. Somehow, she had to patch things up with Gideon. Even if it was a temporary fix, she had to do it for Sherry's sake.

The ping of a text made her jump.

Lara, please call me. We still need to talk.

Lara debated with herself, but then called him back. This time, Gideon sounded subdued. Not himself, but not combative either. He agreed to call her the next day so they could talk things out. Maybe they'd both have "clearer heads" by then, he offered.

Lara didn't like the implication. Was he saying that, up to this point, Lara hadn't been thinking clearly?

"Fine. I'll wait to hear from you."

"Okay. Love you," Gideon mumbled.

Lara didn't bother responding. Gideon had already disconnected.

Chapter 15

At the coffee shop the next morning, Sherry was a bundle of excited chatter. So much so that she was mixing up orders.

Lara giggled when she gave one customer a cranberry muffin instead of the blueberry he'd asked for. He happily accepted a second muffin free of charge. Another customer seated at the counter got pancakes instead of waffles. He shrugged affably, drowned them in maple syrup, and dug in with gusto.

Luckily, Jill, their sole employee, was there to pick up the slack. With her short dark hair, a ruby-colored jewel jutting from one pierced eyebrow, she waved at Lara from a distance. A tray of dirty dishes balanced on one shoulder, she shoved her way through the swinging door into the kitchen.

"So, tell me, what's happening?" Lara said when her friend took a breather.

"First of all, David and I have an appointment with Pastor Folger at five this afternoon. I only spoke to him for a few minutes on the phone, but I got super good vibes from him."

"Sher, that's great!" Lara sipped from her warm coffee mug. "Anything else?"

Sherry grinned. "You bet. Last night, David and I looked at that fortune cookie Web site. Oh my God, the choices! We chose the ones we wanted and ordered them. They'll be here by next Thursday! Plenty of time to make up the favor boxes."

Sherry's news was good all around. Lara was thrilled for her. "Don't forget, I'll help you put the favor boxes together if you want."

"I'm counting on it," Sherry said. Her gaze softened, "Lara, I can't tell you how many people have called me about the invitation. One of Mom's buds is even going to have hers framed. David and I will treasure ours forever."

Lara had hand-painted, in watercolor, each of Sherry's twenty-six wedding invitations. It was a labor of love, and the results had been spectacular. It was the one thing she'd been able to do for her bestie that was unique and special.

"That's nice to hear, Sher. I really enjoyed doing them." Lara popped the last bite of her blueberry muffin into her mouth and swallowed. "I won't be able to linger today. Lots to do at the shelter." *Not to mention a drive to Bakewell to meet Tina.*

Sherry frowned. "You okay? Your eyes look a little weird today."

Yup. She spotted the puffy eyes.

"It was one of those nights," Lara said. "Not much sleep. A lot on my mind, I guess."

Sherry lifted one hand to her hip. "Just remember your promise. None of that girl detective stuff, okay?"

"I remember," Lara said, hedging her answer. "Love to your mom!"

She waved goodbye to Jill, gave Sherry a quick hug, and scooted out the door.

The temperature had made it into the thirties—a heat wave compared to the prior several days. Kayla had decided to take Wednesday off, promising to return on Thursday. With her classes out this week, she wanted a day to catch up on her own projects. Lara suspected she was hoping to spend it with the new man in her life.

Every Wednesday afternoon, Lara and Aunt Fran joined Mary Newman, a local merchant, and Brooke Weston, a high school student, for their classics book club. Initially they used to meet at the coffee shop, but now they met at Aunt Fran's. Brooke was an occasional volunteer at the shelter, but these days she spent most of her free time babysitting to earn money for clothes.

This week they'd be discussing Ray Bradbury's *Fahrenheit 451*, so Lara wanted to be sure to get home in time for the meeting.

"Shall I pick up some snacks for book club?" Lara asked Aunt Fran as she was leaving.

Her aunt was seated at the kitchen table, a cat—Dolce—in her lap and her laptop set up in front of her. "It's Mary's turn to bring treats, but if you see something irresistible in your travels, don't hesitate to buy them."

"Gotcha," Lara said. "How's the book coming?"

Aunt Fran grinned. "Slowly, but I love these quiet winter mornings to write. I feel inspired." Her smile faded. "Lara, you look a bit worn out today. Is everything all right?"

Lara forced back a lump in her throat. "Truth be told, everything's a big jumble right now. Gideon's mad at me for wanting to help Megan."

"That's because he's worried about your safety," her aunt said quietly. "Lara, why is it that you want to help her? Is there something you're not telling me?"

Lara lifted her tote higher on her shoulder. How could she explain the kinds of strange things that had been going through her head?

Her dreams the night before had kept her awake half the night. She kept seeing a sea of people crowding Bakewell's quaint town center. She remembered feeling alone and isolated. Desperate to find someone she knew to give her comfort, she'd searched the faces. But the moment she spotted a familiar one, it morphed into someone different. No one was who they seemed.

She knew they were only dreams, that she shouldn't read anything into them. But she couldn't seem to evict them from her head.

"It's complicated, Aunt Fran. Let's just say, I'm getting vibes from beyond this realm."

Her aunt mulled that for a moment, then said, "Blue?"

Lara nodded, and a tidal wave of guilt drenched her. She hadn't told her aunt where she was headed, only that she had a few errands to run and would be at least a few hours. Maybe it was time to 'fess up.

"Aunt Fran, I'm not really doing errands this morning. I'm heading to Bakewell to meet Tina Tanaka at the diner. She called me last night and wants to talk to me about something. I have no idea what it is. The diner's a public place. Nothing's going to happen."

"Oh, Lara." Her aunt looked stricken.

"I know, but—" She shook her head. "I wish I could explain it better. Something about Bakewell is drawing me there, and it's not just Megan. I think the murder is only part of it."

There. She'd said it.

The thoughts that had been getting under skin since last night's crazy dreams.

"I thought Tina Tanaka was angry with you?" Aunt Fran said.

"She was, but I guess she checked me out and decided I was a good guy, not a bad guy. I have no idea what she wants to talk about. I can only guess it has something to do with Wayne Chancer's death."

Aunt Fran held up both hands, palms out. "I'm not going to try to talk you out of it. I'll say what I always say—be aware of your surroundings. Keep your cell phone on you at all times."

Lara chuckled. "Aunt Fran. I'm not going into a war zone. I'm only going there to find out why Tina wants to see me."

"I know." Her aunt lifted Dolce and set him gently on the floor. Then she rose from her chair, went over to Lara, and hugged her. "I am on your side, no matter what. Always remember that."

Tears sprang to Lara's eyes. "I know you are. Believe me, I know."

Growing up, it was Aunt Fran who'd always been there for her. Who'd nurtured her love of art and taught her to care for cats. Lara's own mom, Brenda, had envied their close bond. It'd had a sad effect on their family dynamics.

"I'll call you after I leave Bakewell," Lara promised. "And I'll be back in plenty of time for the book club."

* * * *

The ride to Bakewell took less than forty minutes this time. Knowing the route, and exactly where to turn, had helped shorten the drive.

Lara spotted Tina the moment she stepped inside the diner. Tina waved to her from a booth at the far corner of the restaurant.

The place itself was adorable, with cozy red-vinyl booths along one side and a counter lined with stools that stretched along the other. Bright red cardboard cupids had been stuck willy-nilly on the walls, and a line of foil hearts had been strung up above the workspace behind the counter. A few elderly men sat at the counter, nursing mugs of coffee while they perused folded newspapers. A thirtysomething, ponytailed woman working the grill turned and beamed at Lara. "Sit anywhere you like. Someone'll be right with you."

"Thank you. I'm meeting someone." She hurried toward Tina's booth and slid onto the bench opposite her.

"Hey, you made it." Tina smiled at Lara. "Right on time."

Lara was relieved to see Tina smiling. They hadn't exactly parted on good terms the day Lara left the bridal salon.

"I think the drive over was easier the second time around." Lara pulled off her gloves and unbuttoned her jacket. "It's actually a very pretty ride."

"It's really pretty once the winter grime melts and the trees start to bud," Tina said.

Another server, this one in her sixties with a wrinkled face and sporting circular earrings the size of Hula-Hoops, sidled over to take Lara's order. She set down a glass of ice water in front of her. "Coffee?"

"You bet," Lara said. "With cream, please."

"Anything else?"

"Not right now, thanks."

The server rolled her eyes and scuttled away.

Tina had already ordered coffee. She took a sip from her mug and winced. "Ach. Still too hot. I can't stand super-hot drinks."

Lara's gaze was drawn to the folder sitting on the table next to Tina. Whatever Tina wanted to talk about, she'd apparently brought visuals. Lara looked around to see if anyone was within earshot. She assumed Tina intended their conversation to be private.

"Don't worry. No one can hear us." Tina waited until Lara's coffee came, then she leaned closer and said, "I told you this wouldn't take long, so I'll get right to the point." She opened the folder and slid out several sheets of paper. Even upside down, Lara saw that they were copies of newspaper articles. Tina turned them around so Lara could see them.

Lara swallowed a gasp. "These pictures…are all of me," she said, taking the sheets in her hand. She flipped through them.

The first article, over two years old, was from the weekly Whisker Jog newspaper. A photo of Lara standing behind her aunt's home, her arm linked through Aunt Fran's, had graced the front page. A wily killer had been caught, and Lara had been largely responsible.

Confused, Lara glanced at Tina, who nodded at her. "Keep going."

The next photo was from the same newspaper. In a dramatic confrontation at the home of legendary actress Deanna Daltry, Lara had gotten help from an unlikely source to stop another killer from getting away with murder. The pic showed a smiling Lara standing in front of the actress's stone mansion. In each of her hands was a kitten. She remembered when the photo was taken. The reporter had insisted on having Lara pose with the kittens, since it was she who'd helped them settle into a loving home.

The remaining two articles were similar. Each photo of Lara was accompanied by an account of the capture of a killer. In every case, Lara had been the catalyst.

Or *cat*-alyst, she thought dryly.

Lara felt her blood pound in her ears. Tina had certainly done her homework on Lara. But why was she showing her these?

"Tina, I've seen all these before, obviously. I'm not sure why you're showing them to me." Lara pushed them back toward Tina, but the young woman stopped her.

"I want you to look at them again," Tina said in a soft voice. "Carefully, this time. I know you're an artist, so you pick up on details."

Lara stared at her, then pulled the articles over in front of her again. She examined each one, then shook her head. They were typical grainy newspaper photos, made even grainier by printing them off a copier. There was nothing unusual about them. "I don't know what I'm supposed to be seeing."

Tina removed a pencil from the flowered purse resting on the bench beside her. Using it as a pointer, she went to each photo. "There," she said. "A tiny pinpoint of light, almost at your feet."

Lara looked again. Tina was right. The sunlight had apparently beamed off a small object in the grass. Either that, or it was a glitch of the camera.

Tina flipped to the next photo. This one had been taken in bright daylight, so the dot of light was less obvious. But it was there, almost on Lara's shoulder.

The other two photos had similar dots of light, both very close to Lara.

She tried to recall if the same photographer had taken each of the photos. The first had been taken by the editor of the paper with a regular camera, but the second two had been taken with his cell phone. The fourth, she couldn't remember.

A weird feeling gripped Lara in a vise. She rubbed her hands over her eyes.

"Lara," Tina said quietly, "you managed to put away four killers. You can't deny that. Even the police gave you credit. No, wait, it was five killers. One of them was very low-key, so your involvement was kept out of the papers."

At my request, Lara remembered dismally.

"How do you know all this?" Lara said curtly. "What did you do, study me?"

Tina nodded. "Yes, I did."

"But…why?"

Tina folded her hands. Her fingers were slender, almost like the pencil she'd used as a pointer. Her shiny black hair reflected a swatch of morning sunlight coming through the window of the diner.

"Lara, something else was going on, wasn't it?" Tina's gaze met Lara's. "Something only you could see. Something you weren't able to share with the police."

It was impossible. There was no way Tina could know about Blue.

"Tina, these pinpoints of light." Lara picked up the articles and fanned them out. "They're from the sun. If you'll notice, three of them were taken outside. Only one was inside the shelter, and it was on our back porch, which has a bank of windows. There's always stray light coming from somewhere."

Tina shook her head. Tears welled in her eyes. "I'm disappointed in you, Lara. I really thought you'd be honest with me. You seem like a straight shooter."

Straight shooter. Lara disliked the phrase.

"Maybe you should tell me what you expected me to say." Lara took a sip from her coffee mug. The stuff was powerful, but delicious.

Tina turned and stared out the window, her lips pressed into a thin line. For a moment, Lara thought her face was going to crumple. Then she whipped her cell phone out of her purse and went to her saved photos. She showed the first one to Lara.

"There. Look at that. It's me and my mom at our restaurant, back when it was still open."

Lara pulled Tina's phone closer. In the picture, Tina stood behind a chair at which a fiftysomething woman was seated. The woman in the chair had high cheekbones and stunning, wide-set eyes. Both women smiled into the camera, joy evident in their expressions.

"Your mom's lovely," Lara said, smiling. "You and she could almost be sisters."

Tina nodded. "Do you see anything above my right shoulder?"

Lara looked again. In the pic, a small dot of light hovered a few inches above Tina's right shoulder. "I see the spot of light," she said, "but it only proves my point. There's stray light everywhere. The camera just happens to catch it."

But even as she said it, she knew it wasn't the truth.

A lump formed in Lara's stomach. Had a total stranger stumbled onto her secret?

Tina took her cell phone back and swiped her way through several more photos. With each swipe, she held up the phone and extended it toward Lara. Most of the pics looked like selfies. A few had been taken in the bridal salon, probably as promotional photos. In every picture of Tina, a small dot of light floated above her right shoulder.

Lara's fingers felt suddenly ice cold, and she rubbed her hands together.

Tina stuck her phone back in her purse. She spoke in a soft, almost childlike voice. "When I was eight years old, my grandma got very sick. She'd always lived with us, so I was especially close to her. She had a cat— Jade—a gorgeous Siamese kitty. Jade was sweet, vocal, and devoted to my grandmother. The cat loved everyone, but my grandma was her world."

"I've known cats like that," Lara said. "My aunt's cat Dolce almost never leaves her lap."

Tina nodded and then took in a quiet breath. "Anyway, my grandma died a day before my ninth birthday. Sucky luck, especially for a kid who'd practically been counting the minutes to her birthday party."

"I'm so sorry," Lara said.

"Thanks. Her death was awful. I didn't go back to school for a week. We all just…missed her so much, you know? She left a hole in our hearts." Tina pressed her fingers to her eyes. "As hard as we took it—Mom, Dad, and me—it was worse for Jade. She wasn't exactly a young'un herself—she'd recently turned fifteen. She just…lay there, almost comatose. She didn't eat or drink. It was like she was telling us, 'That's it, I'm done. *Mata ne.*' That's like, *See you later.*"

Lara felt a boulder lodge in her throat. At some point, every cat had to cross the bridge, but knowing that didn't ease the sadness.

"Jade crossed over one week to the *minute*, and I mean minute, Lara, from the time of my grandma's death. I was there. I felt it. A huge ball of warmth, like a heating pad, suddenly rested on my shoulder. At first it felt heavy, but then it changed. It became soft and comforting. A little while later the warmth faded. But the light—that pinpoint of light that shows up in every picture of me—it means Jade is always there. She's part of my grandma, watching over me."

Tina's dark eyelashes were damp with unshed tears. Lara felt herself beginning to cry, but she forced it back. She glanced around to see if anyone noticed them, but the diner was nearly empty.

There was no way Tina could've known about Blue. Only someone with her own feline guardian could recognize the signs.

"Why don't you be honest with me, Lara?" Tina urged. "Why don't you tell me the truth? You have a spirit cat watching over you, don't you?"

And with that Lara broke down. She told Tina everything.

Chapter 16

Tina listened without speaking, absorbing every word.

Lara began with the day she first saw Blue. It was the day she'd arrived at her aunt's after a sixteen-year estrangement.

Aunt Fran had been tutoring Brooke Weston's little brother, Darryl, who'd struggled to read aloud. Whenever his teacher called on him to read to the class, the poor little kid panicked. That day, Blue appeared at Darryl's side, and the child began to read the words as if he were a high school student. But her aunt insisted she never had a Ragdoll cat, so Lara quietly let it drop.

After that, Blue seemed to materialize whenever Lara needed her. The cat's intervention when Lara was threatened by killers had been nothing short of miraculous.

"I knew it," Tina whispered triumphantly, after Lara had finished. She suddenly looked troubled. "Lara, does anyone else know about Blue?"

"Only three people. My friend Kayla, who adores cats. And my aunt and my, um, significant other."

Tina's face brightened. "You have a boyfriend, and he believed it? Wow, I'm impressed."

I thought he believed it. I'm not so sure anymore…

"Maybe there's hope for me, then," Tina went on. "I *so* want to confide in Mom, but I'm not sure how she'll react. We're super close, but she's a practical lady. She's likely to tell me I'm dreaming it. She always says my head is in the clouds." Tina smiled, but Lara saw the worry in her eyes.

"Only you can decide who to tell," Lara said. "But don't try to rush it. The day will come when you know that the time—and the person—is right."

Listen to me, giving advice. My own life is falling apart.

"Unlike you, I never see Jade," Tina explained. "But I feel her warmth and her weight on my shoulder, and I sometimes hear the *teeniest tiniest* of purrs. It usually happens when I'm super stressed about something. After a while she fades away, and I always feel more at peace afterward."

Their server came by again and refilled Lara's mug. Tina shook her head at her.

"Lara, thank you for being open with me," Tina said, after the woman had strode away. "And believe me when I say my lips are sealed. I will never reveal to anyone what you told me." Tina wiped away an eyelash with the tip of her finger. "I'm sorry I snapped at you the other day. I really thought you were trying to get a bead on me, you know? But after I read more about you, I realized how many people you've helped. You're one of the good guys. I get that now."

I was *trying to pick your brain*, Lara thought, but didn't say it out loud. The old adage "let sleeping dogs lie" popped into her head.

"Plus, you don't just own cats," Tina went on. "You rescue cats. I read all about your shelter when I was checking you out."

Lara smiled at her. "Most of the credit for that goes to my aunt Fran. I learned my love of cats from her at an early age. Plus, if it weren't for her, we wouldn't even have a shelter." She glanced at her watch. She'd been with Tina almost forty-five minutes. There was still plenty of time before she had to get home for the book club. She still wanted to ask Tina about Wayne Chancer.

The young woman must have been a mind reader.

"You want to know about Megan and that slug, Chancer, don't you?" Tina said.

Lara admitted she did. "I have no right to ask you, but something is drawing me to this town. I don't know if it's Megan, or you, or—"

Tina leaned forward and spoke in a whisper. "Is there a cat somewhere in the mix?"

Lara honestly wasn't sure. "I think so, but I don't think that's all of it."

Something else was drawing her to this town. It was a nagging feeling, and not a comfortable one. It was the sense that something bad was about to happen. Lara had no idea what it was.

"Lara, I can't tell you whether or not to help Megan. In my opinion, she's kind of a sad sack, you know? She has only one real enemy—herself. I wish her aunt and uncle would make her get some help." Tina took a sip of her now-cold coffee.

"Sounds like you know her pretty well," Lara said.

"Not really. Her aunt and uncle used to eat at the Japanese Garden kind of regularly. That's how I got acquainted with her. When I found out who her boss was, I started giving her the cold shoulder. I feel bad about that now, but I didn't know if she was spying for him or not, so I wasn't taking any chances."

"She told me how she crashed Chancer's party the night he died and yelled threats at him."

Tina looked away, her cheeks going pink. "Yeah, I heard about that. I guess the whole town's heard about it."

"Do you think she'll be arrested? Have you heard any rumors?"

Tina laughed. "In this town? The rumor mill is grinding away, as it always is. I'm sure it's the same where you live. Small towns thrive on gossip, whether it's truth or fiction."

"That's for sure."

"As for Megan being arrested, I guess it all depends. Chancer wasn't exactly Mr. Popularity. In fact, he was a creep. For him, it was all about excess. Money, women, food, booze…"

"Um, Megan told me what happened to your parents' restaurant. I'm so sorry."

Tina's slender features went taut. "That pig ruined my folks' livelihood— and their reputation. They'll never be the same."

"I'm sorry," Lara said. "Do you think they'll ever open another restaurant?"

"I doubt it. If they do, it sure won't be in this town. Right now, I'm working as hard as I can to help them out. I juggle two jobs, and I recently started my own business. I'm living with them for the time being, but I'm dying to move out and get my own place."

"I bet. When did you start your fortune cookie business?"

Tina's eyes shot open wide. "You know about that?"

"I do. My friend Kayla and I were in the Peach Crate on Monday, right before we went to the bridal salon. She bought a bag of your fruit fortune cookies for her nieces and nephews. I tasted one—it was yummy."

"Thank you." Tina snapped her fingers and pointed at Lara. "Hey, did you refer someone to me? A woman named Sherry went on my Web site last night and ordered fortune cookies for her wedding. Is that the wedding you bought the shoes for?"

Lara felt herself blush. "Guilty as charged. Sherry's my bestie. She has been since we were kids. She wanted something special for her favor boxes, but we were both coming up empty. After I checked out your Web page, I had a feeling she was going to go crazy for your fortune cookies. Turns out she did."

"Wow. Well, thanks for the referral." Tina beamed. "Word of mouth is my best advertiser."

"I'm curious, Tina. Why fortune cookies?"

She smiled. "From everything I've read—and I've done a ton of research—fortune cookies were originally introduced by the Japanese."

"Really?" Lara shoved her now-empty mug to one side. "I guess I learned something new today."

Tina nodded. "Over the decades—centuries, actually—there's been a good deal of dispute over the fortune cookie's origin. I won't bore you with the history, but if you Google it, you'll find some interesting articles about it. To me it doesn't matter. I've always loved the silly little cookies. They're crackly and tasty, even without a fortune inside. But the fortune makes them extra fun, right?"

Lara laughed. "Absolutely. I always look forward to reading my fortune. Not that they ever come true."

"I want to make my company grow," Tina said. "I want my folks not to have to worry about money, ever again."

"They're lucky to have a daughter like you," Lara said.

Tina shrugged. "Thanks, but I feel like I'm not doing enough."

Lara glanced again at her watch. "Tina, I should be going. I'm glad you invited me—"

"Tina?" came a voice from behind Lara.

Tina glanced over Lara's shoulder, and Lara turned to see a sixtysomething, balding man. He came over and stood beside their booth. The scent of stale cigarette smoke clung to his camel-colored coat.

"Hey, Gary. How's it going?" Tina said, her expression neutral. "Gary, this is my friend Lara. Lara, Gary Becker."

The man nodded at Lara. "Pleased to meet you, Lara. Hey, sorry to interrupt, but I wanted to give you some good news for a change. I think we've got a nibble on the restaurant."

"Really? Did you get an offer?"

"Not yet, but I think it'll be coming in a day or two." His thin lips flatlined. "They're gonna lowball us, Tina. You and your folks need to be thinking about the lowest price you'll accept. The building needs updating badly, which you already knew. A savvy buyer is gonna be looking for a deal."

Tina sagged. "I know. Do the best you can, and I'll talk to Mom and Dad." She looked over at Lara. "My folks are trying to unload the restaurant. It's been sitting vacant for a few months, and the taxes and upkeep are killing them. Gary is our Realtor."

"Are you in the market to buy a home, Lara?" Becker asked. With two fingers he pulled a business card out of his coat pocket. "I've got some nice little places I can show you."

Lara smiled and took his card. "Thanks, but right now I'm all set. But I'll keep your card in case I'm ever looking."

His smile fading, he nodded but said nothing. *No sale, no smile.*

"Um, Lara," Tina said, "Gary is Karen Chancer's dad. Gary, Lara is a friend of Megan Haskell."

"I'm more of an acquaintance than a friend," Lara said quickly. She didn't want anyone to get the wrong impression.

Becker fixed his gaze on Lara, as if trying to decide if she was friend or foe. "Well, then, let me tell you something, Lara. I feel sorry for Megan, but if she killed that bum Chancer she did the world—and my daughter—a favor." His fingers twitched. "I know that sounds harsh, but I'm too old to mince words. My daughter put up with that scumbag for too many years. I'm glad it's over."

It was an odd thing to say, given that his own daughter was a possible suspect. Lara wondered if he realized it.

"Gary, you'd better not let the cops hear you say that," Tina said, looking nervous.

He coughed, a phlegmy sound that made Lara cringe. "Too late for that," he barked out. "I already laid my cards on the table with the police. Chancer and I had bad blood, and they all know it. No point trying to hide it now."

"Is your daughter taking his death hard?" Lara asked him.

Becker narrowed his eyes at her. "Actually, she's been pretty stoic. Poor kid. I should've stopped that marriage a long time ago, before it ever took place. Given what I knew—" He broke off and hacked out another raspy cough.

Lara wanted to press him, but she was afraid he'd clam up if he thought she was getting too curious. Either that or hack out a lung. There was one thing, though, that she needed to know.

"Mr. Becker, were you at the birthday party that night?" She was pushing her luck, she knew, but this might be the only opportunity she'd get to question him.

"First off, Lara, it's Gary. Let's not stand on formalities, okay? And no, I was not at the party. I was about a hundred twenty miles away, at a Realtor's conference in Maine. I was supposed to be there all weekend, but given what happened, I had to cut it short. Any particular reason you ask?"

"Oh no. I just wondered if you might've heard what Megan said to Wayne Chancer that night. You know, if it was as bad as she said it was."

Gary studied her with tired eyes. "You're very inquisitive, Lara. Are you working for Megan Haskell? You're not a lawyer, are you?"

"Oh my, no," Lara said with what she hoped was a disarming giggle. "I feel bad for her, that's all. She seems so down on her luck."

Gary shrugged. "She made her bed when she went after Chancer. You know what they say—you lie down with dogs, you get fleas."

"What do you mean, 'went after Chancer'?" Lara asked.

"Exactly what it sounds like. Megan Haskell had a thing for her boss. That's the main reason he fired her. He couldn't get her to leave him alone."

Stunned, Lara sat back against the booth. If what Gary said was true, then Megan had been deceiving her from the start.

"Hey, don't get me wrong," Gary added darkly. "Wayne cheated on my daughter, all the time. But not with Megan. I think she was a little too off-kilter, even for him."

Looking more uncomfortable by the minute, Tina piped in, "Gary, I thought I saw Karen's car at Felicia's shop this morning."

"Yeah, she's there now." He coughed. "She got sick of reporters calling her, trying to interview her. She sneaked out through the garage and drove over there. She said being at the store with Felicia gives her the most comfort right now. She's just praying none of those pushy reporters spots her car there."

The door to the diner opened. A group of three women toddled in and immediately sought out a booth.

"It's starting to get busy in here," Tina said, glancing at the wall clock. "A lot of people come in early for lunch."

"I should go, anyway," Lara said. "Lots to do at home." She stuck Gary's card into her tote and buttoned her jacket. She pulled a ten out of her tote and tucked it under her empty mug. "I'd like to treat, okay?"

Tina smiled. "Sure, as long as I can treat next time. But you know you're leaving way too much, right?"

"That's okay. I really enjoyed our chat. I hope we can do it again soon. It was great meeting you…Gary."

Gary moved aside and held out an arm, as if ushering her out of the booth. "You too, Lara. I'm gonna stick around and gab with Tina for a bit. We have some details to work out."

Lara took the hint. She grabbed her tote and her gloves and slid out of the booth. "Tina, it was so nice talking to you. And thanks again for giving me the deetz on the fortune cookies. I think I know what I'm going to do now."

With a conspiratorial wink, Tina said, "You got it, Lara. Any time."

Chapter 17

Lara sat in her car and started the engine, her mind reeling with everything she'd learned.

Had Megan really developed a "thing" for her boss? If what Gary said was true, it added a whole new layer to Megan's potential motive. More disturbing was that Megan had lied. To Lara, and possibly to Gideon.

Tina Tanaka had been a surprise—a pleasant one. She was sharp and intuitive, and in tune with cats. Even Lara—who was adept at spotting details—had never noticed the pinpoints of light on the photos of herself.

Lara still couldn't believe she'd revealed her secret about Blue to a near stranger. Something about Tina had been so genuine that she'd spilled the entire story without giving it a second thought. Lara had also been relieved that Tina wasn't angry with her. They'd probably never be friends, but she admired the young woman. And yet, Tina had withheld the information about Megan having "chased after" her ex-boss. Was she trying to be discreet, or did she think it wasn't worth mentioning?

As for Karen Chancer's dad, she didn't know how to read him. Gary Becker's bluntness in front of a total stranger had astounded her. Lara couldn't stop thinking about the comments he'd made. He'd clearly known something bad about Wayne Chancer before his daughter married him. If he hadn't had a sudden coughing fit, would he have told them what it was?

Now that she thought about it, she wondered how accidental her meeting with Becker had been. Could Tina have orchestrated the timing? Had she already planned to meet Becker, and decided to add Lara to the mix? If so, why? What had Tina hoped to gain?

Questions, questions. Not a whole lot of answers.

Lara gazed through her windshield as her car warmed up. Bakewell really was a cute little town. Several of the storefronts had striped awnings, making the shops look warm and welcoming. Up ahead was the Peach Crate, the gourmet shop owned by Felicia Tristany. Lara and Kayla had enjoyed browsing there, especially with all those homemade goodies to drool over. Karen Chancer's dad had mentioned that his daughter was there today, trying to evade reporters.

Lara remembered the cherry fruit spread she'd bought there. She'd planned to use it to make something special for Gideon. Maybe muffins or scones. Thinking of him made her feel glum all over again. The last time they'd spoken, he'd sounded disappointed in her. The thought made her sad and angry at the same time. She knew Gideon loved her and cared about her, and that he worried about her safety. But her tendency to stumble onto murders seemed to be wearing on him, and Lara fully understood that. Still, she was entitled to her feelings, and to her opinions. If he didn't share them, so be it. At least he could respect them.

Lara shoved the gearshift into Drive and headed for the Peach Crate.

The store's parking lot had only three cars. Lara pulled in next to a spotless white Lexus. Karen Chancer's car? She couldn't imagine how the car stayed so clean in the dead of winter. Aunt Fran's Saturn was coated in road grime. Lara had been meaning to run it through a car wash, but with all the hullabaloo over Megan, she hadn't had a chance.

"Good morning, Lara," a voice trilled the moment she entered the shop.

Lara glanced toward the back. Felicia was waving at her from the adorable checkout counter—the one designed to look like a peach crate. Today the proprietress wore an appropriately peach-colored cable-knit sweater over gray slacks.

"You remembered me. I'm impressed." Lara smiled at Felicia.

"Oh, how could I forget such a lovely customer?" Felicia said. "Lily remembers you, too, don't you, sweetie?" She bent and retrieved the small white dog from underneath the counter. Felicia lifted the dog's paw in a wave at Lara.

Lara removed her gloves and shoved them into her pockets. She went over and took the dog's paw in her hand. "Hi, Lily. Were you taking a snooze? Did I interrupt your nap?"

The dog licked Lara's hand, then rested her head against Felicia's shoulder.

"Aw, she's mummy's best girl, isn't she?" Felicia cooed to the pup.

Lara thought it was so sweet the way Felicia adored her dog. She wished every pet owner could be as kind.

"Are you back for more goodies?" Felicia asked, a smile lighting up her face.

"I'm sure I won't leave here without some treats," Lara assured her. "When I was here with my friend the other day, we were on our way to an appointment. I don't think I got to see everything."

"Well, you take your time and browse all you like. But before you do, would you like a taste of my raspberry coconut tea? So perfect for a chilly winter day. I created the blend myself, and I have to say, I'm quite proud of it."

Lara had already had her fill of coffee. She didn't know if she could squeeze in even a drop of tea. "Normally I would, but then I'm afraid I'd have to find a bathroom. I've had a lot of coffee this morning."

"That's not a problem. There a restroom right behind me. Someone's in there now, but she shouldn't be long." Felicia tilted her head slightly behind her and winked at Lara.

"Well then…sure," Lara said, wondering if the "someone" was Karen Chancer. Was that her Lexus parked in front? She didn't see anyone else in the shop. "But just a small taste, okay?"

For Felicia's sake, she could manage a few sips. The woman looked as fragile as a hummingbird. Lara wondered if the seventysomething lived alone with her dog.

"Excellent. Lemon or cream?"

"Just lemon, thanks."

Felicia scuttled off through a rear doorway. She returned a minute later with a delicate china mug rimmed with white bell-shaped flowers. "Here you go. I only filled it halfway, and I squeezed in a pinch of lemon. Let me know what you think."

Lara blew on the steaming liquid, then took a small sip. "Wow. This is delicious! My aunt Fran would love this. Do you sell it in the store?"

"Oh, you bet I do. My tea blends are in the far corner near the window."

"Great. I'll grab a basket after I finish this and do a little shopping."

Lara drank the rest of her tea and set the empty mug on the counter. She started toward the front of the store, where a stack of wire baskets rested. The door to the restroom swung open with a bang, and Lara whirled around.

"Sorry. I didn't mean to slam the door," said a thin, thirtysomething woman with red-rimmed eyes. Her light blond hair wrapped into a French twist, she pressed a tissue to her nose and then went over to stand next to Felicia. She started to cry.

"Oh no, honey, please don't cry anymore. Everything's going to be okay." Felicia set down her dog, who shuffled back underneath the counter. She wrapped a bony arm around the woman's shoulder. "Everything's going to work out. I promise."

Lara didn't know what to do. She hated to see anyone hurting. Was the sobbing woman Karen Chancer? She went over to her. "Miss…is there anything I can do to help?" It sounded like a hollow offer, but she didn't know what else to say.

The woman shook her head, while Felicia rubbed her back in soothing motions. "Lara, this is Karen, Wayne Chancer's wife," Felicia explained. "She's been having a tough time since her husband's sad death."

Karen sobbed harder. "I can't stand it anymore. People keep calling, accusing me of killing my husband. What do they think I am, a monster?"

Lara felt for her. The despair in Karen's pale blue eyes was heartbreaking. She spotted a ladder-back chair against the wall behind the counter. "Why don't you sit, okay?" she suggested. "I'm Lara, by the way."

"Thank you, Lara," Karen said, dropping onto the chair.

Lily must have picked up on Karen's dismay. She inched out of her cozy nook under the counter and curled up next to the chair, as if to comfort her.

Karen smiled down at the little dog. "I could probably use another tissue," she said, reaching down to pat Lily.

Before Lara could rummage through her tote for a tissue, Felicia snagged one from a box beneath the counter. "There you go, sweetie." The kindly shop owner spoke to Karen in the same tone she used with Lily.

Karen blew her nose loudly, then sniffled. "I'm okay. I'm better now," she said in a shaky voice. She crumpled the tissue in her fist. "You…you said your name is Lara? That's such a pretty name. Like the woman in *Doctor Zhivago*, right?"

"Exactly." Lara smiled, impressed that Karen had picked up on that. Lara's dad had loved the movie, although her mom, Brenda, had already chosen the name "Monica" for her long before she was born. Then shortly before Lara's birth, the movie came on one of the classic TV stations. Reminded of how much he'd loved the name "Lara," her dad had persuaded her mom to change it.

"You've been awfully sweet," Karen said. "Do you live in town?"

"No, I live in Whisker Jog. I was in Bakewell a few days ago, at the bridal salon. I happened to stop in here, and that's when I met Felicia. I was so impressed with this store! In fact, I bought a jar of your cherry fruit bits."

"Oh, did you like them?" Karen sounded thrilled.

"I haven't used them yet, but I will. My, um, boyfriend loves anything cherry-flavored. I'm planning to make either scones or muffins with them."

"I'd go for the scones, but it's up to you. And use real butter, not the fake stuff." Karen looked up and smiled up at Felicia, who reached down and squeezed her hand.

Without warning, another furry form appeared at Karen's feet. This time it was a cream-colored Ragdoll cat, but only Lara could see her. Blue pressed herself against Lily, then gazed up at Lara with bright turquoise eyes. Lily's ears perked for a second, as if she'd sensed a stir in the atmosphere, but then she settled down and rested her head on her forepaws.

"Feel better now?" Felicia asked Karen.

"Much," Karen said, a thread of steel in her voice. "I have to learn to be tougher. I'm alone now, and I need to work things out for myself. I can't always be depending on others, like you and Dad, to rush to my rescue."

Lara was curious what she meant by that but didn't press her. She was still thinking about Blue, who had already faded. "Karen, is there anything I can do for you?"

"Oh no, you've already made me feel much better."

Felicia beamed at her younger friend. "Karen is thinking of becoming a fifty-fifty partner with me in the store. Isn't that marvelous?"

Lara was stunned. It seemed like an odd time to be talking about a partnership with Chancer's widow. He'd only been dead five days.

"That sounds great. I'm sure you'll both work well together." She didn't have any real reason to believe that, but it was all she could think of to say.

"I've been thinking about it for a while," Karen said. "My home-based business gives me great pleasure, but now I need something more substantial. Maybe the timing is right. Of course, there's still a lot left to do to settle my husband's...estate." She seemed to tiptoe over the word. "But in time it should all work out."

Wow. *Quick change in demeanor*, Lara thought. She couldn't help speculating—had Chancer been in favor of Karen buying in to the gourmet shop? If not, his death had given her the freedom to make that choice. And possibly the funds.

The door to the shop opened abruptly. A pink-cheeked brunette wearing a stylish, red wool jacket with a matching hat skimmed her glance all around. When she spotted the women behind the checkout counter, she grinned and strode toward them. "Come on, Murph. I think she's in here!" She waved at the twentysomething man trailing behind her, a camera the size of a microwave oven propped on his shoulder.

Lara froze when she saw what the woman was holding—a microphone.

"Mrs. Chancer? Karen Chancer?" the woman bleated. "I'm Iris Kelly from the news channel. We've been trying to get an interview with you for days!"

Karen's face paled, and her eyes filled with panic. She opened her mouth to speak, but nothing came out. Felicia looked equally stricken. She twisted her fingers around each other, frozen to the spot.

Lara glanced through the front window of the shop. A TV van was parked sideways in the parking lot, blocking the entrance. Lara recognized the call letters—they belonged to a "wannabe" cable station trying to gain momentum in the state. Rumor had it they were struggling to find enough advertisers willing to hop on board.

Lara bent toward Karen and said quietly, "Karen, do you want to be interviewed?"

Karen shook her head vehemently. "God, no!"

Lara turned back to the reporter and glued on a fake smile. "I'm sorry, Ms.—Kelly, is it? Mrs. Chancer is not interested in being interviewed right now, so she would appreciate it if you would respect her privacy. This is, after all, a place of business. Thank you."

The reporter looked almost gleeful at being challenged. She thrust the mic at Lara. "And you are?"

Lara held up a hand in front of the microphone, careful not to touch it. "I am a friend, and please remove that microphone from my face."

The reporter shifted the mic toward Karen and tried to push past Lara.

"Ms. Kelly, please don't force me to call the police," Lara said, more firmly now. "You're overstepping your boundaries. You've now crossed over the line into harassment territory."

Iris Kelly's nostrils flared. "No, Miss *Whoever-You-Are*, this is not harassment. It's called reporting the news, a term I'm guessing you're not familiar with. Mrs. Chancer," she called out, "is it true that the killer dropped a note next to your husband? Didn't you tell the police you found a note in the snow next to your husband's body?"

Inwardly, Lara gasped. Even Megan hadn't told her that. Was it true, or was the reporter only baiting Karen?

The cameraman, clad in a puffy brown vest and a fleece ballcap, came over and tapped his companion on the shoulder. "Hey, Iris, come on. I don't wanna get in trouble like we did last time. I'm goin' back to the truck. I'll meet you there."

Keeping his face down, he turned on his heel and hurried outside.

Lara breathed a sigh of relief. She didn't think he'd filmed anything yet. In fact, she wasn't even sure his camera had been on.

"I can't believe I have to work with that moron," Iris muttered. She scowled at Lara and pointed a glossy pink fingernail at her. "Don't worry, I'm leaving. But remember one thing. You can't hide from the truth, and neither can the weeping widow." She swiveled on her red high-heeled boots and stormed outside.

Lara felt her pulse race toward her throat. She looked over at Karen, who was crying softly. Felicia fluttered around her, unsure what to do. Finally, Felicia said, "Lara, if you stay here with Karen, I'll go out back and make some more tea. She needs a strong dose of my lemon balm tea with lots of sugar to calm her nerves."

"Sure thing. But what if customers come in?" So far, the shop had been quiet, but Lara didn't think it would last.

Felicia held up a finger. "Good thinking. I'll put up the *Closed* sign temporarily."

Lara grabbed the box of tissues and gave it to Karen. Karen snatched a handful and blew her nose again.

"You must think I'm a helpless ditz," Karen said. She took in a halting breath.

"Not at all. I think you've been through a horrible experience, maybe without much support."

Karen nodded, her eyes redder and puffier than before. "My dad is supportive, and so is Felicia, but I don't have many other friends. Wayne either *didn't* like my friends…or he liked them *too* much, if you know what I mean. Eventually, they all stopped calling me."

Ugh. Lara's opinion of the man had sunk to a new low. But that made her wonder—why had so many people attended his birthday party?

Karen reached over and touched Lara's wrist. "Lara, thank you for telling that awful woman you were my friend. You can't begin to imagine how good that made me feel."

The poor woman, Lara thought. For a small gesture from a total stranger to have meant that much, Karen had to be almost friendless.

Either that or it was a clever act.

The more Lara thought about it, the more she wondered if the police should be taking a closer look at Karen Chancer.

Chancer's death had brought his widow a good deal of freedom. Freedom from being friendless. Freedom from bullying, if Lara had read her correctly. And maybe freedom to invest in a business she'd been eager to become a part of.

Except that it's all speculation on my part, Lara reminded herself. She couldn't prove a thing, nor did she want to.

Felicia emerged from the back room carrying a steaming mug of fragrant, lemon-scented tea. She gave it to Karen, then rested a protective hand lightly on her shoulder.

Something else had stuck in Lara's head. "Karen, do you know what that reporter meant about a note?"

Karen took a sip from her mug and then stared into her lap to avoid Lara's gaze. "There was a note found next to Wayne's body, but the police never revealed it to the public. I don't even know how that terrible woman found out about it."

"May I ask what it said?"

"I suppose there's no harm in telling you. The note simply said, 'I know who you are.'"

"'I know who you are'?" Lara repeated.

Karen nodded and sniffled. Felicia looked at Lara and swallowed.

"Karen, not to pry, but do you have any idea what it meant?"

The young woman shrugged. "I'm guessing my husband had been hiding something from me. Unfortunately, I don't have a clue what it was."

Chapter 18

I know who you are.

The words reverberated in Lara's head. If Karen was right—and if she was telling the truth about the note—there might have been a lot more to Wayne Chancer than anyone knew.

Had he been a fugitive? Running from the law? In a witness protection program? The possibilities were endless.

Except that none of those scenarios made any sense. How could a man be hiding out and still have a thriving business as a personal injury lawyer? Wouldn't a fugitive want to keep a low profile?

Or had Chancer been hiding "in plain sight," as they say? Maybe a plastic surgeon had completely transformed his appearance. With false IDs obtained illegally, he could start over again as an entirely new person.

No, that still didn't work. Chancer had been a lawyer, a member of the Bar. The impostor theory was a bust.

Lara couldn't think about that now. She was already on mental overload. Her allotted shopping time had shrunk, and she really wanted to buy a few goodies from Felicia. It would be fun to bring a bag of Tina's fortune cookies to the book club, plus she wanted to pick out some of Felicia's specialty teas for Aunt Fran.

Felicia went to the front door and flipped her sign to *Open*. Karen hurried through her tea and then hugged both women and left, but not before asking Lara for her cell phone number.

"Thank you, Lara, for being so kind to Karen," Felicia murmured, waving at two women who'd just entered the shop. "If anyone needed a lift, she did."

"I was happy to help, though I don't think I did much." They drifted back over to the crate-shaped sales counter. Lara spoke in a low voice. "Felicia, do you think the Chancers had a happy marriage?"

Felicia frowned. "You know, I always thought they did. At least Karen gave me that impression. But after seeing how she's reacted to Wayne's death, I highly doubt it. I think Karen was putting on an act so her dad wouldn't worry about her. He's not a well man, you know."

"I met Mr. Becker a short while ago, at the diner. I was having coffee there with Tina Tanaka, and he came over to talk to her. He sure coughed a lot."

"Emphysema," Felicia explained. "Bad, too. Gary's totally addicted to cigarettes. He's tried to stop, but nothing works. Wait—you know Tina?"

"Sort of," Lara said. "I met her at the bridal shop when I was looking for shoes for my friend's wedding." Which didn't explain why she was having coffee at the local diner with a near stranger. Fortunately, Felicia didn't pursue it.

A thought struck Lara. "Felicia, what do you think about that note Karen mentioned? Is it possible Wayne had a secret from his past that he'd been hiding from her?"

Felicia eyelids fluttered. She looked troubled by the question. "I suppose anything's possible. How would we know?"

"How, indeed," Lara mused aloud. "It's weird, because her dad said something, too." She wasn't sure how much to share with Felicia, but the woman clearly cared about Karen and wanted to help her friend. "He said knowing what he knew, he should've stopped the marriage before it ever happened."

Felicia gasped. She gripped the counter for support. "Gary said that? Then maybe there was something to that note…" Her words trailed off, as if she was trying to recall something.

"I'm sorry, I didn't mean to upset you," Lara apologized. She seemed to be doing a lot of that, lately. Apologizing, that is.

"No, no, it's obvious you've thought a lot about this," Felicia murmured. "You're a very observant young woman."

Another thought struck Lara. "Felicia, were you at the party that night? You know, when Chancer…?"

Felicia fluttered her hands. "Oh no. I never go out at night. Even if I wanted to, I can't see to drive in the dark. Besides, I can barely make it through *Jeopardy!* without falling asleep." She dipped her head closer to Lara. "Truth be told, my driving issues made a good excuse for my not accepting Karen's invitation. Wayne wasn't my cup of tea, if you get my meaning. But the other thing is, Lily gets very antsy if she's left home alone. She suffers from abandonment issues. That's why I take her with me almost everywhere."

Lara's heart melted, and she hugged Felicia. "You're such a great dog mom. And a lovely person, as well."

Felicia blushed. "Oh, thank you. I sure wish you lived closer. I could picture us becoming fast friends, couldn't you?"

Lara nodded. Bakewell seemed like a close-knit town, where everyone knew everyone else. In that respect it was a lot like Whisker Jog. Either that or Lara had been drawn to the people who'd had a connection to Chancer.

Megan.

Lara hadn't heard from her since Monday. Was she still a suspect? After begging Lara to help her, why hadn't she been in touch?

Her cell pinged with a text. Lara pulled it out of her tote, read it, then smiled. Her aunt was already worrying about her, wondering if she was on her way home. She texted back that she was buying a few goodies and would be heading home in a few.

Lara grabbed a wire basket. She tossed in some of Felicia's tea packets and a bag of Tina's fortune cookies, then paid for her purchases. Felicia hugged Lara this time. She begged her not to be a stranger, but Lara didn't promise anything.

If she were smart, she'd remove herself from any more involvement in Chancer's murder.

If she were smart.

The thought had no sooner tripped through her head when she spotted him. Her nemesis, arms folded over his chest, leaning against her Saturn's front fender with a *gotcha* grin smeared across his handsome face.

State Police Lieutenant Conrad Cutler.

* * * *

"Fancy meeting you here, Lieutenant," Lara said in the most innocent voice she could muster.

"I'd tip my hat, but I'm not wearing one." Cutler unfolded his arms and shoved his hands into his pockets. "Lara, what are you doing here?"

The nerve, questioning her like she was a teenager playing hooky from school!

"I'm shopping for goodies." She held up her bag from the Peach Crate. "What are you doing here?"

"Oh, I'm just wondering why you've been hanging around in a town where a murder took place five days ago. A town you had no prior connection to."

"How do you know I had no prior connection to this town?" Lara said, trying to keep the edge from her voice. *Lord,* but the man was infuriating.

He stared at her without responding.

"And I'm not *hanging around,* as you put it. I came here on Monday to look for shoes for my friend's wedding, and this morning I've been shopping for gourmet treats. To use as wedding favors," she added. A tiny fib, but she saw no need to mention the in-between stuff with Tina Tanaka and Karen's dad. "By the way, I did not appreciate you squealing on me to Gideon the other day."

He shrugged and turned his gaze toward the street, as if keeping a sharp eye out for lawbreakers. "Call it squealing if you like, but I was just keeping him up-to-date on our progress. As you know, he's a former... *friend* of Megan Haskell's."

Lara felt like bopping him. Fortunately, she didn't have a violent bone in her body. If she did, she'd already be in handcuffs. "I'm aware of their prior connection, Lieutenant. It's one of the reasons I wanted to help—"

Uh-oh. She'd put her foot in it that time.

"You wanted to help find the real killer?" Cutler said in a steely voice.

Lara felt a flush creep up her neck. The guy had an uncanny way of reading her thoughts. She looked away and opened her car's passenger side door. She tossed her tote and the goodies bag onto the front seat, then slammed the door shut. "That's not what I meant. I'm sorry, but I'm afraid I need to leave now. Book club this afternoon, and lots of cats to care for. Plus, I'm freezing out here."

"You might be curious to know," Cutler said, "that Gideon called me yesterday. He told me he no longer wants to be kept in the loop. He's washed his hands of any involvement with Megan Haskell."

"A wise choice," Lara said, smiling inwardly. "Eventually the police will find the killer anyway. At least I assume they will."

Cutler's eye twitched at the jab. "You assume correctly, Lara. The cause of Chancer's death—especially if it was murder—will not go unsolved."

If it was murder? Was he hedging?

"Good." Lara started toward the driver's side door, then paused. "By the way, Lieutenant, is it true there was a note found near the deceased?"

Cutler's mouth opened. "What?"

"Was there a note found near Chancer's body?"

"Who told you that?"

"Oh dear, I'm afraid I can't reveal my sources," she said, as if it pained her to withhold the name. "So, is it true?"

Chancer moved closer to her. "I'm going to strongly advise you not to breathe a word about that, Miss Caphart. To anyone."

Suddenly, it was "Miss Caphart." Great. Now she'd planted herself on his bad side. She wasn't even sure he had a good side. Either way, she'd gotten to him.

"Oh, don't worry. If there's one thing I'm not, it's a squealer. Bye, Lieutenant. Catch you later!"

Lara hurried inside her car, locked the doors, and started her engine. She shot a look at her rearview mirror before backing out of her parking space. The last thing she needed was to run over Cutler's foot in her rush to escape.

On the drive back to Whisker Jog, her heart refused to stop pounding. Something the lieutenant said about Gideon had stuck in her head. *He told me he no longer wants to be kept in the loop. He's washed his hands of any involvement with Megan Haskell.*

That meant Gideon expected her to do the same. One of the last things he'd said to her was that he wanted them to "reboot." To go back to the way things were before Megan showed up in town.

"I can't, Gideon. I just can't." Lara realized she was talking aloud to herself, but it helped her think. "There's something about this mess with Chancer that's drawing me to that town. Something I'm supposed to figure out."

At least she had a valid excuse for going back to Bakewell. Once her shoes came in, she'd have to return to the bridal salon to pick them up.

Chapter 19

Brooke Weston snapped her fortune cookie in half and extracted the printed message. "Those who work hard shall reap rewards," she read aloud. With a dramatic roll of her big brown eyes, she popped a broken half into her mouth, crunched it between her teeth, and swallowed. "Hey, at least the cookie tastes good. Most of these things taste like cardboard."

Lara grinned. "I knew we'd all like them."

"Can I take one home for Chris?" Mary Newman asked, referring to her husband. With her smattering of freckles and dark brown hair curled upward into a soft flip, Mary could almost pass for a college student, despite being well into her thirties.

"Take a bunch," Lara said. "We have a whole bagful."

Mary slid three of the cellophane-wrapped cookies into her book bag. "Thanks!"

The rousing discussion of Ray Bradbury's *Fahrenheit 451* had ended with a thumbs-up from all four members, though at one point, Brooke's right thumb had wavered. "The thought of burning books gives me the chills," she said. "But the book was amazing, so…yes, I give it five stars."

Lara removed Munster from her lap, where he'd been purring up a storm, and set him on the floor. She rounded up everyone's empty teacups and plates and brought them over to the sink.

"Hey, I'd better run," Mary said in her lilting voice. "I have a new part-timer in the store, and she panics if I'm gone for more than an hour." Mary owned a gift shop in downtown Whisker Jog, adjacent to Bowker's Coffee Stop. Lara had sold several of her watercolors there, and for an excellent price.

Brooke shoved a strand of her burgundy-tinted hair behind one ear. She jammed the Bradbury book into her book bag, then shrugged on her ski jacket. "Mom'll be here any minute, so I'd better hustle, too. I have to finish writing the report I'm doing for Presidents' Day."

"What are you writing about?" Aunt Fran asked her.

"Everyone had to choose a president and describe a key incident in their life that helped shape their destiny. Either that or choose one of their famous quotes and analyze the meaning. I picked Lincoln. 'Course half the kids in my class picked Lincoln."

"That's an interesting assignment," Aunt Fran, ever the schoolteacher, said. "It makes you do a little research, and a lot of thinking. Knowing you, Brooke, I'm sure your report will be excellent."

Brooke blushed and flashed her a smile. "Thanks, Ms. C."

Lara returned to the table with a sponge and swiped it over the stray crumbs. For snacks, Mary had brought mini–chocolate eclairs. They'd all scarfed them down as if they hadn't eaten in days.

"So, which did you choose?" Lara asked Brooke. "Key incident or famous quote?"

"I went with a famous quote. Lincoln had a zillion of them, but the one I picked is 'You cannot escape the responsibility of tomorrow by evading it today.'"

Lara's hand stopped mid-swipe. She repeated the quote in her head.

A horn tooted outside in the driveway.

"See you next week!" Brooke hugged everyone and dashed outside. Mary followed behind her.

Aunt Fran started to lift Dolce off her lap. "I'll put the dishes in the dishwasher."

"No, you sit," Lara said with mock sternness. "It'll only take me a minute to do that."

Her aunt smiled and held up both hands. "Fine. No need to twist my arm."

Lara finished her cleanup duties and returned to the kitchen table. She knew her aunt was anxious to hear about her trip to Bakewell.

Beginning with her meeting with Tina Tanaka, Lara told her pretty much everything. She omitted the part about Tina's spirit cat, and the pinpoints of light on the photos. Tina had told her about Jade in confidence, and Lara respected that. She ended by describing her run-in with Lieutenant Cutler in the parking lot of the Peach Crate.

"My heavens, you've had quite the day," Aunt Fran said. "You seem to be getting closer to some of the players in Wayne Chancer's life." She said it noncommittally, but Lara knew it troubled her.

"I know," Lara admitted. "And I can't say it was totally accidental. I'd be lying if I did."

Her aunt sighed. "I'm not trying to pry, but does Gideon know you went to Bakewell today?"

Lara shook her head. In a way, the question irritated her. She was under no obligation to provide Gideon with her itinerary. "He texted me once, this morning, but that was it. Aunt Fran, I think he's really mad at me. And with Sherry's wedding coming up, the timing couldn't be worse."

Aunt Fran pulled Dolce closer. "Lara, tell me honestly. What is it about this, well, *matter* that's so important to you?"

"I wish I could explain it, but I'm not sure myself. It's not even about Megan anymore. Who, by the way, hasn't been in touch with me since Monday. And now that I know she probably lied to me, I don't want to see her ever again."

"I, for one, take that as a positive sign," Aunt Fran said. "You said she has her own lawyer, so let them deal with her situation."

A headache was beginning to work its way across Lara's forehead. She rubbed her fingers over it. "You know what was weird? It was the way Blue curled up against Felicia's little dog, Lily. I didn't know if she was trying to tell me something, or if she was only letting me know that Karen was 'okay,' so to speak."

Aunt Fran smiled. "Or maybe she just liked Lily."

"Maybe." Lara gave her aunt a half-hearted smile. "I read too much into things, don't I?"

"Only sometimes," her aunt said tactfully. "Lara, why don't you try to get in touch with Gideon. I think you'll both feel better if you talk things through."

But we already talked, and it only made things worse.

Lara rose from her chair and kissed her aunt's cheek. "You're probably right. I'll go into my studio and give him a ring."

"What about supper? I'm in the mood for a nice veggie omelet."

"Omelets sound great, as long as we add cheese."

"Good. I'll chop up some onions and a sweet red pepper. And I think there's some corn bread in the freezer."

Lara smiled. "I love it when you plan supper."

* * * *

Lara closed the door to her studio, then pulled her cell out of her pocket. She didn't see any missed calls from Gideon, so she pressed his number.

"Lara?" His voice sounded perky, and her spirits instantly lifted.

"Hey, I've missed talking to you today."

"Yeah, me too. Crazy-busy, as usual. I'm still finishing up some closing documents for tomorrow. Thank God for Marina. Honestly, I don't know how I ever functioned without her. How was your day?"

"Busy. Active. I—I went back to Bakewell today. Tina Tanaka called me last night and asked if I'd meet her at the diner there."

His tone chilled noticeably. "Tina Tanaka. Isn't she the woman who was so rude to you at the bridal shop?"

"She was rude, initially. But she researched me online and decided I was a good guy, not a bad guy." Lara laughed slightly, but Gideon remained silent. "Anyway, turns out Tina has her own side business making fortune cookies. Sherry's already ordered some to give out as wedding favors."

Gideon's voice was tight. "How did we go from Tina Tanaka practically throwing you out of the bridal salon to making fortune cookies for Sherry's wedding? Something isn't adding up here, Lara. What is it you're not telling me?"

This was not going well. Lara couldn't reveal Tina's private discussion about her spirit cat, even if he'd be inclined to believe it. She'd promised Tina she wouldn't breathe a word to anyone, and she intended to keep that promise.

"We chatted about a few other things," Lara said, more quietly now. "She talked a little about Megan—who, she believes, did not kill Chancer. While we were having coffee, the broker who's selling Tina's folks' restaurant came in. He turned out to be Karen Chancer's dad."

Lara could almost hear Gideon slapping his head. For at least a full minute, there was dead silence. "Gid...are you still there?"

After a long sigh, he said, "Lara, this conversation isn't getting us anywhere. I'm meeting David for a beer this evening to go over all the 'best man' stuff. Maybe you and I should get together tomorrow and settle things once and for all."

Settle things once and for all. His words had a note of finality that made Lara's heart squeeze in her chest. And she hadn't even gotten to the part about meeting Karen Chancer at the Peach Crate.

"Okay. Pick a time and place and I'll be there," she said, unable to stop the chill from creeping into her own voice.

"Marina's working till noon tomorrow," Gideon said. "Why don't you come to my office around one?"

Lara swallowed. "Shall I bring sandwiches?"

"If you'd like."

"Okay, see you then. Love you."

Gideon disconnected.

Lara felt tears push at her eyes. How did things get this bad, this quickly? Only a week before, she'd had the feeling he was going to ask her to marry him.

She had to hold it together for Sherry and David's sake, but especially for Sherry's.

Barring any last-minute plans with Gideon, she'd planned to work on Amy's watercolor this evening, but her heart wasn't in it. She was grateful that her aunt had suggested omelets for dinner. It was an easy meal with minimal cleanup.

The photo of Amy's farmhouse rested on the corner of her worktable. She remembered Blue standing on the picture, as if she'd been trying to tell Lara something.

Lara picked up the picture and examined it. Again, nothing stood out. She turned it over. On the flipside, someone had written in blue ink, *February 2011.*

The photo was almost ten years old. Why hadn't she noticed that before?

Amy had told Lara that she bought the farmhouse in 2018. Why hadn't she given Lara a more recent photo to work from—one that was taken after she'd moved there?

Probably because nothing had changed, Lara told herself. And because this particular pic was a perfect depiction of the farmhouse in winter. The prior owner had probably taken the photo when they were putting the property on the market.

I have to stop reading too much into everything. I have to stop overanalyzing everything I see.

Lara booted up her tablet and drafted a quick email to Amy. "Hey, it's only me. I'm just wondering if you want me to work with a more recent photo of your farmhouse. The one you gave me was taken in 2011. Let me know! I'll have some preliminary sketches for you to look at soon."

She signed off and set aside her tablet. Aunt Fran knocked lightly on her door, then poked her head in. "Ready for dinner?"

"Oh!" Lara glanced at her watch. It was five forty-five. "Yeah, but why didn't you wait for me to help?"

Her aunt smiled. "Nothing to help with. Took me ten minutes to throw it all together. Come on in the kitchen before your omelet gets cold."

Over fluffy omelets and buttered corn bread, they chatted about Sherry's upcoming wedding. Aunt Fran had bought a dress—a knee-length forest-green chiffon to complement her eyes—and a pair of matching heels.

Police Chief Jerry Whitley would accompany her to the wedding. Their relationship had grown closer than ever, despite the chief's mild aversion to cats.

Lara avoided any mention of Gideon. She didn't want her aunt to know how abruptly he'd ended their phone call. When Aunt Fran finally asked about him, Lara told her only that she was meeting him at his office the next day, to talk.

"Talking is good," was all her aunt had to offer.

Lara wasn't so sure. They last few talks they'd had hadn't ended well.

Strolling over to sit next to Lara's chair, Munster gazed up at her and then reached up with a paw.

Lara patted her lap and grinned. "Come on, you cute little pumpkin. If you promise not to be greedy, I'll give you a tiny bit of egg. No onions, though."

Munster leaped onto Lara's legs and rested his chin on the table, his nose nudging her plate. Lara knew she was encouraging bad manners, but at that moment she didn't care. She cut off a smidgeon of her omelet and let him eat it from her palm. Munster licked his lips, then curled into a circle in her lap, content.

Her aunt smiled over at them. "No one can say we don't spoil our cats."

"We spoil them, but we take excellent care of them." Lara lightly kissed Munster's head, then set him down on the floor. "You made dinner, so I'll do cleanup duty."

Aunt Fran didn't protest.

While her aunt went into the large parlor with her constant companion, Dolce, Lara finished up the dishes, then went back into her studio and closed the door.

She was beginning to feel discouraged. By now, she thought she'd have made better progress on Amy's watercolor project. Although Amy hadn't set a deadline for the painting, it depressed Lara that she hadn't even completed the preliminary sketches.

Lara turned on her tablet and plugged Wayne Chancer's full name into Google's search box. She'd checked him out before, but only to get his background info. Maybe it was time to check him out a little further.

Almost instantly, his obituary popped up. A photo of a smiling man with a wide face and a head full of lush sandy-colored hair stared back at her. She had to admit, Chancer had been fairly good-looking. But something about his charming smile didn't ring true. How many people had been fooled by that fake grin?

She continued reading.

Wayne Thomas Chancer had been born in Peasemore, Massachusetts. On the day he "died suddenly at home," he had just turned forty-three.

Suddenly at home. Not exactly a cause of death. His death certificate had to be more specific than that. What, precisely, had he died from?

The obit went on to describe Chancer's "illustrious career" as a personal injury lawyer, as well as his "deep commitment to local charitable causes." Oddly, none of those causes had been listed. Lara sensed that whoever had written the obit had struggled to find glowing things to write about the man. She hated to be negative about Chancer, especially in light of his unexplained death, but everything about him screamed *phony.*

Chancer was survived by his "loving wife" of five years, Karen Becker Chancer, and by his mother, Julia Harper Chancer Stevens, and stepfather, Dennis Stevens, both of Ithaca, New York. Plans for a memorial service would be announced at a later date.

With nothing to latch on to in the obit, Lara tried Googling him again. Several articles came up, the one about his triumph in the Japanese restaurant lawsuit being prominent.

The claimant had been a man in his late fifties—Perry Owens, of Madison, New Hampshire. He'd suffered "undue pain and suffering" along with gastrointestinal problems after consuming a bowl of miso soup at the Japanese Garden. Owens claimed that the restaurant's owners had become "defensive and arrogant" when he pointed out the bloody Band-Aid in his bowl after he'd already swallowed half the soup. To avoid going to trial, the Tanakas had agreed to a settlement that Owens claimed he could "live with." Lara suspected that between legal fees and costs, about half the amount ended up in Wayne Chancer's pocket.

Lara clicked on several other links, but nothing raised any red flags. She thought back to Gary Becker's cryptic remark about "knowing what he knew" before his daughter ever married Chancer, and how he should have halted the wedding then. Whatever it was, it had to have happened before the Chancers got married.

Fatigue burning her eyes, Lara set aside her tablet. Her heart wasn't in doing much of anything. Her powers of concentration were at an all-time low.

After saying good night to her aunt, Lara headed to her room, Panda trailing at her heels. He'd been leaning against the door to her studio, waiting for her. She'd almost tripped over him when she opened the door.

In her bedroom, she found Amber resting on her favorite perch on the cat tree. Sienna was curled up with Munster at foot of her bed. As gloomy as Lara felt, she couldn't help smiling. The cats always made her feel better, no matter what murky thoughts were weighing on her mind.

She went over to Amber and tickled her under the chin. The sweet girl closed her eyes blissfully but didn't purr.

Lara showered and put on warm pajamas, then tucked herself into bed with Panda, Sienna, and a mystery she'd borrowed from the library. Her mind wandered off the page so many times that she finally put aside the book.

The moment she turned off her bedside lamp, Gideon's face floated into her vision. It was the face of the man she loved, and who she'd thought loved her. Over the past month or so, as Sherry and David's wedding approached, he'd dropped a few not-so-subtle hints about "following in their path." Lara knew he'd been hinting that it was time they got engaged, but no proposal had been forthcoming. Had he been worried that she'd refuse? That she'd say she wasn't ready?

Tomorrow would be D-Day—decision day. They'd either agree to continue their relationship and work out their issues, or make the sad decision to end it. Lara was terrified that it might be the latter.

With worries over Gideon straining her brain, it was Abraham Lincoln's message of over a century and a half ago that she couldn't eject from her head.

You cannot escape the responsibility of tomorrow by evading it today.
If only she could figure out what that responsibility was.

Chapter 20

Sherry's joy shone from her face the moment Lara stepped inside the coffee shop. "Guess what?" she squealed. "Pastor Folger is going to co-officiate our wedding ceremony! He told us that we were one of the most compatible couples he's ever met!"

Lara smiled, genuinely thrilled for her friend. She went over and gave Sherry a hug. "That's great news, Sher. Have you and David shared the news with Loretta yet?" She dropped onto her usual stool and lowered her tote to the floor.

"Not yet." Sherry snatched a mug from beneath the counter and poured Lara a cup of coffee. "We're taking her to dinner tonight and telling her then. Who knows? She might not even be impressed. With Loretta, anything's possible."

"Call me an optimist, but I think the news is going to please her."

Sherry grinned. "Yeah, I think so, too. After dinner, David and I are taking her over to see our new apartment. David picked up the keys yesterday. Oh God, Lara, I can't wait to move in. Do you realize I've never lived anywhere except with my mom? And now, David and I have our own beautiful place. The carpeting is spotless, and the kitchen has all new appliances. I'm dying to show it to you."

"And I can't wait to see it," Lara assured her. "Remember, I promised you a watercolor. You still haven't told me want you wanted."

"I know. That's one of the million things on my list. David and I make all these decisions together."

Lara smiled, wondering how long that would last. She knew Sherry was the dominant partner in the relationship, and that David usually deferred to her judgment.

Holding the coffeepot aloft, Sherry stared hard at Lara. "Are you coming down with something? Your face looks way too pale. Don't you dare get the flu before the wedding."

"I'm fine. I promise. I've just got a lot on my plate."

"Well, start getting some rest," Sherry ordered. "We're officially in countdown mode. The wedding's only a few weeks away, and I want to see you rosy-cheeked and as chipper as a sparrow."

Lara laughed. "'Rosy-cheeked and as chipper as a sparrow'? How did you come up with that one?"

"Made it up." Sherry winked at her. "I'll get you a muffin."

Lara let out the breath she'd been holding. She had to pull herself together.

Jill zipped out of the kitchen holding a massive tray loaded with breakfast platters. She lifted a hand and waved at Lara, and for a moment Lara thought the tray was going to sail off into space. Fortunately, Jill was a pro at juggling. She managed to deliver the orders intact to a table of waiting customers.

Lara ate her muffin as quickly as she could, then made a thousand excuses for why she had to rush home. She prayed Sherry wouldn't mention Gideon. If she did, Lara wasn't sure she could keep her expression neutral.

Luckily, Sherry's head remained firmly planted in the clouds. She waggled her fingers at Lara as she pushed through the door into the kitchen.

Her scarf tucked securely around her neck, Lara hurried home. The sun was bright and the sky nearly cloudless, yet the temps remained in the twenties. When she reached their driveway, she saw a car parked next to the Saturn. Her heart plummeted.

It was Megan Haskell's red Honda.

* * * *

In the kitchen, Aunt Fran was putting on a kettle. Three mugs were lined up on the counter, along with a package of marshmallows. Her aunt nodded silently in the direction of the large parlor.

Megan sat on the sofa, her eyes looking sadder than they had during her prior visit. Panda rested atop her skinny thighs, his long white whiskers a contrast to Megan's candy-pink sweater. The cat stared up at Lara but remained where he was—content and cozy in the comfort of their visitor's lap.

Dark smudges rimmed Megan's lower lashes. Her sweater bore a blob of something she'd spilled—either spaghetti sauce or ketchup, Lara guessed.

She couldn't help thinking of the elderly woman Megan had screamed at in the pizza shop for getting sauce on her blouse.

"Megan, what are you doing here?" Lara pulled off her scarf and jacket and tossed them over a chair.

Megan's lower lip quivered. "I know, I should have called first. But I was afraid you'd tell me to leave you alone. I'm sorry, Lara, but this time I want to come clean. I realized you can't help me if I don't tell you the truth."

"I can't help you anyway," Lara retorted with a firmness that made Megan flinch. "I'm not a lawyer, and...my God, Megan, I barely know you. You need to work things out with your attorney, not with me. I really think you should go."

Megan's eyes filled, and she swallowed. "Okay, but...can we talk just for a minute? Please?"

Lara huffed out a frustrated breath, just as Aunt Fran came in with a tray bearing three mugs of marshmallow-topped cocoa and a pile of napkins. "I'll take mine into the kitchen," she said. "Why don't you two go in the meet-and-greet room, where you can talk privately."

Thanks a lot, Aunt Fran.

Lara took the tray and motioned to Megan to follow her.

Megan gently moved Panda to the sofa. They went into the meet-and-greet room and Lara closed the door. The cats would only distract Megan and keep her there longer, so she didn't invite them in. She set the mugs and napkins on the table and motioned to Megan to sit.

"I know I've caused a lot of trouble," Megan said meekly, twisting her hands in her lap. If a cat had been there, she'd no doubt have woven her fingers into the fur.

Lara lifted her mug and blew on her hot chocolate, sending chocolaty waves rippling through the marshmallow. When she lifted her gaze to meet Megan's, she was startled by the anguish she saw there.

"Okay, look," Lara said softly, setting down her mug, "why don't you go back to the beginning, when all of this started. Why did you really go to Gideon's office last Friday? Something tells me it wasn't about getting fired."

Megan snatched a napkin off the tray and blotted her eyes. "You're right. It wasn't. Not totally, anyway. I did get fired, but it was my own fault. The thing is, I just wanted to see Gideon again. Is that so awful?" She sniffled hard. "He was always so sweet to me, so kind and courteous. He's one of the few gentlemen left in the world, you know?"

Lara smiled. "That he is," she agreed, though she knew a lot of men who were "gentlemen."

"It was wrong of me to make up that story about being fired for incompetence," Megan went on. "I just…when I got there, I was afraid to tell him the truth, that I was fired for harassing Wayne while I was working for him." Megan sagged on her chair. "All I'd really wanted to do was reconnect with Gideon, I guess. I was hoping he might want to do the same. Instead, he looked super annoyed to see me. He was polite, like always, but he was different, too. I realized afterward why that was." She pointed a finger at Lara. "He's head over heels in love with you."

Megan's words made Lara's heart float up in her chest. "Is that why you made up the story about being fired for incompetence?"

"Exactly." She wiped her eyes again with the napkin. "Frankly, it was the first thing that came to mind. I needed an excuse for why I'd gone there without calling him first."

In that moment, Lara realized that she would never be able to trust Megan. Anything Megan told her would have to be taken with a grain of salt and a healthy dose of suspicion.

"Megan," Lara asked softly, "were you in love with Wayne Chancer? Did you have a crush on him?"

Megan nodded and sniffled. "I fell for him, Lara. Stupid me, getting the hots for my boss. So cliché, right? I've never had much of a love life, and Wayne had a powerful personality. He flirted with me, paid me all sorts of compliments. I took it the wrong way. I realized later he does that to every woman he finds attractive, but at the time I thought it was only me. I–I started calling him after hours, suggesting that I might be available to have a drink with him."

A drink that might lead to other things, Lara thought.

In truth, Lara pitied Megan. She'd been lonely and looking for love. It'd been easy for her to mistake Chancer's flirtations for sincere interest.

"I know now that he was a creep and a phony," Megan said in a shaky voice, "but at first I was really flattered."

"Megan, when did things escalate to the point where he fired you?"

"I overheard him talking to someone on the phone one night when I was working late at the office. I'd stayed to catch up on a few things, and he didn't know I was still at my desk. I'd hoped, maybe, when he noticed me working late, that he'd want to reward me and take me out to dinner. Instead, I overheard him talking to someone on the phone about me, calling me names like 'wacky pants' and 'crazy chick.' I knew then what he really thought of me. I was crushed." She cried softly into a napkin.

Lara waited until she'd composed herself. "So, what did you do?"

"I stormed into his office and confronted him. I told him I was going to have a nice little chat with his wife about all the women he was always carousing with. That's when he blew up and fired me. He grabbed my arm, pulled me over to my desk, and threw an empty box on the floor. He watched while I cleaned out my desk, then ordered me never to come back."

"How long ago was that?" Lara asked.

"It was right after Thanksgiving, so like, a few months ago? Thank God my aunt and uncle have been so good to me. They said I can stay with them as long as I want."

"Megan, what did you say when you crashed Wayne's birthday party? I mean, what did you *really* say that night?"

Megan inhaled sharply. "I told him he was a womanizer, a skirt chaser, and a low-down piece of…crap. I said a few other things, but I don't really want to repeat them." Her cheeks flushed a deep pink.

"Did a lot of people hear you?" Lara asked. "I mean, other than Wayne?"

"I don't know. I guess so. People were standing around in groups, talking and munching on goodies. Karen Chancer had hired Bakewell Custom Catering to do the food, and they kept coming out of the kitchen with trays of appetizers. There was also a huge tray of shrimp, which everyone was attacking." She shuddered. "I don't know how people eat that stuff, but to each his own, I guess."

"Back to the real issue. How did Wayne react when you started yelling at him in front of his guests?"

Megan covered her eyes with her hands. "He laughed at me, Lara. The pig stood there and laughed at me and said I was delusional. He threatened to call the police if I didn't leave." She took a fortifying sip of her cocoa.

"What about his wife? Was she close by?"

Megan nodded. "I think she was in the kitchen, but she heard me screaming and came in to see what all the commotion was. She stood there, staring at me like I had three heads. But she didn't say anything. She just turned and hurried away into another room. I felt bad because I'd always liked Karen. Anyway, I was standing near the shrimp tray, so I grabbed a handful and tossed them in Wayne's face."

A thought struck Lara. "Megan, could Wayne have been allergic to the shrimp? I know of a woman who died from a severe allergy to shellfish."

"No, he loved shrimp. Far as I know, he wasn't allergic to anything. Except honesty and human decency," she spat out.

"What happened next?" Lara asked quietly.

"There was a man there, a cousin of Wayne's. I'd met him once. He took my arm and kind of, you know, propelled me out the door. By that time, I realized I'd made a horrible spectacle of myself. I was so mortified. I got in my car and raced back to my aunt and uncle's house. I was crying so hard I almost couldn't see the road."

Oh, Megan. You really are your own worst enemy, Lara wanted to say.

"Megan, tell me honestly, why did you crash the party that night? What did you think you'd gain from it?"

Once again, tears filled Megan's eyes. "I don't know. After I found out Gideon had met his one and only, I suddenly felt so alone, so unwanted. Anyway, I thought crashing Wayne's party would make me feel better. I was wrong, wasn't I?"

"You were," Lara said, the words "*his one and only*" clinging to her heart. "But you were hurting, and you weren't thinking straight." After a lengthy pause, Lara said quietly, "Megan, tell me about the tattoo."

Megan gave her a surprised look, then her shoulders sagged. Her voice grew soft. "When I was sixteen, a boy at school invited me to the prom. I'd never really dated, so it took me kind of by surprise. He was sort of cute, though, in a nerdy way. Anyway, I said yes, even though I knew my father would probably go bonkers."

"He didn't want you to date?"

She shook her head. "He never trusted me. He always assumed the worst, that I'd get myself into trouble." Her eyes filled. "I wasn't that kind of girl, Lara. My own father didn't even know me."

"What about your mom?"

"Secretly she was on my side, but she was afraid to speak up to him. Looking back, I realize what a bully he was. When he finally agreed I could go to the prom, he insisted on driving to the mall with Mom and me to pick out my prom dress. He wanted to be sure it was suitable for a girl my age."

"Oh, Megan."

Megan took in a deep breath. "Anyway, when we got inside the mall, we happened to pass by a pet shop. In the window was this adorable black-and-white kitten. All alone, he was meowing his little heart out. I bent down to talk to him through the glass, and he reached up with his paw and clawed at the window." She swallowed. "I couldn't help myself. I started to cry. I begged my father to let me adopt him. I told him I'd skip the prom if I could just have the kitten."

Lara was afraid to hear the rest.

"He laughed at me, literally. Told me he wasn't going to have some filthy animal living in his home. He said cats belonged in barns, killing mice. And then"—she swallowed—"he flicked his fingers at the glass to frighten the kitten. The poor little thing flinched. The look on that sad little face broke my heart. I ran out to the car, bawling my eyes out."

Lara felt her own eyes filling with tears. *What a horrible man.*

"The next day, I went to the only tattoo parlor I knew of and asked if I could get a small tattoo of a kitten on my wrist. It was my first attempt at defying my father. They refused, though, because I wasn't eighteen. So, on my eighteenth birthday, I went back there and got this tattoo." She held out her wrist. "It's like, a tribute to that sweet kitten I saw that day. It's also a reminder of the promise I made to myself, that someday I'll have a kitten just like this one."

Lara went over and hugged her. "Megan, thank you for sharing that with me. I'm sure it wasn't easy. But when you finally got your own place, why didn't you adopt a kitten?"

Megan shrugged. "Seems like every place I lived they didn't allow pets. The one place where they did allow them, I had a roommate who was allergic."

"That's too bad," Lara said. She couldn't help thinking of the resemblance between Panda and the kitten tattooed on Megan's wrist.

Megan gulped down the remaining dregs of hot chocolate in her mug. "I'd better go. I won't darken your door again, I promise." She gave out a little laugh.

Lara rose and escorted her back to the large parlor. Megan had left her coat on the sofa next to her purse, and Panda had made a cozy little bed from it. He gazed up at Megan and yawned.

"Oh, gosh, he looks so cute, doesn't he?" Megan said. She leaned down and hugged the cat, then slid her coat out from under him.

Lara smiled. "You're definitely one of his favorite visitors," she said, hoping to make her feel a little better. "Megan, before you go, have the police found out anything new about Wayne's cause of death? Was it definitely poison?"

Megan stuck her arm in a sleeve. "I guess it's looking that way. My attorney said they've ruled out most of the food, since so many other people had shared it. If he was poisoned, someone had to have added it directly to whatever he ate. Knowing Wayne, that was probably just about everything. The only thing he indulged in that no one else did was the cigar he smoked after the party. He'd gone outside to smoke it—Karen was a stickler about that. She didn't allow smoking in the house."

"Interesting," Lara said. "Did he already have the cigars, or were they a birthday present?"

"You're pretty sharp to ask that," Megan said. "Turned out the cigars had been delivered that morning, wrapped in a beautiful container. They're being tested at the state police crime lab now."

"Was there a note with the cigars?"

"I've told you everything I know, Lara," Megan said, sounding exasperated now. She buttoned her coat and grabbed her purse off the sofa, then her shoulders drooped. "I'm sorry, I didn't mean to snap. You and your aunt have been very nice to me. Whatever happens, I won't forget you, either of you."

Lara walked her to the door and wished her luck. The words "*if there's anything I can do…*" lingered on her tongue, but she snatched them back. Megan looked as if she wanted to hug Lara, but then quickly turned and left.

Peering through the front window, Lara watched as Megan trudged out to her car. With her head down and her arms wrapped around herself, she looked like a lost soul.

Lara went back to the meet-and-greet room and tidied up the table. It was almost eleven. She'd promised to meet Gideon at his office at one.

Even if she started now, there wasn't enough time to whip up a batch of scones with the cherry fruit spread inside. She'd have to save that for another day.

If there was another day.

A feeling of doom fell over her. Her meeting with Gideon was going to be pivotal. After today, their relationship would turn in one direction or another.

There would be no in-between.

Chapter 21

Before she headed to Gideon's office, Lara made up two ham and cheese sandwiches with lettuce and tomato. She stuck them in a grocery bag, along with two wrapped dill pickle spears and a large bag of chips. Gideon always had water and coffee in his office, so she didn't pack any drinks. Remembering the shortbread cookies she'd bought at Felicia's store a few days earlier, she added those to the bag as well.

Ten minutes later, she knocked lightly on the door to Gideon's office and poked her head inside. "Hey," she said, when she saw him hunched over his desk.

He looked up sharply but didn't smile. "Lara, I didn't even hear the front door open." He rose quickly and dashed over to take her bag and her jacket. "Still freezing out?"

She smiled, a gesture he did not return. "Well, it made it all the way into the thirties, so I guess that's progress. It was seventeen degrees when I woke up. You looked like you were lost in thought there. Busy day?"

He nodded. "Isn't it always?"

My, we're chatty today, aren't we?

It seemed as if things were devolving even before their conversation began. She took a seat in the chair opposite Gideon's desk and set her tote on the floor.

"I hope you're hungry," she said, trying to sound upbeat. "I made two huge ham and cheese sandwiches, and I also brought along some shortbread cookies."

"Shortbread?" He looked perplexed. "Did you make the cookies?"

"No, I bought them." She decided not to reveal where. So far, Gideon's demeanor hadn't been too encouraging.

His face reddened. "Um, actually, Lara, I already had a quick bite for lunch. Marina grabbed a tuna wrap from the coffee shop for me before she left."

Lara's stomach dropped. Hadn't she mentioned she'd be bringing sandwiches? Or had she left it vague? She couldn't recall now.

"That's okay. Save them for a snack later, or for supper if you'd like."

Gideon didn't bother asking Lara if she was hungry, or if she wanted one of the sandwiches. He plunged right in. "I understand you had a visitor this morning."

"I…we, how did you know?"

He released a long sigh. "I decided to stop by your house around nine thirty. I thought maybe you'd had a few free minutes, and we could talk there instead of here."

A few free minutes? Did he think that was all it would take to resolve their differences?

"But," he went on, an edge to his tone, "I saw a familiar red car in your driveway, so I didn't bother to stop."

Oh no. Talk about lousy timing.

"She stopped by uninvited, Gideon," Lara said, unable to keep the snark out of her own voice. "We talked, and I told her that I couldn't help her. She opened up about a few things she'd lied about. I guess she wanted to get everything off her chest, so to speak. Bottom line, I don't think I'll be seeing her again. Besides, I'm not even sure she's a prime suspect anymore. Plenty of other people hated Wayne Chancer."

Gideon met her gaze with a level one of his own. For the first time since she'd arrived, Lara realized how tired and drawn he looked. Even his eyes were a bit bloodshot. She felt a sudden urge to leap off her chair, rush over to him, and wrap him in a hug.

But something else, some unseen force, kept her rooted to her seat—the sinking feeling that no matter what she said, or did, it was not going to move him.

"'Plenty of other people'," he repeated, his voice taut. "How do you know that? Who else have you been talking to?"

Anger, mixed with disappointment, rose inside her like a rogue wave. "I already told you who I talked to, Gideon. Tina Tanaka asked me to meet her at the diner because she wanted to talk about a matter totally unrelated to Megan, or to Wayne Chancer. I'm not going to tell you what it was, because I promised Tina I wouldn't. It's private, and it's confidential. As a lawyer, you should understand that."

Gideon's jaw lowered slightly, and his face paled. He couldn't have looked more shocked if Lara had physically slapped him.

More quietly now, Lara said, "I happened to meet Karen Chancer's dad when I was chatting with Tina, but it was totally inadvertent. I went back to the gourmet food shop because I wanted to buy a few more things—the goodies there are mind-boggling. When Kayla and I were there on Monday, we didn't really have enough time to browse."

Even as she said it, Lara realized how lame it all sounded. And she hadn't even mentioned her encounter with Karen Chancer yet. Should she spill everything? Or had she done enough damage to their relationship?

Gideon looked away, his gaze fixed on the watercolor Lara had painted for him. Was he thinking this was the end? That they wouldn't be seeing each other anymore?

He turned slightly and folded his hands over his blue desk blotter. "I appreciate your being up front with me, Lara, but I still think you're holding something back." His voice was hoarse. "You've gone to Bakewell twice, now, and I suspect you'll go back again. This isn't just about shoes, or about gourmet treats, is it? Something else is going on."

Lara closed her eyes, contemplating her answer. When she opened them, she said, "Think about it, Gideon. If I hadn't gone to Bakewell on Monday, I'd still be looking for shoes to go with my dress, and Sherry would still be agonizing over her wedding favors. As it is, we've resolved both problems—minor though they were in the scheme of things. All I'm saying is, things happen for a reason. You and I have talked about that in the past."

"Yes, we have." He blew out a breath. "So, what's next?"

"What's next? I'm not even sure what you mean by that." She thought about telling him that Pastor Folger was going to co-officiate Sherry and David's wedding ceremony, but she held back. With the attitude he was displaying, he didn't deserve to know. "Right now, I'm focused on doing everything I can to help Sherry with her wedding prep."

His smile was flat. "Which includes going back to Bakewell to pick up shoes and fortune cookies. How convenient."

Lara felt her stomach do a backflip. "That's so unfair of you, Gideon. I can't even believe you said that."

He lowered his head but said nothing. Lara saw his eyes water.

"When you feel like talking—I mean, *really* talking, which includes listening—please let me know. You know how to reach me."

She bent down and grabbed her tote, then went toward the door.

Gideon came after her. Her hand was already on the doorknob when he gently took her arm. "Lara, wait. Before you go, I need to say something. I love you, more than I've ever loved anyone. More than I've been able to express." His voice faltered. "I'm just so afraid that one day something will happen, like before, and I won't be able to get there in time to help you. It's my worst fear."

Something inside Lara melted, and a tear leaked from her eye. "I totally get that. Honestly, I do. I know I've gotten myself into a few...scrapes in the past."

"'Scrapes'?" He gaped at her as if she'd sprouted horns. "Is that what you call them?"

"Okay, it was worse than that," she admitted. "But think of the good that came from them. Think of the bad guys sitting behind bars right now who might otherwise be walking the streets."

He shook his head. He released her arm, and with his thumb blotted the tear crawling down her cheek. "I'm sorry, Lara, but I just can't see it that way. I don't understand why you have to be a one-woman crusader for justice."

"My God, is that how you see me?"

He held out his arms and shrugged. "Okay, maybe that was too strong. But please, Lara, *please* try to see things from where I'm standing." He took her hand in his. "Just try, okay?"

She closed her eyes, but not to do as he asked. She had to figure out where to go from here.

Lara squeezed his hand and pulled in a calming breath. "After the wedding, we'll have plenty of time to sit down and work things out. Right now, I don't want to see anything happen that could spoil Sherry's special day. Can we at least agree on that?"

Slowly, he removed his hand from hers and gave her a brisk nod, his eyes full of pain. "Yes, we can," he said quietly.

Afraid of bursting into tears, Lara kissed him lightly on the cheek and hurried outside. She thought she heard him calling her name, but if he did, it was too late.

He'd asked her to try to see his point of view and she'd blatantly ignored him. If he'd done that to her, she'd be furious.

Lara drove back to the shelter, slowing to a near-crawl to allow for her blurry vision. The moment she pulled into the driveway, her phone pinged with a text. She dug it out of her tote, praying it was from Gideon begging her to return to his office.

Her stomach clenched when she saw the name.

Karen Chancer.

Lara read the text.

> *Lara, would you mind if I called you? I want to*
> *ask a favor from you.*

Her finger hovered above the text. *Delete it*, she told herself. *Pretend you never saw it.*

She tapped the Reply box.

> *Sure. Call any time.*

Chapter 22

Lara groaned and dropped her head on the kitchen table. "Oh God, Aunt Fran. She wants me to go to her husband's memorial service with her on Monday. When I saw her at the Peach Crate yesterday, she never even mentioned a service." In her lap, Munster let out a squeak of alarm. "Sorry, sweetie, did I scare you?" She bent and kissed his furry orange head. He closed his eyes and purred to let her know he was okay.

"But why?" Aunt Fran asked. "You only met her once, and you're not a friend of the family. I really think she's taking advantage of your generous nature."

"I know. I *know*." Lara moaned again, this time careful not to disturb her lap cat. "She said that half the town thinks she poisoned her husband. She's afraid everyone will be gossiping about her and pointing fingers at her."

Aunt Fran pushed her laptop aside and took a slow sip of her fragrant tea—one of the specialty flavors Lara had picked up at the Peach Crate. "But her dad will be there, won't he? Isn't that better than having a near-stranger accompany you?"

Lara sighed. "She said her dad will be 'running interference,' as she put it. She wants me there for moral support. I get the sense that she doesn't have a huge support group of friends."

The more Lara thought about it, the more she wished she'd grown a backbone and refused Karen Chancer's request. No way did she want to attend that memorial service. Besides, she had no right to be there. She never knew the man, and so far, she hadn't met anyone who'd had a kind word to say about him.

"Maybe between now and then the police will have caught the killer," Aunt Fran said.

"That would be wonderful," Lara said, "but I'm not hanging my hopes on it."

"Lara, not to bring up a touchy subject, but how did things go with Gideon this morning?"

Lara shook her head. "Not good. He said he didn't understand why I had to be a 'one-woman crusader for justice.' That's exactly how he worded it."

"Oh, Lara. This breaks my heart."

Mine, too, Lara thought, but didn't dare voice it for fear of spilling more tears.

"We agreed that we'll let things stay in a lull until after the wedding. But then, we have some serious things to work out." *If they can ever be worked out.*

Aunt Fran absently stroked the black cat nestled in her lap. Her expression grew pensive, as if she was debating with herself whether or not to speak her mind. Then, "Lara, there's something I never told you about my husband's death."

Lara stared at her. "I always assumed it was too difficult for you to talk about it."

"The memory still hurts, but not as much as it once did. Brian died in the midst of a raging snowstorm. He stopped on the highway to help a stranded motorist and a plow hit him straight-on." Her eyes welled.

"I'm so sorry, Aunt Fran." Lara had heard that much of the story before, but no one, not even her dad, had ever shared the details.

"I was in our apartment studying for an exam when I heard the doorbell ring. We lived just off campus, close enough for me to walk to classes, but an easy commute to the school where Brian was teaching." She blotted one eye with the corner of a napkin. "Anyway, I hurried to answer the door—I thought maybe Brian had forgotten his key. I didn't want him standing out there in the frigid cold any longer than necessary. But it wasn't Brian. It was a police officer."

Lara closed her eyes and shook her head.

"After he told me what had happened, I think I actually passed out for a few moments. When I came to, I was sitting in a chair, crying. Sobbing, actually."

"I can't even imagine," Lara said hoarsely, feeling tears slide down her cheeks.

"But…the reason I'm telling you this is that earlier that day, as we were rushing through breakfast, Brian and I had a terrible argument. I'd felt he was running himself ragged taking on too many projects at school. He, on the other hand, wanted to help pay down my student loans as quickly as possible, which is why he started doing some athletic coaching on the side. It didn't pay a lot, but every cent he earned from it he put toward my loans. As for me, I was young, newly married, and studying hard to earn my degree. I felt as if Brian and I never had enough time to spend together."

Lara thought back to her own college experience. Her dad had paid most of her art school tuition out of his own pocket. Any money Lara earned for books and incidentals came from working part-time in bakeries or coffee shops. She realized, now, how lucky she was to have had such a supportive family.

"Well, I won't bore you any more with details," Aunt Fran went on quietly, "but here's what I want to emphasize. When that policeman told me Brian had been killed by a snowplow, my whole world fell apart. We'd made so many plans for our future. In one horrible moment, in an accident that was beyond his control, his life was cut short."

Lara set Munster on her chair, then went over and hugged her aunt tightly. "I never knew."

"All I could think of"—her aunt swallowed—"was that the last words we'd spoken to each other were harsh ones. I was anxious for him to get home that night so I could apologize and set things straight. And then—" She bowed her head and squeezed Dolce.

Lara took in a deep breath to keep herself from bursting into tears. It wasn't hard to figure out what her aunt was trying to tell her.

She needed to make things right with Gideon.

She understood better, now, why her aunt wanted to write a novel. It was cathartic for her. It helped her to deal with the feelings of guilt and loss she'd carried all these years.

Lara went back to her chair, where Munster had sprawled into a furry orange rug. She lifted him gently and set him in her lap again.

Aunt Fran sat up straight. "Lara," she said firmly, "let's get back to the present. It's not too late to change your mind about going to the memorial service. Tell Karen the truth—that you don't feel comfortable attending a service for a man you didn't even know. Explain that you have a lot going on right now, and that you can't add one more thing to your schedule."

Lara shook her head, and a curly strand of copper-colored hair fell over her eye. She pushed it back. She had an appointment with Kellie at Kurl-me-Klassy the following week. She wanted to get her hair trimmed as close as possible to Sherry's wedding day, so she'd gone without a haircut for way longer than usual. "I can't, Aunt Fran. It's too late for that. I gave her my word. Oh Lord, if you could've heard her on the phone. She sounded so…pathetic."

"She could have been acting," her aunt pointed out. "She also could've poisoned her husband. Who else would be in a better position to do it?"

The thought that Karen might have killed her husband gave Lara a mental jolt. The more she ran it through her mind, the more she saw the possibility.

Why did Karen throw her husband a birthday party in the first place? It wasn't a milestone birthday, like his fortieth. It was his forty-third birthday. And from everything Lara had learned about Wayne Chancer, he'd made more enemies than friends over the years.

Maybe Karen had been trying to rescue a faltering marriage. Maybe she'd wanted to give him the party as a gesture of love and faith.

Or maybe she wanted to set him up for being poisoned with a few dozen potential suspects present.

"I should have told her no, shouldn't I?" Lara pushed her empty mug to the center of the table.

"In my opinion, yes," her aunt said. "But as you said, you gave your word. Would you like me to go with you?"

Lara smiled. "You're such a darling aunt. That's sweet of you, but I'd feel as if I were subjecting you to torture. I'll go, and I'll get through it just fine. After that, I'm done. If I have to go back to Bakewell to pick up my shoes, I'll drag Sherry along with me."

She kissed Munster's head, then set him on the floor. After cleaning up the table, she went into her studio. So many things were bouncing around in her head. She found it almost impossible to decide what to do next.

In less than a week's time, her life had turned upside down. Only a week before, she'd been sure that becoming engaged to Gideon was a near certainty. Now, she was in danger of losing him altogether, and she wasn't even sure why.

Her tablet was sitting where she'd left it, on her worktable. She was booting it up when she spied movement out of the corner of her eye.

The photo again—the one of Amy's farmhouse. Somehow it had landed on the floor. Which was strange, because Lara distinctly remembered having tucked it safely under her cat-shaped marble paperweight. Now, a fluffy Ragdoll cat sat on the photo, gazing up at Lara with her intense turquoise eyes.

Lara spoke aloud to the cat. "What are you trying to tell me, Blue? Do you want me to look at the picture again?"

Her tablet came to life, just as Blue faded into the ether. Lara checked her email. She'd gotten a response from Amy with two photos attached.

Hey, are these any better? I took them yesterday with my phone, so you might want to stick with the original pic. I'm not the world's best photographer (giggle). Up to you! Feel free to omit that crummy old wicker chair on the porch from the painting, unless you think it makes for a vintage look. I'll be throwing it out in the spring. Cheers! Amy.

Amy's short message made Lara smile. With all the sad things Amy saw every day in her veterinary practice, she always maintained a bubbly, positive attitude.

Lara clicked open the first pic. Amy's farmhouse was shown against a backdrop of dazzling blue sky, a wisp of pale smoke puffing out of the brick chimney. The snow was linen-white, stretching across the old cow pasture in gently rolling mounds. In front of the house, dried patches of frozen leaves huddled against the cold.

Not seeing much difference between the original photo and the one she'd just viewed, Lara opened the second pic.

Aw, look at that. In between shots, a male cardinal had landed on the porch railing. The bird was a startling red, a gorgeous burst of color against the seemingly endless snow. Funny that Amy hadn't mentioned him. She'd probably taken the photos quickly and hadn't examined them too closely.

Lara had once read that cardinals were a symbol of loved ones who've passed on. They appeared when you needed them most, especially in times of trouble. Her dad had died from colon cancer years before, and she still missed him. Time had softened the ache, but it was always there.

Was that why the cardinal had appeared suddenly in the photo? Was it a reminder that her dad was watching over her?

Whether or not it was true, the thought gave her comfort. After placing two sheets of photographic paper into her printer, Lara printed out each one.

She set all three photos next to one another and examined them. Not much difference. She kind of liked the old wicker chair on Amy's front porch. Coated with patches of snow, it added a sense of peaceful realism to the scene. For sure, the cardinal would stay.

What else? Was there a subtle difference she wasn't picking up on?

It had to be the cardinal. Maybe it was Blue's way of reminding her that her dad was always with her. But how did Blue know that a cardinal would appear in a new photo?

She jumped when her cell rang, and she set aside the photos. She grabbed the phone from her pocket, hoping to see Gideon's smiling face appear on her screen. Instead, it was an unfamiliar number. "Lara Caphart."

"Oh, good," a woman's voice said. "I wasn't sure I had the right number. This is the cat shelter, right?"

"It is," Lara said, putting a smile in her voice. Since the shelter was currently closed, the calls were being forwarded to her cell. "What can I help you with?"

The woman went on to explain that she'd seen a cat on the High Cliff Shelter's Web page that she might be interested in adopting. She had a tabby of her own who was FIV positive, and she'd been hoping to bring a furry friend into his life.

"That's our Sienna," Lara said. "She's a beautiful girl with a sweet personality. Adoption hours start at one tomorrow. Can you come by tomorrow afternoon to meet her? If not, we have adoption hours on Saturday, too."

"Shoot. I was afraid you'd say that." The woman sounded distressed. "I'm sorry, I haven't even introduced myself. I'm Jeannie Jennings. I own a catering company, so Fridays and weekends are my busiest days. I don't suppose, I mean, is there any chance you could make an exception for me? If you're going to be there, I could drive over this afternoon."

Lara didn't even have to think about it. They agreed that Jeannie would come by around two that afternoon.

Excited over the prospect of Sienna finding her forever home, Lara ran into the kitchen to tell her aunt.

Chapter 23

"I am like, so sick of being a frozen Popsicle. Is this cold ever going to end?" Kayla pulled off her scarf and tugged off her jacket, dropping both on a free chair in the kitchen. Her nose was red, and her glasses were fogged. She whipped them off and blotted them with a corner of her jersey top.

Lara smiled. "Hey, it's New Hampshire, and it's winter. Need I say more?"

"Yeah, yeah." Kayla waved a hand at her.

"Hot chocolate?" Lara asked.

"Yes!"

Lara put on the kettle, then set up two mugs with hot chocolate mix.

Kayla sat down and rubbed her hands together. "Where's Ms. C?"

"Upstairs. She said she hadn't cleaned her bedroom in ages, and there's enough cat hair in there to crochet a new cat. But…I think there might be another reason, too."

"Uh-oh."

Her aunt hadn't said anything, but Lara had been reading between the lines.

"Twinkles has been failing. He doesn't come downstairs much anymore. We've been keeping him comfortable upstairs, but I see him getting weaker every day. I think Aunt Fran likes to sit up there with him and read, to let him know that he hasn't been forgotten. Sometimes"—Lara choked back a lump—"sometimes I hear her reading out loud in her room, but quietly, in a soothing voice. I think she's reminding Twinkles that she's there for him, always."

Kayla looked heartbroken. "As if any cat in this household would ever be forgotten. I'm not ready to lose Twinkles, Lara."

"I'm not either. But I have other news, and it's good." She told Kayla about the woman who was coming by that afternoon to visit with Sienna.

"Oh, that is good news! If she works out, that is. She still needs to be approved."

"I know, but I have a good feeling about her." Lara poured boiling water into Kayla's mug, then into her own. "Shall we work on finishing that editorial today?"

"Sounds good to me." Stirring her hot chocolate, Kayla stared across the table at Lara. "You're looking a little pale yourself. Are you okay?"

Lara shook her head. Kayla knew her too well and was adept at reading her moods. "Gideon and I have been struggling over a…particular issue. Right now, we're sort of at an impasse."

Kayla's eyes flashed. "Hmmm, a particular issue. Anything to do with Blue?"

"No," Lara said, but then wondered if Kayla might have hit upon something.

Gideon had always assured her that he believed in Lara's spirit cat. Enough crazy things had happened to her that couldn't otherwise have been explained.

Still, it took a huge amount of faith to believe in a cat no one could see. No one except Lara, that is—and even then, she only saw brief flashes of Blue. Looking at it from Gideon's point of view, she could understand a bit of skepticism. If she was honest with herself, there were many times when she'd doubted her own sanity. When she'd wondered if Blue was a figment of her overworked imagination.

Other times, she knew the Ragdoll cat was real. Blue had been there when Lara needed her most. In a physical sense, she'd rescued her on more than one occasion.

"Lara?" Kayla waved a hand in front of her. "Are you sure it's not about Blue?"

"I'm pretty sure," Lara said. "He's not thrilled that I've gone to Bakewell twice. He thinks I'm—"

"Wait a minute," Kayla interrupted. "You went there again?"

Lara sighed. "Yeah, yesterday. It's kind of a long story, but Tina Tanaka wanted me to meet her at the diner. She apologized for being so rude to me at the bridal shop. Evidently she checked me out more thoroughly and decided I was one of the good guys."

Kayla looked surprised. "That's good, I guess. Couldn't she have apologized over the phone, though? Seems like a stretch to ask you to drive over there just for an apology."

Lara felt her face flushing. She hated lying, but Tina had revealed her secret about Jade in the strictest of confidence. If anyone would be inclined to believe the story, it was Kayla. Still, Lara had no intention of breaking her promise to Tina.

"I know, but we chatted about a few other things. One thing I learned for sure, she loathed Wayne Chancer."

Kayla's eyes narrowed, then she sat back in her chair. "Oh my God. You're investigating the murder, aren't you? That's why Gideon's so bummed."

Lara winced. "No, not…not really. I just keep stumbling onto things that are leading me down that path." She squeezed her fingers over the bridge of her nose. "It's so hard to explain, Kayla, but something is drawing me there, and I don't think it has anything to do with Megan."

For at least a minute, Kayla was silent. Then she took a sip of her cocoa and dabbed a napkin to her lips. "I don't know what to say except, what can I do to help?"

"Probably nothing. Just put up with me until all this stuff passes, okay?" Lara gave Kayla a half-hearted smile.

"Agreed." Kayla's face beamed suddenly at the black-and-white cat strutting toward her. "Hey, I wondered where you were." She patted her lap and Panda jumped on board. Kayla rubbed her nose against his face, and he purred like a contented tiger.

For the next few hours, Lara and Kayla worked on changing litter, washing food and water bowls, and grooming the cats. Lara put out a fresh table runner in the meet-and-greet room to prepare for Jeannie Jennings's visit. Sienna was perched on the cat tree in the large parlor, gazing out at the frozen landscape in between snoozes. Lara prayed that Jeannie might be the perfect mom for her.

Lara was giving the windows in the meet-and-greet room a once-over with glass cleaner when a little green car swooped into the parking area reserved for the shelter. A woman wearing a hat with knitted ears that made her look like a brown bear hopped out of the car. She hoisted a large, rainbow-patterned handbag onto her shoulder and strode up to the door. Before she had a chance to ring the bell, Lara opened it.

"Jeannie?"

The woman, who looked to be in her mid-twenties, flashed a bright white smile. "Yup. In the flesh." She stuck out a gloved hand. "Are you Lara?"

"I am. Come on in. Can I take your coat?"

"Nah. I'll keep it on for now." Jeannie's gaze bounced all around the room, and her smile widened. "Whoa. This place is so cool." Tugging off her gloves, she ambled over to the bulletin board, where photos of the shelter's successful adoptions were posted. She pointed at a photo of a trim, seventyish woman clutching two darling kittens. "Hey, I recognize her. She's a famous actress, right?"

"That's right," Lara said. "Deanna Daltry. Those kittens—Bogie and Bacall—are fully grown now. They have the run of her mansion."

"Awesome."

Kayla came into the room, and Lara introduced them to one another. "Lara told me you're interested in meeting Sienna," Kayla said.

"I am." Her expression grew serious. "My little guy, Bunny, is FIV positive. I've been hesitant to adopt another cat because of that. The thing is, I know Bunny would love a feline companion. And I would love another cat."

Lara waved her over to a chair, and they all sat down.

Jeannie set her gloves on the table and continued. "My vet assured me that the only way another cat could get infected by Bunny is if he *bit* the other cat. Which is never gonna happen. No way. But I've still been a little worried about getting another cat. The thing is, my job keeps me tied up for long hours, especially on weekends. I want Bunny to have a buddy when I'm gone."

Lara suspected that Jeannie had good intentions. Nonetheless, she needed to be sure that Sienna would be as well-loved as Bunny if she became a member of her household.

Lara had done a bit of research on the subject, and she'd also consulted with Amy. FIV positive cats should be examined by their vet twice a year, which included having blood work done. They should also be spayed or neutered and live indoors. At the slightest sign of illness, a visit to the vet was crucial.

"The good thing about a cat who's FIV positive is that it's not the death sentence some people think it is," Lara said. "But there is a higher level of care involved, which I'm sure you know."

As if she'd read Lara's mind, Jeannie began ticking off points on her fingers. "I take Bunny to the vet for a checkup every six months, at which time he gets every test imaginable. He's neutered, of course, and he never goes outside. I feed him exactly what my vet advises, nothing funky or raw."

Lara peeked over at Kayla and saw her smiling. Jeannie was saying everything she wanted to hear.

"Plus," Jeannie emphasized, "I know that at the slightest sign of sickness, I'm supposed to take him to the vet right away. Fortunately, that hasn't happened with Bunny."

"How did you land on the name 'Bunny'?" Lara asked her.

Grinning, Jeannie rummaged through her tote and brought out a plastic sheaf of pictures. She pulled out a photo and handed it to Lara. "Take a look at those ears. Aren't they adorable?"

Lara stared at the photo of a cinnamon-colored cat with alert gold eyes and delicate white whiskers. His large ears gave him the look of being constantly on alert. "Oh my, is he an Abyssinian?"

"Yes, he is. Gorgeous little guy, isn't he?" She took the picture from Lara and gave it to Kayla. "I got him from a woman who'd bought him from a friend who supposedly was a reputable breeder. When she found out the kitty was FIV positive, she had a fit. The so-called breeder"—she made air quotes around the word—"refused to take him back, but the woman who'd bought him definitely didn't want him anymore. I found out about him through a neighbor of mine who knew the woman. If I hadn't adopted Bunny, she was going to have him euthanized. Can you believe it?" The outrage in Jeannie's voice could have been cut with a knife and served on toast.

"She sounds like an idiot," Kayla said harshly, returning the photo to Jeannie. She looked over at Lara and smiled. "Shall I bring Sienna in?"

"Yes! First of all, where are my manners? Jeannie, would you like a warm drink? We have tea, hot chocolate—"

"No, just the cat please." Jeannie smiled eagerly, her soft brown eyes dancing with anticipation.

Kayla left the room and returned a minute later with Sienna nestled in her arms. "Here's our princess," Kayla said.

Jeannie's face lit up. "Oh gosh, she's the most beautiful tortie I've ever seen!" Kayla went over to Jeannie, and Sienna almost fell into her arms. The cat curled up against Jeannie's puffy jacket as if she knew she'd found her forever mom.

Lara crossed her fingers. *Another successful match*, she hoped.

She gave Jeannie time to get acquainted with Sienna, while Kayla went about putting together their standard adoption packet, along with an application.

"This is like, even better than I could've hoped for," Jeannie gushed, her cheek buried in Sienna's fur. "She's so affectionate. I just know she'll make the perfect companion for Bunny. Are you guys okay with my adopting her? Is there some like, protocol I have to go through?"

Lara gazed over at the sole unoccupied chair. A cream-colored Ragdoll with turquoise eyes was staring at Jeannie with something akin to adoration.

She smiled at Jeannie. "Something tells me you and Bunny are perfect for Sienna. We do have an application process, though, and we'll ask for references."

"No problem." Jeannie looked as if she'd just struck a vein of gold in her yard. "I've got a super busy weekend coming up, so the timing might be perfect. I'm catering a Valentine's Day dance at a private high school tomorrow night, and I'm doing two birthday parties on the weekend. By Monday I'll have some free time to buy new kitty supplies and get the house ready for Sienna. Do you think my application might be approved by then?"

"I'm sure it will." Lara's heart jolted in her chest at something Jeannie had said earlier. "Did you say you have a catering company?"

Jeannie's face lit up with pride. "I sure do. If you ever need a gig catered, I'm your gal." Still clutching Sienna, she freed one hand and pulled two business cards out of her handbag. She slid one over to each of them.

Lara took the card and stared at it, her pulse racing. Jeannie Jennings was the owner and proprietor of Bakewell Custom Catering.

"Bakewell Custom Catering. Jeannie, did you cater the birthday party for Wayne Chancer last week?"

Jeannie's expression tightened, and her eyes glazed over. "I did. In all my years of catering, it's the one job I wish I'd never accepted. You probably heard in the news that the police think Wayne Chancer was poisoned at the party." Jeannie twisted her lips.

Lara and Kayla nodded in unison.

"Well, the next morning they summoned me and my employees to the police station—separately, of course—and questioned us for hours. Plus, they took samples of every bit of food and drink we served that night so they could examine it. Don't get me wrong. I'm not complaining. I have the deepest respect for the police. A man died horribly, and they were doing what they had to do. But it was embarrassing, to say the least—not to mention a huge waste of time. A couple of my employees felt like they were being singled out."

"Did the police ever tell you what the results were?" Lara asked her.

Jeannie's smile was tight. "They found nothing—not one iota of our food that could've caused Chancer's death."

Lara mulled that over. "So, have they figured out yet what killed him?"

"At first, they thought it was a heart attack, but the medical examiner ruled that out. I'm not sure I'm supposed to reveal this but—" She looked at each of them, then pulled Sienna closer, eliciting a soft purr from the kitty. "I have a cousin who works at the Bakewell police station. She just happened to overhear a conversation between our chief of police and one of the state police guys. They think whatever poisoned Chancer was in the cigar he smoked after the party."

Cigars! The same thing Megan had mentioned.

"But if that's the case," Lara said, "shouldn't they be able to trace where they came from?"

"My cousin told me they're working on it, but so far they haven't located the source. Apparently, the cigars were delivered rather secretively, either the day before the party or the morning of. In all the hoopla getting ready for the party, Chancer's wife didn't notice when they arrived or who delivered them."

"What about the poison itself?" Kayla asked. "Have they figured out what it was?"

Jeannie shook her head. "Not yet, but whatever it was, it led to heart failure." She gazed down at the cat in her arms, and her voice softened. "Right now, adopting this little girl is my top priority. Can I fill out the application while I'm here and leave it with you?"

"Sure," Lara said. "That would be perfect. How about some tea while you work on it?"

"No thanks." Her cheeks pinked. "But I wouldn't mind having one of those yummy-looking sugar cookies I saw on your Web page."

Lara laughed. "You got it."

"I'll get it," Kayla offered. "Are they in the container in the kitchen?"

"Yep. Same place."

After Kayla left, something occurred to Lara. "By the way, how did you happen to check out our shelter? I'm thrilled that you did, but if I'm not mistaken, there's a no-kill shelter even closer to you, right outside of Bakewell."

Jeannie smiled. "Easy question. One of my employees recommended this shelter. In fact, I think you met her recently. Tina Tanaka?"

A cold chill skittered down Lara's spine. "Tina works for you?"

"She sure does. Part-time, anyway. I've tried to persuade her to buy in to my business and become an equal partner with me, but she's hell-bent on making her fortune cookie company into a national brand."

So, Tina worked for the catering company that had catered Chancer's party. How interesting that she'd never mentioned it.

Interesting or deceitful?

"Jeannie, was...Tina at the Chancer party the night he died?"

"Yeah, she was, but she stayed in the kitchen so she wouldn't have to look at him. She despised Chancer, said he was a creep and a weasel. She didn't want him to see her either, so she stayed out of sight."

If she despised him, why did she agree to work his birthday party? The question perched on the tip of her tongue, but she held it back.

It was just too coincidental, Lara thought. She couldn't help wondering if Tina had wanted to work the party so she could sneak the poisoned cigars into the house. It also made her wonder if Tina'd had an ulterior motive when she'd asked Lara to meet her at the diner. Even more important, why had Tina withheld that information from her? What was she trying to hide?

Only one person could answer that question with any certainty.

Tina Tanaka.

Chapter 24

After Jeannie left, Lara and Kayla managed to complete a decent draft of the editorial they wanted to send to the local paper, encouraging people to bring unwanted pets to a shelter and not to leave them out in the cold. Lara saved it on her tablet. She planned to let it sit for a day and then review it the following morning. Assuming it didn't need any final tweaks, she'd send it along to Chris Newman, the editor at the *Whisker Gazette*.

By ten that evening, after she'd dabbled in a few other projects without making any real headway, Lara still hadn't heard from Gideon. She'd hoped he might have felt bad about the way their meeting had ended that afternoon and called her, or even texted. The idea that their relationship might be over saddened her deeply. She loved Gideon, and she knew he loved her. So, why couldn't they work it out?

The more she thought about it, the more it irritated her. After all, wasn't it *his* old girlfriend who'd started all the trouble in the first place? If Megan hadn't shown up at his office last Friday, Lara never would have heard of Wayne Chancer. His untimely death would never have crossed her radar, and she never would've gone to Bakewell.

Aunt Fran was still sitting at the kitchen table, working on her novel, by the time Lara was ready to head upstairs for the night. Lara kissed her aunt on the cheek. "Still working?" she said.

"Mostly doing revisions," her aunt said, looking distracted. "I can't say I made much forward progress today. Some days my mind is elsewhere."

Lara wrapped an arm around her aunt's shoulder. "You're worried about Twinkles, aren't you?"

Aunt Fran nodded and squeezed her eyes shut. "I don't think he has much longer. I'm keeping him as comfortable as I can."

"It's so hard," Lara said, choking back tears. "But think of all the wonderful years he had here with you. He couldn't have asked for a more loving mom, or a better home."

Her aunt smiled, and she stared at Lara through glassy eyes. "No, I suppose he couldn't." She gave Lara an impulsive hug. "But it's because of you that so many others like Twinkles found their forever homes. I can't imagine the mess I'd be in if you hadn't driven up here on that fateful October day."

If her aunt didn't stop reminiscing, Lara was going to burst into tears herself. "This is the way things were meant to be. Just remember that."

She left her aunt and headed upstairs, planning to make it an early night. Easier said than done when she couldn't shut down her mind. She tossed her tablet onto her bed, then went over to Amber, who was curled up on one of the perches on the cat tree. "Hey, little girl, how are you doing up here?"

Amber closed her eyes and lowered her head to her paws, a sign that she was growing more comfortable with Lara. Lara patted her for a while, then went over to her bed. Panda had already plunked himself onto her tablet, and Munster was trying to pull it away from him.

Lara sat cross-legged on her bed and gently tugged her tablet out from under them. "Sorry, you little monkeys, but I need to check out a few things."

After booting up the tablet, she Googled *Bakewell Custom Catering*. The site popped up instantly, and a colorful array of delectable goodies swirled around the border. The Web page was strikingly designed in muted shades of lavender, blue, and rose. Somehow it made Lara's mouth water—it reminded her of a birthday cake laden with sugary colored frosting.

Lara clicked on the "Meet Our Staff" link. Six faces popped up—the one at the top being that of Jeannie Jennings herself. Beneath her photo was a description of her experience and her culinary degrees, which were impressive for so young a woman. She also volunteered at a food bank and donated her time every Thanksgiving to serving meals at a shelter for veterans in transition.

Knowing more about Jeannie's background made Lara like her even more. She was more convinced than ever that Sienna would be the perfect addition to her household.

Beneath Jeannie's bio, the smiling pics of four women and one man appeared. Only one face was familiar to Lara—that of Tina Tanaka. Lara clicked on her picture and her bio came up.

Tina's vast experience working in a family-owned, Asian-style restaurant was emphasized, as well as her skills at presenting food aesthetically. She'd also created her own style of homemade fortune cookies, which she was hoping to develop into a national brand. That pretty much wrapped up her bio.

Lara went back to Tina's photo, and she spied it instantly—a tiny pinpoint of light that hovered about two inches above her right shoulder.

Jade. Tina's guardian cat.

Lara wanted so badly to trust Tina, but the question remained: Why hadn't Tina told her that she'd worked at Chancer's birthday party? That single omission—a critical one, in Lara's mind—made her both wary and suspicious of her.

She briefly reviewed the bios of the other four employees, but nothing stood out or raised any red flags.

After powering down her tablet, Lara took a fast shower and put on her warmest flannel nightie and a pair of snuggly socks. She slipped under the covers, then fished her e-reader—a recent indulgence—out of her nightstand drawer and turned it on. She'd been seriously enjoying the cozy mystery she'd downloaded about a young woman who gave up her law career to work in her family's Mediterranean restaurant. The food descriptions were delectable, and the mystery was a delightfully complex puzzle that challenged Lara's detection skills.

Tonight, however, her mind was a jumble. She was finding it hard to concentrate on anything. The events of the past several days had worn her out, both physically and emotionally. Her own life was fraught with mystery, and she wasn't having much luck solving any of it.

Faces kept popping up in her mind's eye.

Gideon's.

Megan Haskell's.

Tina Tanaka's.

Wayne Chancer's.

She thought about Aunt Fran, losing her young husband in a tragic accident when their future had just begun. It was obvious why her aunt had told her the painful story about that awful night—she wanted Lara to make her peace with Gideon.

Lara wanted that, too—if only she knew where to begin.

She smiled when Sienna leaped onto her bed and curled up against her chest. Munster and Panda had claimed the foot of her bed and were snuggled in together for the night.

Eventually she gave up on reading and turned out her light. Exhaustion claimed her, and she fell asleep almost instantly.

Chapter 25

The *ping* of a text early Friday morning dragged Lara out of a half sleep. In the next instant she shot awake, hoping it was from Gideon.

She reached over to her night table for her phone, but it was gone. Rubbing the last shreds of sleep from her eyes, Lara sat up and glanced around. Her phone was on the floor halfway across the room. She could only guess which feline culprit had been responsible for its relocation.

Lara was smiling when she hopped off her bed to retrieve it, but her smile died a quick death when she saw who'd sent the text. Not Gideon. Sherry.

> *David and I made another earth-shattering*
> *decision last night. Can't wait to tell you. Stop in*
> *early!*

Any other day Lara would have been thrilled to receive that message. But as she'd drifted off to sleep the night before, she'd already made the decision not to visit the coffee shop this morning. Sherry was a pro at picking up on her moods, and Lara was afraid of alerting her that something was wrong.

Her heart low, she texted back.

> *So much going on today. I'll try to get there.*

It was a cop-out, she knew, but it couldn't be helped. Some days she had to cut herself some slack without feeling guilty about it. This was one of those days.

Oddly, no furry feline faces were around to greet her. Where had they all disappeared to? Lara looked at her phone again. It was after eight! How had she managed to sleep so long?

She threw on her robe and slippers and headed downstairs. The delectable scent of cinnamon drew her into the kitchen like a culinary siren song.

Her aunt smiled when she saw her. "Good morning. I made some cinnamon rolls for breakfast, if you hadn't already guessed."

Lara inhaled deeply, relishing the scent. "I knew it was something with cinnamon. They smell delicious." She grinned at the sight of the cats lined up at their food bowls, chowing down breakfast. "And you fed the cats. Lucky thing, because I'm sure they'd have all starved to death by the time I came downstairs."

They sat down to a breakfast of cranberry tea and frosted cinnamon buns. Lara was surprised to discover how hungry she was. She couldn't remember what she'd eaten the night before, so it couldn't have been too substantial.

"Sherry texted me that she has some news, but I think I'm going to skip the coffee shop this morning."

Aunt Fran took a sip of her tea, then set down her mug and looked at Lara. "I wish I could help you with everything you're going through, Lara, but I suspect this is something you have to work out yourself."

"Thank you," Lara said, forcing a smile. "That alone helps, more than you know. And you know what? It *will* all work out, eventually. I just have to give it time."

Time I don't have. Sherry's wedding day is nipping at my heels!

Aunt Fran's cell rang. She answered in her professional-sounding voice. "Fran Clarkson."

Lara watched as her aunt's expression changed from curious to pleased. "Well, I guess I have a job today," she said after she disconnected. "One of the teachers at the middle school called in sick with the flu, so I've been asked to sub."

"Excellent! I mean, not that the woman is sick, but...oh, you know what I mean." She knew Aunt Fran loved it when she was called in to sub.

Her aunt rose and began quickly cleaning up her dishes. "They apparently called a few other subs first, but all of them were sick as well," she said with a chuckle. "I guess I'm the last one to be asked to the dance."

"Not the last—the best." Lara shooed her aunt away. "Go on. I'll clean up the dishes. You go get ready for school."

Aunt Fran winked at her. "Yes, ma'am. It won't take me long to get ready. But I just thought of something. Do you need the car today?"

"Nope. I have no plans other than hanging around here for adoption day. You go!"

After tidying up the kitchen, Lara dressed and went into her studio. She was determined to complete at least two sketches for Amy to look over. The watercolor, once completed, was going to be one of the best she'd ever done.

She pulled out all the photos Amy had supplied—including several of her three Australian shepherds—and clipped them to her easel. The young male was Bo; his mom and sister were Dotty and Freida. Lara had met all three dogs. They were feisty, friendly, and full of energy. Depicting them dashing across a snow-covered field was going to be a fun project.

Lara worked for about an hour before deciding to take a break. She'd made some progress, finally. One detailed sketch was completed, and she'd made decent headway on the second. Something still bugged her about the older photo of the farmhouse and the two pics Amy had recently emailed.

Her cell rang. *Please be Gideon*, she thought, snatching it out of her pocket. He hadn't texted that morning, nor had she texted him.

Her stomach rolled over when she saw the caller's name. "Lara Caphart," she answered brusquely.

"Oh, um, hi, it's Tina. Is this a good time to call?" No doubt she'd picked up on Lara's sharp tone.

"Yes, it's fine. What can I do for you?"

"Nothing," Tina said, her voice wary now. "I mean, nothing except I wanted to let you know that we got a shipment in this morning. Your shoes came in, and they're gorgeous. I can't wait till you see them."

The shoes—the ones she'd bought to wear at Sherry's wedding. As desperately as she wanted them, Lara was tempted to tell Tina to refund her money and sell them to someone else.

Instead she said, "Fine. Thanks for letting me know. I'll be in Bakewell on Monday. I'll pick them up then, assuming you're open."

Tina's voice tightened. "Yes, the salon is only closed on Sundays. Lara, is something wrong? You sound weird."

"Nothing's wrong, except that I met one of your employers yesterday. Jeannie Jennings."

After a short silence, Tina sighed and said, "I'm the one who referred her to your shelter. What's wrong, didn't you like her?"

"I liked her very much," Lara said. "In fact, she gave your name as a reference. She wants to adopt one of the cats from our shelter, a little tortie named Sienna."

"I know. She told me. Jeannie is a wonderful cat mom. I have only glowing things to say about her. And I've seen her with Bunny. She absolutely adores him."

"Thank you. That's good to know. I'll take that as a positive reference."

Tina sighed again, louder this time. "Are you mad because I didn't tell you I worked for the company that catered Chancer's party?"

"Not mad," Lara said. "Disappointed." She knew she sounded like a stern schoolmarm, but she couldn't help it. "And, to be honest, a little suspect. You were at the party that night, but when you and I were discussing it at the diner, you never mentioned it."

"I didn't know I was required to tell you everything," Tina replied tartly. "The police know I was there, and they interviewed me at length. They're also well aware of how much I despised Chancer. Since I'm not currently in custody, it's obvious they believed me."

Or did they? Maybe they were only biding their time until they can gather enough evidence.

"By the way, why are you coming to Bakewell on Monday?" Tina asked. "Don't tell me you're going to the memorial service for that lowlife."

Lara hesitated. She hadn't wanted to tell Tina about her plans.

"Oh my God," Tina said before Lara could respond. "You're going with Megan, aren't you? She wheedled you into it, didn't she?"

"I'm not going with Megan," Lara said.

Lara wished she could see Tina's expression right now. The young woman tended to wear her feelings on her sleeve. She'd noticed that the day they chatted at the diner. Should she drive over to Bakewell today to pick up her shoes? Talk to Tina in person?

No, today was an adoption day. Plus, Aunt Fran had the car. Even if no one showed up at the shelter this afternoon, Lara still had to be prepared. Besides, she was tired of driving to Bakewell. Monday would be soon enough. After she picked up her shoes and accompanied Karen to the memorial service, she'd say goodbye to Bakewell—forever.

"Lara, look," Tina said, sounding contrite. "I'm sorry I didn't tell you about my being at the party that night. I was afraid you'd think I was guilty of something I didn't do. But believe me when I tell you, Chancer never saw me that night. If he had, he'd have tossed me out so fast my head would've spun. I stayed in the kitchen the whole time, preparing food and setting up trays. He never set foot in the kitchen, and I was careful to stay out of sight."

"But why did you work the party in the first place, Tina? That's what I'm really struggling with."

"I work every job I can," Tina answered quietly. "I'm saving money so I can buy my folks' restaurant property and turn it into a commercial kitchen for my cookie business. They don't know it yet. I'm going to surprise them. But I need enough for a down payment. Every penny I save gets me closer to that goal."

Lara rubbed her eyes. Now she felt terrible for chiding Tina.

"I thought you had a potential buyer for the building?" Lara said.

"It didn't pan out. The offer was ridiculous, but it was a blessing in disguise. I've known for a while what I wanted to do."

"Tina, look, I'm sorry, too. You're right—I'm not a cop, and I had no right to question you. I'll see you on Monday, okay? If you're at the bridal salon, that is."

"I'll be here from noon on. See you then." Tina disconnected without saying goodbye.

* * * *

Kayla swept through the kitchen door at around eleven thirty. "Hey, I stopped at the coffee shop to pick up more cookies. I noticed yesterday we were getting low." She set a large container on the countertop.

"We were?" Lara said. "Thanks. I didn't even notice. I should have been paying more attention."

Kayla pulled off her scarf and gloves and plunked them on a free chair, then peeled off her jacket. "Daisy had two batches all ready for you. She'd been keeping them in the freezer so they'd stay fresh. She really has a nice business going for herself with those cookies, doesn't she?"

Lara smiled. "She does. The timing was good, too. With Sherry and David getting married, she'll need more help in the coffee shop. The extra income from the cookies has been coming in very handy."

A little over a year before, Daisy had landed a gig with a high-end gift basket company in Moultonborough. Every cellophane-wrapped cookie they tucked into their beautiful baskets was baked and decorated by Daisy. Recently, Daisy had added to her repertoire with all sorts of new, fun-shaped cookie cutters. She'd even found one shaped like an antique car, which she used to bake cookies for a gift basket for the opening of a new car dealership.

Kayla's eyes widened. "Isn't Sherry going to work at the coffee shop anymore?"

Lara set down a mug of tea for Kayla. "She is, but she wants to cut back her hours a bit. Who knows, one of these days she and David might decide to expand their family."

"Not too soon, I hope," Kayla said dryly. "Once you have kids you're stuck, literally."

Kayla was a bit jaded when it came to kids. Every weekend, her cousins and their little ones descended on their grandmother's home and made Kayla the de facto babysitter. While she adored her nieces and nephews, Kayla sometimes felt overwhelmed by them. And underappreciated by their parents.

"Um, Sherry was a little bummed that you didn't go there for coffee this morning," Kayla said carefully. "She told me to tell you."

"I figured she would be. It's just that I have so much going on right now, you know? Sometimes I need a little space."

Kayla nodded. "No explanation needed. I totally get it. Hey, did you review Jeannie Jennings's application yet? She sounded like a shoo-in to be Sienna's new mom."

"Yeah, I think so, too," Lara said, smiling. "I have one other reference to check, but then I think we're good. I know she's anxious to pick up her little newbie early next week."

Panda trotted into the kitchen and made a beeline for Kayla, who grinned as the black-and-white kitty hopped onto her lap. "Hey, it's about time you came in to see me." She took the cat's face in her hands and kissed him soundly on the snout.

"You won't believe who called me this morning," Lara said, sitting down with her own cup of tea. "Tina Tanaka."

"Whoa. What did she want?"

Lara related the highlights of their phone conversation, including Tina's bombshell that she'd been at Chancer's party the night he died.

"You've *got* to be kidding me. Why didn't she tell you that before?"

"She was afraid I'd peg her as being guilty of something. Plus, she didn't think it was any of my business, especially since she'd already been interviewed by the police."

"I guess she has a point. So, what do you think? Could she have killed Chancer?"

Lara blew on her tea and then took a sip. "At this stage, I'm thinking anyone could have killed Chancer. I don't think I've talked to one person who had a good word to say about him."

Lara debated whether to tell Kayla about the note—the one Karen Chancer claimed was found near her husband's body. *I know who you are.* She recalled Lieutenant Cutler's warning not to mention the note to anyone. Or was it only a suggestion?

"I keep wondering," Lara said, "if Chancer could have been leading some sort of double life."

Kayla tickled Panda under the chin. "Why would you think that?"

"The day I met Karen Chancer, she told me something strange. She said the police found a note near Chancer's body that read 'I know who you are.'"

Kayla's eyes widened, and a hint of glee danced in her gaze. "*What? Why didn't you tell me that before? Chancer might have been leading a secret other life. We need to do some serious digging on this guy!*"

Lara laughed. She knew Kayla was an aficionado of true crime. Her scrapbook of articles about criminals who'd been nabbed in the Granite State had grown ever larger with each major arrest. "I should have known that would light a fire under you."

"Yeah...well, you know I follow the true crime shows. Especially if they take place in New Hampshire."

"Remember, if Karen was telling the truth, then the police must have the note. I'm sure they've been doing plenty of digging on their own."

Kayla raised her eyebrows and grinned. "Yeah, but the police don't have a spirit cat who knows more than us mere mortals."

"Kayla," Lara said, her tone serious now, "I think it's best we don't talk about Blue. As it is, Lieutenant Cutler thinks I'm a half-baked girl detective who's always poking her nose in everyone's business and getting into trouble. Any mention of a spirit cat, and he'll really blow a gasket."

"I hear you," Kayla said with a slight pout. She lowered her voice. "I'm only wondering if you'd picked up on any clues lately. I won't elaborate more than that."

"No clues, except..." Lara thought back to the day at the Peach Crate when Blue cozied up to Felicia's dog, Lily.

"Except what?" Kayla said impatiently.

Lara told her about Blue snuggling up to Felicia's little white dog at the gourmet food shop.

"I'll bet Lily sensed Blue's presence," Kayla reflected. "Animals are so much more in tune with the spiritual world than humans are."

"Maybe," Lara said.

"By the way, where's Ms. C today? Upstairs with Twinkles?"

"No, the school called her in to sub today. She was thrilled. I think she really misses teaching."

Kayla nodded. "I'll bet she's a great teacher, too. Why doesn't she go back full-time?"

"I think she likes the flexibility of being a sub. She's been seeing more and more of the chief, and sometimes on his days off they enjoy taking day trips."

"Say no more." Kayla grinned.

They finished their tea and set about doing some litter box cleaning and cat grooming. Sienna climbed onto the perch in the large parlor, while Amber stayed in Lara's room in her own favorite spot.

"It's weird," Kayla said, wrapping up a trash bag with a plastic tie. "I don't think we've had this few cats in a while."

"I know," Lara said. "I've been thinking of reaching out to another shelter to see if they'd like us to take one or two of their cats. But with Sherry's wedding, and then…everything else, my mind hasn't been too focused."

The doorbell to the shelter's entrance rang, and Kayla frowned at Lara. "Way too early for adoption hours. Did you make an appointment with someone?"

"Nope."

Kayla trailed Lara into the meet-and-greet room and closed the door behind them. Lara flicked on the light. Through the glass door pane, they saw a man and a woman huddled on the step. The woman peeked inside and waved when she spotted Lara.

Putting on her best smile, Lara hurried to open the door. "Hi, there," she greeted. "Come on in out of the cold."

"Oh, thank you," the woman said, practically tripping over the top step to rush inside. She clutched at the collar of her green wool coat. "I hope we came to the right place. We're here about a"—she shot a look at her male companion and he blinked in acknowledgment—"about a cat."

Lara's guard instantly went up. Why the weird look between them?

She smiled again and ushered them over to the table, where the couple sat down. "If you're here about a cat, then you came to the right place. Why don't you both have a seat? I'm Lara, and this is Kayla."

"Pleased to meet you," Kayla said, shaking their hands. Her expression was wary, and Lara knew she'd picked up the same strange vibe from the pair.

"We're the Emersons," the woman said. "Sally and Art."

Without being asked, they simultaneously unbuttoned their coats and draped them over the backs of their chairs. Apparently, they planned to hang for a while.

Lara guessed them to be somewhere in their sixties, but there was a stodginess about them that aged them well beyond that. The woman wore her dark-brown, chin-length hair in carefully curled waves. Her pearl earrings were clip-ons, and a matching pearl brooch in the shape of a butterfly rested on the collar of her pink turtleneck sweater. Her husband, attired totally in shades of beige and brown, had pale brown eyes set deeply into a slightly pudgy face.

"Can I get you anything?" Kayla asked. "Something to drink?"

"Oh no, we wouldn't want you to go to any trouble," Sally said hesitantly.

"You know what?" Kayla said brightly, "why don't I bring in a pot of tea with some mugs, and we can all help ourselves." She dashed out of the room before anyone could protest.

Lara addressed the couple. "So, tell me, how did you hear about our shelter?"

Art cleared his throat and folded his hands on the table. "I'll be right up front. It was our niece, Megan Haskell, who told us all about you."

Zing.

Lara's mental antennae shot straight out of her head.

"I see," she said stiffly. "So, you're not really here about a cat, are you?"

"Oh no, we are," Sally was quick to correct her husband. She fussed with the sleeves of her sweater. "Oh my, I'm not handling this well at all, am I?"

"Dear." Art reached over and touched his wife's wrist. "Why don't you explain first about Megan."

"You're right. Of course." Sally lifted her chin and looked at Lara. "Megan is my brother's daughter. For the last several months, she's been living with us in Bakewell."

"Megan did tell me she was living with her aunt and uncle," Lara acknowledged.

Sally nodded, then continued. "You have to understand about Megan. She's such a lovely, smart girl. It's a shame she had to grow up the way she did." She shook her head sadly.

"What do you mean?" Lara said, feeling her gut clench.

Sally pressed her fingers to her lips, and her husband picked up on the cue.

"Her father, my brother-in-law," Art piped in, "was not a very loving father. He'd wanted a boy, and their only child turned out to be a girl." He frowned in disapproval. "I don't think a day went by when he didn't let her know it."

Sally pulled in a deep breath and picked up the thread. "Nothing our niece did was ever good enough for him," she said. "If she got an A on a math test, he'd demand to know why she hadn't scored an A-plus. One time—oh, it was awful—he even demanded that the teacher show him a list of the test scores of all the other students in the class. He wanted to see how they compared to Megan's."

Lara nearly gasped. "The teacher didn't do it, I hope."

"No, of course she didn't. She had more integrity than that, and she saw exactly what my brother was trying to do—humiliate his own daughter."

Lara felt suddenly heartsick. It confirmed what Megan had implied about her dad, that he was a controlling bully. "What about Megan's mom? Didn't she have any say in all this?"

Sally gave her husband a pained look, and then, "No, I'm sorry to say she was as bullied by my brother as Megan was. We tried to gently intervene whenever we could, but we had to be careful. With my brother, it would've been easy to make matters worse."

"Truth be told," Art said quietly, "we'd have raised Megan ourselves, if we could have."

"Art and I were never able to have children," Sally added.

"At one point, we even consulted an attorney," Art went on. "The problem was, as we were told, her father's treatment didn't rise to the level of abuse. He was strict and demanding, but he only wanted the best for his daughter. Plus, Megan excelled in school, so her parents' upbringing didn't throw up any red flags."

Megan was trying so hard to please them, Lara thought sadly, *she didn't dare* not *score good grades.*

"Once or twice, we tried to gently suggest having Megan come and live with us." Sally's lips pursed. "The look my brother gave us would've stopped a charging bull in its tracks."

"Does Megan ever see her mom and dad? I mean, do they live close by?"

Again, the exchange of looks.

Finally, Sally spoke. "They moved to Hollis several years ago, but Megan rarely sees them. In fact, she spends all her holidays with us. Her parents don't even invite her anymore. They're too busy trying to impress their fancy friends." Her words, spoken through tight lips, had an undertone of bitterness.

How awful, Lara thought. "She's not even close to her mom?"

Art spoke this time. "Her mom is—how can I put this—a *puppet* of my brother-in-law. He controls the strings. She dances."

Kayla appeared in the doorway carrying a tray. Lara suspected she'd overheard at least part of their conversation. She came in and set down a flowered teapot, along with mugs, spoons, cream, sugar, lemon wedges, and a small pile of napkins.

"Oh, this looks lovely," Sally chirped. "You didn't need to do all this."

"We're happy to do it," Kayla said, sliding onto the one free chair. "Please, help yourselves."

Sally fixed herself a cup of tea with sugar and cream, but her husband declined. Kayla made up a mug for both herself and Lara.

"Mr. and Mrs. Emerson—" Lara began.

"Please, it's Sally and Art." Sally took a tiny sip from her mug.

"Okay. Sally and Art, I'm sorry to hear about Megan's troubles as a child, and I can see how much she means to you, but I'm still not sure why you're here."

Art's face flushed. "I'm sorry. We didn't mean to ramble."

"As you know, Megan is living with us now," Sally said, then smiled. "We'd have her live with us forever, if we could, but it's not what's right for her. For her own sake, Megan needs to make her own way in the world, find her own brand of happiness."

Such kind, good people, Lara thought. She couldn't help wondering, if Megan had been raised in their household, would she have developed more self-esteem? Lara suspected that Megan's self-destructive tendencies were, at least partly, the result of her stern upbringing.

It was Sally's turn to flush. "Lara, we…have a confession. We *are* here about a cat, but we have some news to share first."

Art sighed. "Around eleven o'clock last night, the police caught Megan snooping around Wayne Chancer's locked office. She was arrested and charged with unlawful entry."

Chapter 26

"*What?*" Lara said. "Did they hold her?"

Art shook his head. "No, fortunately. They released her to our custody. Here's the thing—technically, Megan had a key to the office, since she used to work there. When Chancer fired her, he didn't think to ask for it back."

"Megan mailed the key back to him about a week later, but before she did, she had a copy made."

Not good, Lara thought. Megan was getting herself in deeper trouble, when she should be trying hard to do the opposite.

"Did she say why she did it?" Lara asked wearily.

"She said she was looking for something, a phone number," Art explained. "She remembered a call Chancer had gotten shortly before he fired her. Something the caller said had scared him, badly, and Megan wanted to find that number. She was hoping it might still be on the caller ID. If she could find it, she thought it might help lead to his killer. She told the police she was only trying to help them."

But Megan worked as a paralegal. She had to know that was the wrong way to go about it.

"Did she take anything?" Lara asked, dreading the answer.

"No, thank the Lord." Art smiled weakly and crossed himself. "That worked in Megan's favor. Her lawyer's working on getting the charges dropped, so probably nothing will come of it. Problem is, it gives the police yet another reason to look more closely at her for Chancer's death."

Lara felt as if her head was going to explode. What Megan was doing to herself was bad enough. But with every day that passed, she was dragging Lara further into the nightmare that was Wayne Chancer's death. She couldn't help wondering if she was being manipulated. Did Megan send these kindly people here to lobby on her behalf?

Sally must have sensed Lara's frustration. "Lara, I know we've rambled on for a long time, so we'll get to the real reason we're here." She waggled a forefinger at her husband's shirt. "Show her the pictures, hon."

Art reached into his shirt pocket and pulled out a folded envelope. He extracted a short stack of photos and gave them to Lara. "This is our old cat, Maisie. She died back in, oh, let's see, was it two thousand thirteen, Sal?"

"That's right," Sally confirmed. "She'd been living outside until we took her in. Our vet's best guess is that she was fourteen or fifteen when she died." She blinked back tears.

"The other photos are of our other cats. They go way back."

Lara smiled at the photos. Maisie had been a pure black cat with large gold eyes. The pictures of the other two cats were fuzzy, but one was clearly a calico.

"Lara," Art said, "I'll cut to the chase. We, Sally and I, would like to adopt your black-and-white cat, Panda."

The mouthful of tea Lara had just swallowed rose up in her throat. Choking, she grabbed a napkin and coughed into it, trying to get back her breath. She was surprised to feel a small but firm hand clapping her on the back.

"There, there," Sally said. "Are you okay now?"

Lara nodded. "Sorry. I must've choked on something."

Sally sat down again. "I think something went down the wrong pipe."

Kayla gave Lara an alarmed look. Lara didn't know if it was because she'd nearly choked, or because the Emersons wanted to adopt a cat they hadn't even met.

Where to begin.

While Lara didn't doubt the couple's sincerity, she was wary of their motive. She smiled at the pair. "May I ask why? You haven't even met Panda, and I'm afraid I can't help wondering about the timing."

Sally nodded, and Art reddened and cleared his throat. "We understand, totally," he said. "But we've had cats before, and I know the vet we used in the past would vouch for us. We...we want to do it for Megan's sake, as well as for our own. She's taken quite a liking to Panda."

Lara floundered for a response. Finally, she said, "We'll be glad to introduce you to Panda, but forgive me for asking: Would Panda be your cat or Megan's?"

Sally and Art shot each other another odd look. "He would be ours, certainly," Sally said, hedging a bit. "The thing is, at some point in the future, if Megan can get her life together and find a good job, we'll help her find a nice place of her own to live. If she does, we'd be willing to let Panda go with her. It would help her emotionally, and we know she'd give him a loving home."

Lara suppressed a groan. So many things were wrong with this scenario.

She didn't doubt for a moment that the Emersons were gentle people who could give Panda a loving home. The issue was that they wanted to adopt him for the wrong reasons. By their own admission, they'd be willing to uproot the kitty and turn him over to Megan to help her get her act together, so to speak.

The kitten tattoo on Megan's wrist suddenly popped into her mind. Its resemblance to Panda had been startling. Lara remembered the sadness in Megan's expression when she'd related the tattoo story. But Lara's first responsibility was to Panda. She needed to be sure he went to a stable home.

"Art, Sally," Lara said, "I really have to give some thought to this, and I'd like to talk to my aunt as well. She's the co-owner of the shelter."

Sally's face fell. "You...don't think we're good enough to adopt Panda?"

"Oh no, I do, absolutely," Lara said, feeling terrible that she'd offended them. "It's just—"

In the next instant, a flutter of movement caught Lara's eye. She looked over to see Blue sitting placidly at Sally's elbow, her turquoise gaze fixed on Art. Lara started to say something, but the words got trapped in her throat and she lost the thread of her thought. She saw Kayla staring at her with a worried expression.

For several seconds, time seemed to freeze. Then, with a flick of her furry tail, Blue was gone.

"Lara," Art said, sending a silent message to his wife, "we understand your hesitation, honestly we do. We don't have to meet Panda today, but please give some thought to our request. We're well aware that this"—his lip curled—"*situation* with Chancer isn't over yet. But when it is, and the police find the real killer, we're going to see to it that Megan gets all the help she needs to start over. We only want the best for her. We always have."

"I know you do," Lara said, believing it with all her heart. These were good people dealing with a dicey situation.

As Art and Sally began shrugging on their coats, something jingled in Sally's pocket. Looking at her husband, she fished out an old-fashioned flip phone and opened it. When she saw who the caller was, she paled slightly. "Hello?"

Her husband watched her anxiously as he buttoned his coat.

"That's…interesting news," Sally told the caller, "I actually can't talk right now. Can I call you back in an hour or so?"

After several more seconds, Sally closed the phone and slipped it back into her pocket.

"Was that Meggie?" Art asked her, looking concerned. "Is she okay?"

"No, it wasn't Megan. It's nothing important. I'll tell you in the car."

Lara's heart wrenched. These two people loved Megan so much. They'd do anything for her—she felt sure of it.

Sally hugged Lara and Kayla before they left. "We'll be in touch," she whispered in Lara's ear.

After the Emersons had pulled out of the driveway, Kayla dropped her head on the table. "My God, that was excruciating."

"I know." Lara cupped her hand over her forehead. "Megan's lucky to have such a caring aunt and uncle, but she's still doing crazy things."

Kayla lifted her head and shrugged. "Maybe. Or maybe it wasn't so crazy." She swallowed the last dregs of her tea. "Tell you the truth, Lara, if I were in her place, I might've used my key to check out Chancer's office, too."

"Seriously?" Lara said, shocked. "Kayla, she's getting herself in deeper and deeper. She needs to let the police do their job. That's the only way the murder is ever going to be resolved."

"Come on, even you don't believe that." She plunked the dirty mugs and spoons onto the tray and rose from her chair.

Lara groaned and followed her into the kitchen. Munster, who'd been loitering near the door to the meet-and-greet room, trailed behind them.

"Kayla, I'm not getting any more involved in this," Lara said with more conviction than she felt. "I'm done."

"What are you talking about? You're involved up to your eyeballs! You've been to Bakewell twice, and now you're going to the memorial service."

Lara remained silent. Everything Kayla said was true.

While Kayla finished up the dishes, Lara added a few treats to each of the cat bowls. Panda, with his bat-like hearing, came running into the kitchen.

Kayla dried her hands on a paper towel. "Lara, I'm sorry if I sounded like I was attacking you. I guess I can be a little blunt at times."

Lara shook her head. "You weren't attacking me. If there's one thing I can always count on from you it's honesty, and I appreciate that. But this murder business, it's getting old, you know?"

"I know," Kayla said softly. "Hey, I didn't mean to be so flip about Blue before. I won't mention her again."

Lara smiled at her. She and Aunt Fran had grown so close to Kayla. Kayla had started out as a shelter assistant, and then turned into a friend, both to her and Aunt Fran. Now she was more like a member of the family. "Kayla, you can mention Blue any time you want. It actually helps me to feel, you know, validated—like I'm not going totally nuts."

"You're not going nuts. Don't ever think that." Kayla shot a glance at the clock. "Shoot. I forgot to tell you, I have to leave at three today. There's a memorial mass for my grandpa tonight at six, and I have to take my gram."

"Not a problem," Lara said, then an idea struck her. "Since no one's here right now, can I get your thoughts on something? It won't take very long."

"You bet," Kayla said.

"Great. Be right back."

Lara went into her studio and retrieved the photos Amy had sent her of the farmhouse. She returned to the kitchen and spread them out on the table, then pushed the first one toward Kayla.

"This is the photo Amy gave me when she first asked me to do the watercolor for her."

Kayla sat down and pulled her chair closer to the table. Panda scooted underneath the table and slipped silently onto her lap.

"Oh, I just love Amy's house," Kayla gushed. "That's my dream, you know, to live in a big old farmhouse where I can adopt cats to my heart's content."

Lara laughed. "I can absolutely picture that." She slid the other two photos over to Kayla. "These two pics are more recent—Amy took them a day or two ago. All three photos were taken in the winter, but there's something in the first one that's different. I can't put my finger on it."

"Hmmm." Kayla studied the photos, her brow wrinkled in concentration. Then her eyes lit up. "Did you see the cardinal in this one? He's not in the others."

"I did see it," Lara said. "Isn't it amazing the way he appeared suddenly the second pic?"

Kayla nodded slowly, studying all the photos. "The only thing I can think of, and I might be imagining it, is that the patches of dried leaves along the border of the house look different in the first picture. Although it's hard to really see that through the bits of snow cover. My eyes might be playing a trick on me."

Animated now, Lara snatched the photos back and turned them around. "Good glory, I think you're right." She held up a finger. "Be back in a sec."

Lara went back to her studio and returned holding up a magnifying glass. "My handy-dandy spyglass." She sat down again and examined the photos.

Kayla rubbed Panda's head, triggering a turbo-charged purr. "Can I ask why it's so important?"

Lara sighed. "At least twice, now, Blue has tried to make me look harder at the first photo."

Kayla sat up straighter, and her eyes flew open wider. "Okay, now we're getting somewhere. In one of these photos, there has to be a clue she's trying to get across to you."

Gazing again through the magnifying glass, Lara studied the original photo. "I think you're right. The leaves are different in this one. They're just a *tad* larger." She moved the magnifier over to the other two photos. "In these two pictures, the leaves are smaller, but the frozen stems are more visible."

"Yeah," Kayla said. "They remind me of my gram's petunias last October, after the frost finally did them in. She should have dug them out of the flower boxes sooner, but she never got around to it, and I'm not much of a gardener."

With an exasperated sigh, Lara set down the magnifier. "Listen to us. We sound like a couple of characters out of a kids' detective story." Lara laughed and gathered up the photos. "Hey, thanks for your input. I don't see how the dried leaves can mean anything, but I'll ask Amy about it anyway."

Kayla glanced at the clock again and made a face. "I guess I'd better go. Adoption hours are almost over, anyway. What do you think you'll do about the Emersons?"

"I seriously don't know. I want to talk to Aunt Fran about it. There's no reason why we have to make an instant decision."

Unless someone else wants to adopt Panda in the meantime.

After Kayla said goodbye to all the cats, she hugged Lara and left. Anytime now Aunt Fran should be getting home from school.

Lara remembered all those years as a kid when she spent every afternoon after school at her aunt's. Either homemade blondies or cookies would always be waiting on the table for her, along with a sketch pad and a packet of colored pencils.

Because Aunt Fran was a teacher, she got home earlier than Lara's working parents did. The arrangement worked out perfectly—Lara's dad would pick her up on his way home from work each day, and Lara's mom would have supper waiting when they got home. Usually. Occasionally her mom would deem that it was "pizza night" and send her husband back out to get two cheesy pies.

Lara checked the time—it was almost three thirty. There wasn't enough time to whip up a batch of brownies before Aunt Fran got home, but she could certainly have tea and cookies ready for her.

Using some of the orange spice tea packets she'd bought from Felicia's shop, she prepped the teapot and set a kettle of water on the stove. It was a treat to use a real teapot on occasion, instead of just plunking tea bags into mugs. She'd wait until she heard her aunt pulling into the driveway, then turn on the burner.

Cookies. They still had some of the shortbread cookies she'd bought at the Peach Crate. Lara found the package and arranged several of the buttery delights on a pretty plate. She set out two of Aunt Fran's favorite mugs, along with spoons and napkins.

No sooner had she completed the task when she heard the slam of a car door outside. The sound didn't come from the driveway, though. It came from the shelter's parking area on the other side of the house.

Another late visitor, hoping to adopt a cat?

Lara hurried through the large parlor and into the meet-and-greet room to welcome the newcomer. But when she peered through the door pane, her stomach dropped to her knees.

A little red Honda was parked outside. Megan Haskell was climbing out of the vehicle.

Chapter 27

Fuming that Megan had the nerve to show up unannounced—again—Lara was sorely tempted to wave her away and refuse to allow her in. She stood at the door, arms folded over her chest, prepared to send Megan on her sorry way.

But as Megan approached the steps, Lara's resolve crumbled. The young woman looked so scared and frozen that Lara couldn't turn her away. She swung open the door. "Megan, what are you doing here?"

Megan shivered on the doorstep, her hands bare, her eyes red and puffy. "C-can I come in? I promise, I'll only stay a few minutes."

With an audible sigh, Lara waved her arm and ushered her inside. "You look frozen," she said, as if scolding a child. "Where're your gloves?"

Megan choked out a tiny sob. "I left them in Wayne's office when I"—she swallowed—"when I went in there last night. Stupid, right?"

"Nothing about what you did last night was smart." Lara waved a hand at a chair. "Sit down for minute. At least get warm."

With a forlorn nod, Megan did as Lara instructed.

Lara cautioned herself against feeling sorry for her. In her opinion, Megan was the designer and editor of all her own problems. She needed to help herself before anyone else could help her.

"You sent your aunt and uncle here to beg for Panda, didn't you?" Lara said, a bit more harshly than she'd intended.

Megan shook her head vehemently, "No. *No!* They did that on their own, because they care about me." She sucked in a hard sniffle, and tears slid down her cheeks. "I hate it that I've made so much trouble for them. They're the only ones who *ever* cared about me. I don't deserve them."

If Megan was acting, she was doing a terrific job of it.

Lara still didn't trust her. How could she? By her own admission, Megan had lied before. Lara suspected she'd been manipulating the truth since she was young girl, as a way of surviving her stern upbringing.

She thought of her own dad, Roy Caphart, the most loving dad anyone could have asked for. He'd rarely scolded; most often he'd praised. He'd been a role model and a wonderful dad—always there to cheer Lara on. Would Megan have developed more self-esteem, more confidence in herself, if her dad had been more like Lara's?

"Megan, everyone deserves a family who loves them," Lara said softly. "The thing is, you're too smart a woman to do some of the stuff you've been doing. Going into Wayne's office late at night? What were you thinking?"

Megan swiped at her tears with her fingertips. "I had a good reason for doing that, Lara. That's why I came here. The police don't take anything I tell them seriously anymore."

Lara felt like ripping out her hair in frustration. "But, Megan, you have an attorney, right? He's the one you should be talking to. I can't help you."

"I did talk to him. And he talked to the police. But they still aren't getting it."

The faint sound of a car door slamming drifted from the other side of the house. "Megan, stay here for a minute, okay? My aunt just got home. I want to let her know I'm in here."

"Sure," Megan said meekly.

Lara went into the kitchen and greeted her aunt. "Hey, how was your day?"

Aunt Fran beamed. She peeled off her coat, scarf, and gloves and set them over a chair. "Fabulous. I really do miss teaching. I'm thinking seriously of going back full-time next year, if there's an opening."

"I want to hear all about it, but right now"—she tilted her head toward the other side of the house—"I've got Megan Haskell in the meet-and-greet room."

Her aunt frowned. "Again? Oh, Lara. Did you know she was coming?"

"No, but it's a long story. I'll tell you everything later."

Aunt Fran glanced at the kitchen table. "What's all this?"

"Well, I was going to have tea and cookies ready for you when you get home, but—"

"I know. The best-laid plans." Aunt Fran smiled. "That's okay. We'll have tea and cookies after your visitor leaves."

Lara headed back to the meet-and-greet room. She was only half surprised to find Panda curled up in Megan's lap, purring up a thunderstorm.

"He came in on his own," Megan said defensively. She curved one slender hand protectively over the cat, as if she expected Lara to snatch him away from her.

"That's fine. I'm not worried about Panda." The little cat really did love cozying up to Megan.

Megan reached into her coat pocket and pulled out a small notepad. "I know you want me to leave, Lara, so I'll tell you this quickly. About like, two weeks before Wayne fired me, he got a phone call late in the afternoon. I took the call, but the caller wouldn't identify himself. He said he wanted to speak to Wayne, that he was an old friend and wanted to surprise him." She paused, as if waiting to see if Lara wanted to hear more.

"Okay. Then what?"

"The door to Wayne's office was open, so I popped my head in. I told him there was a man on the phone for him, but that he wouldn't give his name." She paused again. "Wayne took the call, but after a few seconds his face got real gray, like, the color of his cigar ash. I'd never seen him look like that before, so I knew it was bad. I kind of just stood there, unsure what to do." Her face flushed. "I was still, you know, kind of infatuated with him, and I thought he might need help."

"Did Wayne say anything?" Lara asked her.

"Not right away, but then I heard him mumble the word *overdose*—just that one word. At that point he must've noticed I was still standing there, because he barked at me to get out and shut the door."

Lara waited.

"So, I did, and when I went back to my desk, I saw that the line was still lit up. They talked for about another three minutes. I know, because I timed it. I should have thought right then and there to make a note of the phone number, but I didn't. The only thing I noticed was that it was an out-of-state area code."

"Megan, by any chance, did you pick up the extension and listen to any of the conversation?"

She gave Lara an odd smile. "No, but I can't say I wasn't tempted. The thing is, I knew if I got caught that it would've been the end of me, job-wise. I couldn't risk it."

Lara sighed. "Okay. Tell me the rest."

"After the call ended," Megan went on, "Wayne stayed in his office for a long time. When he finally came out it was after five. I was packing up my things to leave for the day. He asked why I was still there, and I told him I was worried about him. Then I made the mistake of asking who his mysterious caller was. He told me it was none of my freakin' business, only he used a slightly different word." Her lips pursed.

Nice way to talk to his employee, Lara thought.

"After that he stormed out, leaving me alone to close up the office. But before I left, I went into his office. His yellow legal pad was on his desk, so I looked at it. He'd written only one thing—the letters 'O.D.' in big letters at the top. O period, D period."

"O-D. Overdose," Lara said.

She nodded. "I locked up the office and left right after that. It was only a few weeks later when he fired me." Megan's face crumpled.

"Megan, can I ask you a question?" Lara said quietly. "Why did you wait until now to reveal this? Your ex-boss died a week ago, and now suddenly you're remembering a weird phone call from an unidentified man? The timing doesn't add up."

Megan blushed and looked down at the cat curled contentedly in her lap. Was she stalling? Trying to concoct a fib she hoped Lara would swallow?

"I figured you'd say that," she murmured after a long pause. "That's why I decided to go to Wayne's office last night. I wanted to look at the caller ID on the phone to see if the number might still be there."

"Was it?"

Megan shook her head. "No, the caller ID didn't store numbers that far back. But that's when I stupidly, *stupidly* remembered something else. The morning after Wayne got that call, I couldn't stop thinking about it. Wayne was still acting strange, biting my head off at the drop of a hat. By lunchtime, I couldn't stand it anymore. That's when I remembered the caller ID. I checked the phone, found the number, and wrote it down on one of my business cards. I shoved the card under my file folders in the bottom drawer of my desk."

Megan's story was getting stranger, and more convoluted. Lara wasn't sure she believed a word of it. It almost seemed as if she was making it up as she went along.

"Lara, last night…I found the card," Megan said. "It was right where I'd left it. Wayne hadn't even bothered to clean out my files after he fired me."

"So, you have it, then?" Lara said, her curiosity ignited.

"No. I shoved it in my jacket pocket so I could take it to the police. But—first I wrote down the number." Her eyes alight now, Megan pushed her notepad over to Lara.

Lara looked down and stared at the number. "The area code is four-oh-one. That's Rhode Island, isn't it?"

"I think so," Megan said.

"Did Wayne ever mention knowing anyone in Rhode Island?"

"Not that I recall."

Lara rested her elbows on the table. She felt as if she were playing a losing game of Twenty Questions. "How did the police happen to catch you last night?"

"That," Megan said sharply, "was unfortunate. Someone spotted my flashlight beam bouncing around in Wayne's office and called the cops."

"Can you blame them?"

Megan shook her head, and her eyes drooped. "No, I suppose not. The cops scared me half to death when they charged into the office. My God, one of them had his gun drawn. I told them the truth, about why I was there. I wasn't sure if they believed me, but I gave them the business card with the phone number on it. Thank God I'd written it down first. They took me to the station and booked me. Luckily, after they heard my whole story, they called my aunt and uncle and allowed me to go home with them."

Something else occurred to Lara. "After you got home, I don't suppose you thought to Google the phone number?"

Megan quirked an odd little smile at her. "No, but I did even better. I called the number."

"*What?* Megan, what if the caller was the guy who poisoned Wayne? You could have been putting yourself in danger!"

Megan reached over and lightly touched Lara's arm. "Please don't worry. No one answered the phone. I got some generic voice-mail message. Whoever the caller was, he hadn't bothered to set up a personal greeting."

"But your number will show up on *his* caller ID!"

"So what? He can't find me with a phone number, can he?"

In truth, Lara wasn't sure. Probably not, but who knew? If the caller was someone sleazy or underhanded, he might have ways to find out.

"Please, Megan, *please* stop doing all this stuff on your own. Let the police, and your attorney, handle it. They're the professionals."

Megan lifted her chin and met Lara's gaze head-on. "But you've caught murderers, Lara. Don't deny it, you have. I Googled you, and I know all about you." Her voice was so childlike that it squeezed Lara's heart.

From the other side of the house, another car door slammed. Was Aunt Fran leaving? Or had someone else stopped by? Lara's heart thumped at the thought that it might be Gideon.

An idea struck her. She picked up Megan's notepad and tore off a sheet. She went over to the display of the shelter's successful adoptions and grabbed the pencil balanced on top of it. When she sat down, she wrote five words on the paper: *I know who you are.* She showed the paper to Megan.

Megan stared at it for a moment, then shot Lara a look of confusion mixed with anger. "What are you talking about? You know who I am—I'm Megan Haskell. Are you implying I'm someone else?"

"Never mind," Lara said, feeling hugely relieved. She was certain that if Megan had written the note found next to Chancer's body, or knew who had, she'd have reacted differently.

"I think you just want me to leave," Megan said, her voice trembling, a hurt expression in her blue eyes. "Which is exactly what I'm going to do. And don't worry, I won't darken your door ever again. This time I mean it." She gently lifted the black-and-white cat snoozing in her lap, kissed his head, and set him on the floor.

"Megan—"

"One more thing. I didn't come here to beg for Panda. I know I'm not ready to adopt a cat yet. But when I am, I'll go to a regular shelter."

She stalked out, leaving her notepad on the table.

Chapter 28

Still reeling from Megan's reaction, Lara scooped up the notepad and slipped it into her jeans pocket. Voices drifted from the kitchen. Feminine voices, to Lara's disappointment. She stopped short when she saw who was sitting at the kitchen table chatting with Aunt Fran.

"Sherry! I didn't know you were coming over."

Her friend rose from her chair and hugged her. Sherry's eyes glowed, and her skin gleamed with a rosy hue. *The look of a happy bride-to-be*, Lara decided.

"Well, you didn't stop into the coffee shop this morning, so I had to hunt you down." She plopped her hands on her hips.

Lara swatted her arm playfully. "I know," she said, a wave of guilt swishing over her. "I just have so much going on right now. I needed a break. Don't worry. It's only for a day. I'll be back tomorrow."

Sherry's eyes narrowed, and she studied her friend. "Can we talk? Privately?"

"Um, sure!" Her voice rose on a higher pitch than she intended.

Aunt Fran, picking up on the cue, jumped in and said, "Lara, I'm heading upstairs to check on Twinkles. You gals stay here and gab to your heart's content." She squeezed Sherry's arm and trotted out of the kitchen.

"Did Aunt Fran make the tea—" Lara started to say, but Sherry interrupted.

"I don't want tea and I don't want cookies, Lara. I want to talk to you."

Lara felt her pulse spike. Something was up.

"*Okaaay.* Sit. Let's talk."

Sherry took her seat again. "Marina came into the coffee shop at lunchtime today to pick up a tuna sandwich for Gideon."

"She's a great assistant," Lara said. "Gideon always says he doesn't know how he ever got along without her."

"Don't change the subject," Sherry said, her expression somber. "This isn't about Marina. It's about you. And Gideon. I want to know what's going on, Lara. Have you two split up and you're not telling me because you think it'll spoil my wedding?"

Lara swallowed. "I—no, we haven't." *Have we?* "Why would you ask that?"

"Because Marina said Gideon hasn't been himself for days. He's distracted. He forgets to return calls. He showed up fifteen minutes late for a closing yesterday and threw the seller into a tizzy. The seller needed the proceeds for the house they were buying the same day."

Oh Lord. That wasn't like Gideon at all.

Lara folded her hands on the table, avoiding Sherry's gaze. "I don't know what to tell you, Sher. Gideon's *really* upset with me because I've gone to Bakewell twice. He thinks I'm trying to help Megan, but that's not why I went there."

"Then what is it? Why are you doing this?" Sherry asked quietly.

Inwardly, Lara groaned. There was no way to explain what was going on in her head. And it definitely wasn't the right time to tell Sherry about Blue.

"Sher, I'm going to explain it as best I can, but I don't think it's going to make any sense to you. For some reason I feel drawn there, but I don't know why. I've met people there—I told you about Tina."

Sherry nodded. "And I'm thrilled that I found the perfect wedding favors through her. But I'm sure that's not the reason you feel *drawn* there. It's something else, isn't it?"

Lara dropped her face into her cupped hands. She shook her head, then linked her fingers together on the table. "It's as if…as if something else is going to happen. Something I'm supposed to know about. Something I'm supposed to figure out."

Something I'm supposed to prevent.

Sherry's face went from rosy to pale. She spoke firmly. "You have to stop this, Lara. Just wipe Bakewell off your mental map and stay away from there. Because, look—I'll tell you the truth. I'm starting to get a bad feeling, too. A feeling that something's going to happen to you. If someone hurts you, I'll have to kill them myself, and it's not the way I want to start off my marriage."

Lara looked over at her bestie—the most wonderful, loyal friend she ever could have asked for—and saw her lips parted in a wicked smile.

"Got it?" Sherry said. "Are we clear?"

Lara nodded, but then shook her head. "I told Karen Chancer I'd go with her to her husband's memorial service at eleven o'clock on Monday. After that I have to pick up my shoes at the bridal salon, and then I'm never going to Bakewell again. That's a promise."

Lara waited for Sherry's scream, but it never came.

"I'll accept that," Sherry said with a slow nod, "but you have to do something else. You have to make things right with Gideon. You two belong together the way David and I belong together."

Tears pricked at Lara's eyes. "I'll do my best, Sher. But I might have already messed things up for good."

"You haven't. Not according to Marina. Gideon just wants to understand, Lara. He's terrified of losing you, terrified that you'll put yourself in danger—again. Please, *please* talk to him. I think he's waiting for you to make the next move."

The dam broke. Lara felt hot tears sliding down her cheeks. Sherry hopped off her chair and wrapped her in a hug.

"Oh God, I'm so sorry, Sher. My problems are interfering with your wedding plans, and that's the last thing I wanted."

Sherry gripped her shoulders. "Listen to me. My wedding plans are coming together beautifully, and that's largely because of you. No matter what else happens, David and I will be fine. It's you I'm worried about. Now, you get your act together and talk to Gideon. Don't make me call out the flying monkeys."

Lara laughed through her tears. "God, no, don't bring out the monkeys. I've seen your monkeys. They're frightening." She wiped her face with a napkin. "By the way, you said you had good news. What is it?"

Sherry's face brightened. "Oh yeah, I almost forgot. After David and I get settled in our new apartment, guess what we're going to do?"

"I'm afraid to guess," Lara said warily.

"Okay, then. I'll tell you. We're going to adopt a cat."

Lara's eyes shot wide open. "Honestly?"

"Don't look so surprised. The only reason I couldn't have one until now is because of mom's allergies."

"Sher, that's great. And David's totally okay with it?"

"Totally. I told you right after I met him that he loves cats, didn't I?" She snatched a shortbread cookie off the plate on the table. "Now, why don't you get that tea going?"

Feeling perkier than she had all day, Lara turned on the burner under the kettle. She grabbed another mug for Sherry, along with the specialty tea bags she'd bought at the Peach Crate. She popped another tea bag into the teapot.

"Whoa. These cookies are really good," Sherry said, wiping crumbs from her fingers. "I'm so used to having Mom's sugar cookies that I never try anything different. You got these at that place in Bakewell?"

"I did," Lara said. "It's called the Peach Crate. Very cute shop." She thought of Felicia Tristany and her sweet little dog, Lily. And then of Karen Chancer, who was hoping to buy in to the business and become partners with Felicia.

The kettle boiled, and Lara prepared the teapot. Excusing herself, she went upstairs to her aunt's room, the door to which was slightly ajar. "Want to join me and Sher for tea?"

Aunt Fran was sitting in her rocking chair, her gaze distant, Dolce nestled in her lap. Twinkles rested at the foot of her bed, deep in a soundless sleep. Lara went over and gently kissed his head. Twinkles opened his eyes briefly, then drifted back to dreamland.

"Sure. I'd love to join you."

"Let me carry Dolce," Lara offered, going over and lifting the black cat into her arms.

In spite of her aunt's successful knee replacements, Lara still worried about her when she navigated stairs, especially going down. The staircase in Aunt Fran's old Folk Victorian was steeper than most modern ones, and it also had shallow risers. Lara had almost slipped a few times herself popping downstairs in her stocking feet.

Sherry had already poured the tea. The fragrant aroma of orange and cloves filled the kitchen. "I love this," she said with a grin. "A ladies' tea party. Now, tell us what happened with that Megan chick, Lara. We're dying to hear everything."

They all sat down. Munster trotted in and claimed Lara's lap. Not to be outdone, Panda padded into the kitchen and leaped onto Sherry's knees, prepared to settle in for the long haul. Sherry smiled and rubbed his furry head. "Did Lara tell you David and I are going to adopt a cat?" she asked Aunt Fran.

"Not yet."

"I haven't had time. You just told me!"

They all laughed and talked about cats for a while. Then Lara related the highlights of her conversation with Megan.

"Forgive me for saying this," Sherry said with a scowl, "but I think the woman's a little warped. I mean, come on, are you telling me she doesn't have any other friends? All of a sudden she's latching on to you like static cling, and you're telling me that's normal?"

"I never went *that* far," Lara defended.

"I know." Sherry reached for another cookie. "I was being rhetorical."

"Either way," Aunt Fran put in, "it's my opinion that Megan Haskell has been taking advantage of Lara's good nature."

While the two chatted between them, Lara's mind wandered off.

I know who you are.

Who had dropped the cryptic message near Chancer's body? Did they do it before or after he…passed on?

And the phone number—the one with the Rhode Island exchange. Did it have anything to do with Chancer's death? Or did it belong to a disgruntled victim from one of Chancer's sketchy lawsuits? The possibilities were endless—so much so that it was impossible to narrow them down.

The phone number. It was burning a hole in the pocket of Lara's jeans. She itched to go to her tablet and Google it.

"Lara, what planet are you on right now?" Sherry demanded, waving a hand in front of her. "Because I think you left Earth a long time ago."

Planet Crazy, Lara wanted to say. "Don't worry. I heard everything you said. Well, almost everything."

"Did you hear me say I'm leaving?" Sherry tested her.

"Sorry, no." Lara rubbed her eyes.

Sherry rose off her chair and handed Panda to Lara. "Take charge of this cat. He might be mine one day. And don't forget what I said about a certain lawyer, okay?" She slipped on her coat and gloves.

But this is Megan's cat, Lara almost protested.

Whoa. Where had that come from?

Baffled by her own nutty thought, she started to get up to see Sherry to the door when Blue appeared suddenly at her feet. If she'd been a real, flesh-and-blood cat, Lara would have tripped over her.

"Don't worry," Lara said, aware that Sherry was gawking at her. "I'm going to call Gideon shortly. You have my word."

Blue faded before Lara could even wonder why she was there.

Through the door pane, she watched Sherry march down the porch stairs in her trendy black leather boots.

Chapter 29

"Sounds like you had a productive day," Lara said, smiling at her aunt. She cleaned up the table and stuck the dishes in the sink.

Aunt Fran nodded. "Productive, but it also made me rethink my career. Up until now, I thought I'd be happy subbing. Now I'm not sure if it's enough."

"It's a lot to consider," Lara said. "Especially now that you're writing a novel."

Her aunt smiled. "Well, I don't expect to finish my book anytime soon. But you're right. Now that I've got my head into this writing gig, I want to try and make it work. Right now, though, I don't want it to interfere with my day job, should I decide to look for a permanent position."

Lara's cell rang in her pocket, and she dug it out. Her heart smashed against her ribs when she saw who the caller was.

"Gideon?" She looked at her aunt, who immediately signaled that she was leaving to give her privacy.

"Hi, Lara. I've missed you," he said hoarsely. "It's been a long week."

"I've missed you, too. Is everything okay at the office?"

"It's not the office I'm worried about. It's us."

"I am, too," she said in a lowered voice. "So, what should we do?"

"Well, it is Friday, and we do usually grab a bite to eat. I was thinking of asking if you wanted to go to the Irish Stew, but it gets so noisy in there, especially on a Friday night. We wouldn't really be able to talk."

But we'd be together, she almost blurted.

Except that he was right. Most times Lara didn't mind the noise level at the Stew—it was part of the pub's ambience. Tonight, though, they needed to talk. *Really* talk.

"Do you have something else in mind?"

"I do," he said. "It just so happens that Marina made me a pan of her wonderful lasagna, all ready to bake. I think she was hoping I'd share it with you," he added quietly. "I've got salad fixings, and I'm pretty sure I've got some frozen rolls. Besides, Pearl and Orca miss you."

"I miss them, too. I have only two questions. What time would you like me to be there, and can I bring anything?"

"How about seven? And the only thing you need to bring is you."

"See you then."

After they disconnected, Lara hurried upstairs. Aunt Fran had retreated to her bedroom. Lara found her in her rocking chair, reading with Dolce in her lap. Twinkles was still on her aunt's bed, but he'd moved closer to the pillow.

"Hey, I'm heading over to Gideon's for dinner around seven."

"Oh, good," her aunt said, visibly relieved. "I'm so glad."

Lara took a quick shower, then went into her bedroom to get ready for her date and figure out what she was going to wear. Most times their Friday nights were casual, a way to wind down and relax after a long week. Tonight, though, she wanted to pretty things up a little.

She perused her closet, flipping through item after item, not landing on anything special. And then it caught her eye—the dress she'd picked up the day she and Sherry had chosen her maid of honor dress. It'd been on the sale rack, marked down about a zillion times, until it became an irresistible buy.

The dress was navy, with small white polka dots and bell sleeves. Stylishly understated but not terribly formal, it was perfect for a quiet evening with the man she loved.

She glanced at the clock on her bedside table. It was five forty, which left plenty of time to get ready. Still wrapped in her terry-cloth robe, she dropped down on her bed and fired up her tablet. From her high perch, Amber gazed down at her. Eyes wide, the shy kitty looked almost ready to join Lara, but then settled in and contented herself with simply watching.

Lara had already removed Megan's notepad from her jeans pocket and set it on her bedside table. She found the phone number Megan had written down entered it into Google's search box.

A string of links popped up, but nothing that gave her a name. Not surprising. If the caller had been as secretive as Megan claimed, he didn't want to be identified. Lara wondered if the number belonged to a burner phone—a prepaid throwaway registered to no one in particular.

Munster leaped onto the bed and leaned into her side. "What do you think, Munster?"

The cat's response was to raise a leg in the air and lick it thoroughly.

"Yeah, that's what I thought. You're not going to be any help at all, are you?"

Lara needed to get dressed, but first she couldn't resist Googling Chancer's name. She'd done it before, shortly after Megan had been taken in for questioning, and about a thousand links had popped up. She'd scrolled through the most promising ones, even clicked on a few to see if they might disclose any useful tidbits. But nothing had struck her as being of any help, so she hadn't pursued it any further.

Once again, pages of links appeared on her screen. Those five ominous words—the message supposedly found near Chancer's body—scrolled through her head.

I know who you are.

Strange, considering that everyone already seemed to know who Chancer was.

He was a husband to Karen Chancer, formerly Karen Becker, a woman who ran her own small but successful gourmet food business.

He was son-in-law to Gary Becker, a local real estate agent.

He was the former employer of Megan Haskell, a sensitive young woman who'd become enraged when he ignored her flirtations.

Chancer's reputation as an attorney had been well-established in local circles. If everything Lara had heard was true, he'd been a ruthless personal injury lawyer. She couldn't help thinking of Tina Tanaka's parents, feeling forced to shut down their restaurant over an incident that might well have been staged.

There has to be something else, Lara told herself.

Something beyond the obvious.

Something that went further back in Chancer's past.

Lara sighed and turned off her tablet. She didn't have time for this now. Later, after she got back home, *if* she got home, she'd spend more time looking into Chancer's background.

Right now, she had only one thing on her agenda.

Gideon.

* * * *

"I can't believe how delicious that lasagna was," Lara said, dabbing her lips with her napkin. "Be sure to thank Marina for me."

"I will. She was hoping you'd be sharing it with me. I was, too," he added softly.

Gideon spoke carefully, almost as if they were strangers. The entire dinner conversation had consisted of the same polite chatter. They'd tiptoed around each other's words as if they'd only just met. It was enough to make Lara's heart crack in two.

Gideon gazed over at her, then raised his wineglass and drained it. Dark pouches hung beneath his eyes, and his face looked drawn from lack of sleep.

"Gid, we need to talk," Lara said, hating the tremor in her voice. "*Really* talk."

"I know. We do." He cleared his throat. "Lara, as far as I'm concerned, nothing has changed. I love you as much as I always have. More, if that's even possible."

"I feel the same," she said, but it came out in a shaky whisper.

He rose from his chair, kissed her temple lightly, and carried their plates over to the sink. "Why don't you go in the living room and visit with Pearl and Orca. Give me a minute to stick these in the dishwasher, then I'll join you."

Normally Lara would protest at letting him clean up the dishes on his own—they usually worked in tandem. Tonight, she was too stressed and too weary to argue.

Five minutes later, Gideon joined her on the sofa. Pearl was sprawled in her lap, her huge double paws extended in a lazy stretch. Orca, perched on the back of the sofa, was chewing on a strand of her hair.

Gideon laughed. "Lord, what a picture you all make. Best thing I've seen all week."

Lara smiled at him and patted the sofa. "Join us."

He sat down close to Lara, and they played with the cats for a while. When Orca and Pearl finally trailed off and climbed onto their window perch, Gideon snugged in closer to Lara. Time fell away, and they reminisced over some of their first dates, breaking down into giggles over some of the crazier things.

"Have you talked to Uncle Amico this week?" Lara asked.

Gideon's uncle was currently living in a nearby assisted living facility. He enjoyed their visits tremendously, especially when Lara had time to bake something for him, like his favorite blueberry buckle. She'd grown so attached to the sweet, elderly gent that she thought of him as her real uncle.

"Gosh, I forgot to tell you. I talked to him Wednesday, and he had this funny lilt in his voice." He squeezed Lara's hand. "When I pushed him a bit, he admitted that he was getting sort of friendly with a woman who'd recently moved to the facility."

"Honestly? Oh, that's great," Lara said with a grin. "I hope we can meet her one of these days." Her smiled faded. "We still haven't talked about the elephant in the room, have we?"

"Elephant?" Gideon said soberly. "I think of it more like a tiger."

"Tiger Lara." She reached over and took his hand. "That's what you called me in grade school, remember? You got it from Tiger Lily in *Peter Pan*."

"Of course, I remember. Did you think I would ever forget that?" Looking pained now, he said, "Lara, can I speak first? Then you can say anything you want, okay?"

Her heart slipped gears and went into overdrive. Was he going to give her an ultimatum? "Sure. Go ahead."

I'm ready. I hope.

He took in a long breath, then spoke earnestly. "Lara, everything about you is what made me fall in love with you. The way you treat people with kindness and respect, your devotion to Fran, your passion for helping cats—not to mention how you use your artistic talent to help others."

Lara felt a flush creep up her neck. "Now you're making me sound like Joan of Arc."

He grinned. "Did she rescue cats, too?"

She gave him a light swat on the knee.

He got serious again. "But I want to add this because it's important. I don't want you to think for one moment that I ever doubted you about Blue. During one of our conversations, I had the feeling you were thinking that. You didn't exactly voice it, but I was reading between the lines. Anyway, I just want you to know—Blue is as real for me as she is for you. The only difference is that I can't see her."

Lara sagged against the sofa with sheer relief. She reached up and hugged him, but he gently took her arms and released her.

"Our only point of contention, it seems, is this strange involvement you have with murderers. I don't know why—to this day I don't get it—but they just seem to keep stumbling into your path."

Inwardly, Lara winced. She couldn't explain it herself. How could she expect anyone else to understand it?

"I don't think 'involvement' is the right word," she defended. "I don't attract murderers, but if they threaten people I love or care about, then I have to do everything in my power to stop them."

He nodded. "I understand. And that's exactly what you've done, and what I'd expect you to do. The thing is, after the last time, I really thought that would be the end, you know?" His voice dropped off and he swallowed hard, and Lara saw that he was struggling.

"This is different, Gideon. It's almost as though—how can I say it? As though I'm *supposed* to help someone, and I don't even know who that someone is."

Gideon shot her a confused look. "I thought you were trying to help Megan," he said bitingly. "God knows she's bothered you enough." He shifted on the sofa and crossed one leg over the other.

Lara leaned back and closed her eyes. "I don't know if it's Megan or not, but her aunt and uncle came over today."

"*What?*"

Lara related the highlights of her conversation with the Emersons, ending with their tale of Megan's arrest the night before.

Gideon threw up his arms. "Good God, what's she going to do next?" he said heatedly. "You know, I'm starting to realize something. All of this is my fault. You never would've heard of Megan Haskell if it hadn't been for me. I'm taking the blame for all of this."

"It's no one's fault, Gideon. This isn't about fault. Besides, after today, I'm pretty sure Megan will never speak to me again." She explained how Megan got offended when Lara showed her the slip of paper that read: *I know who you are.*

"I know who you are. Why did you write that?"

Here goes...

"The day I met Karen Chancer, she told me that the police found a note near her husband's body that said, 'I know who you are.'"

"But you don't even know if that's true. She might have made that up."

Lara looked at him. He had a good point. What if Karen had invented the story about the note to cover her own guilt? What if she'd written the note herself to throw the police off her trail?

Except that when Lara had mentioned the note to Lieutenant Cutler, he'd seemed incensed that she knew about it. He'd gone so far as to warn her not to breathe a word of it to anyone.

"I'm pretty sure there was a note," Lara said. "I mentioned it to Cutler the day I ran into him and he acted weird about it, like he was ticked that I even knew about it." She pulled in a calming breath. "I—I have something else to tell you, too."

She explained how Karen Chancer had acted so needy when Lara met her at the Peach Crate. "She called me and asked if I'd go with her to her husband's memorial service on Monday. I tried to say no, but she sounded desperate."

Gideon's face reddened. "You know that's ridiculous, don't you? She has a father, she has friends—"

Lara didn't appreciate his tone, but she let it go—for now. "She said the few friends she had have pretty much ditched her since her husband's death. I know that's not what you wanted to hear, but I gave her my word. But I will promise you one thing, and this is a firm promise. After Monday, I'm done with Bakewell. Totally. Forever."

He sat back, his face pinched. "I have no choice but to accept that, I guess."

The mood had shifted, like a seismic wave of roiling emotion. Lara knew that it would be folly to spend the night at Gideon's.

"Can I ask you one last thing?" he asked, as if he sensed the same thing.

"Of course," Lara said, terrified to hear the question.

"Something must have triggered this…this feeling you have that you're supposed to help someone in Bakewell, whoever that someone is. What was it, Lara? Was it something someone said?"

You cannot escape the responsibility of tomorrow by evading it today.

"It was," she said. "And it was Abraham Lincoln who said it."

Chapter 30

Lara dreaded going to the coffee shop on Saturday morning. The moment Sherry saw her, she'd know immediately that Lara hadn't resolved things with Gideon.

When she arrived, however, she was surprised to see Jill scurrying around behind the counter instead of Sherry. Lara dropped onto her usual stool and waved at her.

"Hey! We missed you yesterday." Sporting a pink hoop ring in each of her pierced eyebrows, Jill scuttled over and poured a mug of coffee for Lara.

"I missed you guys, too, but I had a lot going on. One of those days, you know?"

"Yeah, I hear you."

"So, where's our favorite gal today?"

"Kellie's giving her a trim this morning. Sherry didn't want to get it done too close to the wedding, just in case it comes out a bit too short." Jill's eyes lit up. "It's getting *sooo* close to the big day. I'm seriously excited, aren't you?"

Lara grinned. "I am over the moon."

Jill plated a poppyseed muffin and set it down in front of Lara. Normally, Lara would slather it with butter and devour it as if she hadn't eaten in days. Today she skipped the butter and picked at the muffin. It felt like lead going down her throat.

Her appetite had deserted her.

The night before, she'd had a series of baffling dreams. She was in Bakewell again, walking among that same sea of faces she'd dreamt of before. The crowd kept thickening, shoving her aside, and she couldn't seem to make any forward progress. She sensed she was supposed to find someone in that crowd—if only she could figure out whom. The dream—more like a nightmare—then morphed into Gideon driving past her in his sedan. But when she waved at him, he merely looked at her with a deadpan expression, almost as if she were invisible. She'd awakened in a cold sweat, grateful none of it had really happened.

"Not hungry today?"

Lara jumped. She hadn't noticed Jill standing directly in front of her, gawking at her. "Oh, um, not really. I had some raisin toast with my aunt this morning." It was a fib, but she didn't want Jill to sense that anything was wrong. It would get right back to Sherry and then she'd have the devil to pay. "I'll take the rest of the muffin home with me."

Jill nodded, then fetched her a small carryout bag. Lara gulped down the rest of her coffee, paid the tab, and left.

Tote bag on her shoulder, she paused for a moment in front of the coffee shop. The air was crisp, the sky crowded with gray clouds. Since it was Saturday, this was about the time of the morning Gideon would typically be making waffles or pancakes for the two of them. The memory made her throat hurt.

Lara glanced in the direction of Gideon's house. She could be there in five minutes if she hoofed it.

Should I, or shouldn't I?

She hadn't heard from him since she'd left the night before. They'd hugged, but it hadn't felt genuine. It'd felt as if the end was near.

Lara turned and headed home. Kayla had texted her the night before saying she was taking Saturday off. Her new friend, or boyfriend, or whatever he was, was taking her to the planetarium in Concord—a place Kayla had always wanted to visit.

Today was an adoption day. Lara could certainly handle it on her own, plus Aunt Fran would be there. Maybe this was a good day to reach out to a few other shelters to see if they wanted High Cliff to take in a few of their cats.

Aunt Fran was sitting at the kitchen table, tapping away at her keyboard. Dolce rested in her lap. "Still cold out?" she asked Lara.

Lara peeled off her outerwear. "In the high thirties, but kind of raw. I'm wondering if we'll get some rain." She plunked her muffin bag on the counter. Munster was chowing away at one of the food bowls, but Panda was MIA.

Aunt Fran looked at Lara, her face etched with concern. "Lara, I'm not going to press you with any questions, but I'm here, always, if you want to talk."

"I know. Thank you." She kissed her aunt's cheek. "I'll be in my studio for a bit."

Lara hurried into her studio and closed the door. She needed to be alone for a while.

The sketches she'd done for Amy's project were sitting on the corner of her worktable. Lara studied them again, wondering if Kayla had hit on something when she noticed that the shriveled flower beds in the newer pics were different from the ones in the older photo. She sent Amy a quick text, asking her to call when she got a free minute.

Meanwhile, she fired up her tablet. There were at least three area shelters she wanted to get in touch with. She went to the Web page for each one and located the email address for the person who appeared to be in charge. She sent each one a message with an offer of help. High Cliff could easily take in two or three more cats.

It was almost certain that Sienna would be going home with Jeannie Jennings in the coming week. Lara smiled, thrilled that the sweet kitty's diagnosis wasn't impeding her from being adopted by a loving mom.

Her cell rang, and Amy's face popped up on her readout. "Hey, Lara, I got your message." As always, Amy's voice was full of sunshine and cheer.

"Hey, yourself," Lara said. "Thanks for calling me back. I have a quick question. I looked at the recent pics you sent of the farmhouse and compared them to the old photo. This might sound strange, but did you replace any of the flower beds after you bought the house?"

"The flower beds," she mused. "Oh! Gosh, yes, I did. I can't believe you even noticed that. When I first bought the farmhouse, one of the dogs—Freida—kept poking around in the flowers in front of my house. It wasn't until she threw up one day that I made the connection. The beautiful flowers in front of the house were poisonous!"

Lara winced. "Oh no. Was Freida okay?"

"Thank God, yes. But I was mortified that I'd let that happen. Being a vet, I was horribly embarrassed that I hadn't picked up on it sooner. I'd just moved in and was up to my eyeballs in projects, but that's no excuse."

"What were the flowers?" Lara asked her.

"They were lily of the valley. Totally gorgeous when they're in bloom, but they're also quite toxic. Soon as I realized what they were, I ripped out those bad boys and planted petunias. It's a cautionary tale, for sure. I lecture all my pet owners about it now."

They chatted for another few minutes before Amy said, "Hey, I gotta dash. We just got an emergency patient in."

Lara thanked her and disconnected.

Lily of the valley. Was that what Blue had wanted her to notice in the photo? She started to Google the flower in question when her cell pinged with a text. It was from Kayla.

> *Did some snooping this morning on Chancer.*
> *Weird, and I don't know if it means anything, but*
> *check out this link. Could he be the unnamed*
> *juvenile? Check out the other links, too.*

Lara sent her back a quick text thanking her and wishing her a great day.

The link referred to an article from a newspaper in Peasemore, Massachusetts, dated October 17, 1993. Two teens and a juvenile had been arrested for throwing a softball-sized rock off an overpass onto the highway below. The rock smashed through the windshield of an SUV driven by a local nurse—Olive Dandreau of Lynnfield—killing her fourteen-year-old son.

Frowning, Lara scrolled down further.

The teens, both eighteen, were identified as Richard Mulhaney and Chad Walford, both of Peasemore. The juvenile, who was sixteen, was not named.

As Lara read through the article, a sense of horror washed over her. The perpetrators had been close high school friends, despite the age difference between the older two and the youngest. In a sick, senseless act that took a fraction of a minute, they destroyed a family. The driver, Dandreau, a single mom, suffered multiple injuries. Her fourteen-year-old son, Jarrod Dandreau, was crushed by the rock when it sailed through the SUV's windshield.

Lara clutched her stomach, sickened by what she'd read. A grainy photo of a smiling Jarrod appeared next to the article. With his gap-toothed smile, he looked achingly young, not even close to fourteen. His life had barely begun before it was callously extinguished.

In court, both teens had sobbed before the judge, insisting they'd never meant to harm anyone. Identified as the ringleader, Chad Walford was sentenced to eighteen months in prison. Mulhaney received a one-year suspended sentence, along with community service. Charges against the unnamed juvenile—declared by the judge to be an "unwilling participant" in the horrific act—were dropped.

Lara shook her head, disgusted by what she'd read. But why had Kayla assumed that the unnamed juvenile had been Wayne Chancer?

She scrolled down and saw that Kayla had attached two other links.

The first opened to an article about a trio of teen boys, identified as "lifelong friends," who'd emerged victorious in a game of field hockey in a face-off against the team from a neighboring school. Chad Walford, Richard Mulhaney, and Wayne Chancer were pictured with their arms around each other, grinning into the camera. In an interview, their coach had glowingly described the three young athletes as being "tight as ticks."

Lifelong friends.

Tight as ticks.

Did that mean the three had done everything together? Including tossing a rock off a bridge and killing a boy?

Lara moved on to the third link. This one was an online article about the problems of addiction, and the scarcity of resources for those seeking help. One of the examples given was that of Richard "Rickster" Mulhaney, who'd died several months earlier from an overdose. The article quoted Richard's grieving mother, who'd been shocked that her son had slipped back into addiction after he'd been clean for so long. His death from an apparent overdose had been completely unexpected. "Happy and positive one day, gone the next," she was quoted as saying. "Something's not right. I want answers."

Her heart racing, Lara saved all three links. Had Kayla stumbled on to something?

Clearly the three had been close buds, friends who'd done everything together.

I know who you are.

Lara shivered. The words took on a whole new meaning.

She felt sure Kayla was on to something, and now she couldn't help wondering. Had the unnamed juvenile in the deadly rock-throwing incident been Wayne Chancer?

Chapter 31

On Saturday afternoon, two different groups showed up for adoptions.

The first was a fourteen-year-old girl and her dad. From the surly way the girl spoke to her father, combined with his meek responses, Lara suspected she was a spoiled teen who'd always been allowed to do pretty much what she wanted. The girl had been annoyed when Lara told her they didn't have any kittens. They left right after the teen had scarfed down two of Daisy's cat-shaped cookies.

An elderly couple came in shortly after that. While they seemed genuine, they'd been surprised not to see a few dozen cats from which to choose. They'd evidently thought the shelter was the equivalent of a pet store. The woman, somewhere in her late seventies, Lara guessed, had set her sights on adopting a Siamese cat. When she learned that High Cliff didn't have a Siamese, she heaved a dramatic sigh, then signaled to her husband that it was time to leave.

So much for adoption day.

Late in the afternoon, Lara was tidying up the meet-and-greet room when a call came in. A volunteer from one of the shelters Lara had emailed was interested in learning if High Cliff could take in a pair of female siblings.

"They're very sweet, but very timid," the woman, whose name was Glenna Tyler, said. "They came from a feral community that a local man has been caring for in his barn. But these two," she explained, "didn't really act feral. They seemed more scared than anything, so after they were spayed and vaccinated, they went to a foster home. Problem is, the foster mom is going into the hospital next week. She really needs someone to take them—otherwise they'll end up here."

"I see," Lara said.

"Not that we don't provide good care," Glenna was quick to assure her. "We do. But after being in a real home for several weeks, it would be hard for them to adjust to shelter life. We're afraid it might undo the progress they've made. When I saw your email today, it was like…like a prayer had been answered, you know? I've read about High Cliff," Glenna went on, the smile obvious in her voice, "and I know it's a real home for cats. I think it would be perfect for them. They're both in excellent health, and I can supply their records."

"I think so, too," Lara said, not without a touch of pride. "There is one thing I want to tell you. One of our little girls is FIV positive, but it looks like she's going to be adopted by a wonderful woman early in the week. She hasn't shown any signs of illness, so it shouldn't be a problem."

"That's fine. I'm happy that you found her a great home. Can I drop off Holly and Noella to you tomorrow, or is that too soon?" Glenna ventured.

Holly and Noella. What adorable names! "That'll be perfect," Lara agreed.

"Terrific. I'm dying to see your shelter, too. I think it could be a model for others to follow, if they have the right kind of home and the resources."

They set up an appointment for ten on Sunday morning. Several children had set up times to read to a cat in the afternoon, so the timing would be perfect.

Lara went into the kitchen to tell Aunt Fran.

"Oh, that's marvelous," her aunt said. "I can't wait to meet them."

"Yeah, me, too. The woman from the shelter was so grateful."

For the next half hour or so, Lara prepared the isolation room for Holly and Noella. Glenna hadn't described the cats, so she was anxious to see them. In spite of both cats having clean bills of health, Lara thought it would be best to give them their own space for a few days. That way she could spend some quality time alone with them and assess their personalities. After that she'd introduce them to the rest of the household. She didn't anticipate any problems, unless Panda decided to get territorial.

Lara suddenly realized she was starving. The excitement over the new cats had taken her mind off her troubles, and her stomach.

"Hey," she said to her aunt when she was back in the kitchen, "want to have pizza for supper? I'll have it delivered, so we don't have to trek out in the cold to pick it up."

Aunt Fran pushed aside her laptop. "I've done a lot of work on my book today, and you've made arrangements to take in two new cats. Yes, I think we deserve a pizza."

"Good. It's my treat, so don't start pulling out your wallet."

Her aunt laughed, while Lara called in an order for a pepperoni and onion pizza. They set out plates and napkins, and the pizza arrived thirty minutes later. They both dug in right away so they could eat it nice and hot.

"Have you heard from Gideon today?" Aunt Fran asked, after swallowing a bite of the cheesy pie.

Lara shook her head. "I have not," she said, picking off a pepperoni round. "And honestly, I don't even want to think about it. I've decided that what will be, will be. I'm getting quite fatalistic in my old age." She popped the pepperoni slice into her mouth.

Aunt Fran nodded but kept her expression blank.

They chatted about the incoming cats, and how fun it was going to be to have some fresh feline faces in the house. Then Lara remembered Kayla's text with the links she'd sent earlier. She told Aunt Fran what she'd learned when she followed the links.

"Well, that adds to the picture, doesn't it?" Her aunt's brow furrowed with worry. "All the more reason for you to stay out of it, Lara. If there's any connection to Chancer's past, I'm sure the police are already on top of it."

She was probably right. Knowing State Police Lieutenant Conrad Cutler, he'd probably already examined every detail of Chancer's life, from birth until his sad demise.

But what if he hadn't? The charges against the "unnamed juvenile" had been dropped, she recalled from the article. If that had, indeed, been Chancer, did that mean his juvenile records had been sealed, or that they simply didn't exist? If they'd been sealed, could the police still obtain a copy? Lara would normally pose the question to Gideon, but things between them lately were far from normal.

She was wiping up the table when her cell rang. She dropped the sponge and slid her phone out of her pocket. Gideon's smiling face appeared on the screen.

"Hi, Gideon," she said, hearing her voice crack.

"Hi, Lara, can you talk for a few?"

"Of course. Always," she said, heading into her studio for privacy. She closed the door. "Okay, I'm in my studio."

"Lara, I hate what's happening between us. This isn't right. It isn't us."

She swallowed. "I know. I agree." She pulled in a calming breath. "So, what do we do about it?"

His voice grew quiet. "I called to ask if you would agree to my attending the memorial service with you on Monday."

Lara was stunned. It was the last thing she'd expected him to say. "You want to go with me?"

"I do," he said. "I would feel much better if you didn't go to Bakewell on your own. I know Karen Chancer thinks of you as a friend, so I would, of course, treat her with the utmost courtesy and respect."

"You didn't even have to say that, Gid. I know you would."

Lara thought about it for a moment. Would Karen object if Gideon came along with her? Did she even have a right to object? Not really, since Lara was doing *her* the favor by accompanying her to the memorial service.

"You know what? That sounds good to me. Only thing is, after the service I have to go to the bridal shop to pick up my shoes."

"Not a problem. I'll even treat you to lunch afterward. And I'll do the driving, if that's okay."

In truth, Lara was relieved. Not only that she'd have his company at the service, but that he was anxious for things to get back to the way they were.

"Are you sure you have time for this, Gideon? You don't exactly have a light schedule."

"There's always time for the most important things. I'll go to my office tomorrow and play catch-up on a few things—that'll help. On Monday I'll ask Marina to juggle my schedule. It'll all work out. I promise."

Lara smiled, feeling her heart swell. "Then let's make it a plan."

After she hung up, she felt her entire body relax. The emotional weight she'd been lugging around like a ship anchor lifted from her shoulders. She imagined seeing it float to the ceiling and drift out of sight.

For the rest of the evening, she worked on Amy's sketches. She didn't typically spend so much prep time on a commissioned watercolor, but Amy Glindell was a special friend. She'd helped get them through so many feline crises, it was the least she deserved. By Monday afternoon, Lara would be ready to present the sketches to the veterinarian. After Amy chose her favorite, Lara would begin painting the watercolor.

Chapter 32

Glenna Tyler showed up early on Sunday morning. Petite, with a shock of short black curls and an engaging smile, she had light brown eyes that danced with excitement when she walked into the meet-and-greet room. In one hand she carried a humongous pet carrier.

"I'm *sooo* glad to meet you," she told Lara, giving her an impetuous, one-armed hug.

Lara laughed. "And I'm delighted to meet you." She kneeled and peeked into the carrier. Two darling gold-and-white faces gazed up at her. "Oh, look at them. I'm so glad you brought them here. Come on, I'll show you where they're going to stay for the first day or two."

She led Glenna and company through the downstairs portion of the house, and then upstairs to the isolation room. Munster and Panda followed like furry bodyguards, more curious than worried about any intruding newcomers. It took a few tries, but they managed to get into the isolation room without any feline ushers.

"This whole place is great," Glenna gushed. "The way you care for the cats—it's even nicer than I thought. And I can't believe this room. You've made it so welcoming for them."

Lara had set out an oversized cat bed for the pair, along with food bowls, a fresh water dispenser, and a clean litter box. "This is only temporary. After a day or two I'll introduce them to the rest of the household. I want them to get used to our smells and sounds first."

"Excellent idea." Glenna opened the carrier door. Two pink noses lifted simultaneously, but the cats remained inside. "Let's chat for a few. Give them a chance to check out their surroundings."

The more Lara learned about Glenna, the more she liked her. Aside from holding a full-time day job, she worked tirelessly as a shelter volunteer. Last winter, she'd single-handedly rescued a community of seven feral cats from a dilapidated shed. The cats were now all neutered and vaccinated, and three were living in comfy homes.

A furry face emerged slowly from the carrier, her big green eyes alight with curiosity. She gazed all around, then sauntered over to the food bowl.

"That's Noella," Glenna said softly. "Her face has more gold than Holly's."

"I love the names," Lara said.

Glenna grinned. "You can thank their foster mom for that. She got them last December, hence the Christmasy names."

A minute later Holly followed her sister, joining her at the food bowl. Lara's heart melted at the sight. "I won't try to pick them up right away. I'll let them get used to me gradually."

"Good idea. They're not thrilled about being held, but I think that'll change over time." Glenna gave Lara a worried look. "You'll…you'll make sure they get good homes, right? Their foster mom can't keep them any longer."

"You have my word," Lara said. "And I'll keep you informed, too."

They slipped out quietly and closed the door. After a tour of the rest of the house, Lara introduced Glenna to her aunt, who was reading the paper in the kitchen.

"It's so nice to meet another cat lady," Aunt Fran said kindly.

"Exactly what I was thinking," Glenna said, her brown eyes beaming. "Hey, if it's okay, I've really gotta run. I've got lots of other cat duties today. And…thank you, both. It's obvious I've left Holly and Noella with the right people."

* * * *

Lara and Aunt Fran arrived at Saint Lucy's church in time for the twelve o'clock service. After the final blessing, Lara whispered to her aunt, "Do you mind if I wait until everyone leaves so I can chat with the pastor for a few? I just want to thank him for helping out Sherry and David."

"I don't mind at all."

As the pastor strolled slowly along the aisle, greeting his parishioners, Lara and Aunt Fran waited for him in front of the door leading to the vestibule.

His eyes lit up when he spotted them. "Well, if it isn't two of my favorite people," he said, taking Aunt Fran's hand and squeezing it.

"Good morning, Pastor," Lara said. "I just wanted to thank you again for helping out my friends Sherry and David. They're so thrilled that you're going to be co-officiating their wedding ceremony."

He nodded. "I'm equally pleased. In fact, I'm looking forward to it." He leaned over and in a faux-whisper said, "I do hope the wedding cake will be chocolate."

"Well, you might just get your wish," Lara said cryptically, "but I can't reveal any more than that."

After chatting for a few more minutes, Lara and Aunt Fran headed home. Five children had made appointments to read to a cat that afternoon. They wanted to be ready.

Things are looking up, Lara thought to herself, angling the Saturn into the driveway.

Sherry's wedding plans were proceeding smoothly. Lara and Gideon had patched their differences—at least for now. Their future was still hazy, but she'd deal with that in due time.

Once inside the house, Lara made a beeline for Holly and Noella. Both cats padded over to her the moment she stepped into the room. It was a good sign—they were adjusting well to their new digs. She played with both kitties for a while and gave them a good brushing. Tomorrow, after she got back from Bakewell, she'd open the door to the isolation room and encourage them to explore the house.

In the next instant, Lara remembered the links Kayla had sent her yesterday. Lara hadn't pursued them any further. Maybe a quick look wouldn't hurt before the kids arrived. If she could glean something helpful before attending Chancer's memorial service, she'd be more than happy to turn it over to Lieutenant Cutler.

She fetched her tablet from her bedroom and carried it downstairs. Aunt Fran was busy baking brownies, and a delectable aroma filled the kitchen.

Lara sat at the table. The link she wanted to reread was the one about Jarrod Dandreau's death. She forwarded Kayla's link to her email in-box, and then pulled it up on her iPad.

Jarrod had been a studious but well-liked boy, according to the news article. An avid chess player, he was also a member of his high school's drama club. On the day his life was so tragically taken, he'd been on his way home from his school's production of *Beauty and the Beast*, in which he'd had a minor role. His grief-stricken mother told the reporter that Jarrod was a wonderful, brilliant child whose death would never be forgotten.

Outside, on the shelter side of the house, a car door slammed.

"One of the kids must be here," Aunt Fran said, pulling a pan out of the oven.

Lara glanced at the clock. It was a few minutes before two. "Must be Nathan with his folks. I'll let them in."

The remainder of the afternoon passed by in a blur. Kids came and went, and the cats learned all about *Green Eggs and Ham*, among other delights.

After a hearty supper of veggie frittata and roasted red potatoes, Lara headed upstairs, where she spent more time with Holly and Noella. Both cats were bonding nicely with her. By the time next Sunday rolled around, she hoped they'd be ready to take part in "read to a cat" Sunday.

Lara decided to hit the hay early, since Gideon planned to pick her up at eight forty-five for the drive to Bakewell. She'd already chosen her outfit—her navy pantsuit with a plain white blouse—and her low-heeled leather boots.

She texted with Gideon for a while before turning off her light.

After that, surrounded by cats, she allowed sleep to carry her off into dreamless oblivion.

Chapter 33

Lara glanced at her phone for the tenth time. It was 9:12, and Gideon still hadn't arrived.

"That's not like Gideon," Aunt Fran said, her brow creased with worry. "Did you text him?"

"I did, twice." Lara looked at her phone again. She was just about to call him when it rang. "Gideon?"

"Hi, Lara. Oh boy, I've got some bad news. I'm afraid I won't be able to go to Bakewell with you this morning. I was practically out the door when I got a call from the assisted living place. Uncle Amico fell. He's on his way to the hospital."

"Oh no. The poor man! Is he okay? Did he break anything? It's not his heart, is it?" She was so frantic she didn't know which question to ask first.

She heard Gideon take in a long breath. "Not heart-related, as far as I know, but he might have broken his hip. At this point, they're not sure. Lara, I don't want you to worry. They said he has some pain, but he's in good spirits. He was even joking with the EMTs as they were loading him into the ambulance."

Lara sagged. That much was a relief.

"Honey, listen, I'm not going to ask you to cancel your plans for the memorial service. I know Karen Chancer is counting on you. But please, *please* be careful. And will you do me a favor? If you see Cutler, try to stick close to him. I'm sure he'll be hanging around somewhere. By the time the service is over, I should have more info on Uncle Amico. I'll keep in touch, but you do the same, okay?"

"I will," Lara promised. "Please give Uncle Amico my best, okay? Tell him I'll be there as soon as I can."

"You got it. Love you, Lara."

"Love you, too."

Lara disconnected, feeling immensely frustrated. If only she could get out of going to the memorial service—she could head to the hospital and be with Gideon and Uncle Amico.

With a sinking heart, she was telling Aunt Fran what had happened when her cell rang again. Lara grabbed it quickly, thinking it might be Gideon. She was dismayed to see that it was Karen Chancer.

"Hey, I just wanted to touch base," Karen said in a halting voice. "A limo from the funeral parlor is going to pick up me and Dad at nine thirty. Can you meet us at the Peaceful Valley Funeral Home between ten fifteen and ten thirty? I was going to ask you to come to the house, but that same awful reporter's been haunting me, so we're going to sneak out. The limo's going to wait for us in a neighbor's driveway."

"Karen, I…here's the thing. I—"

"Oh my God, you're still going to the service with me, right?" Her voice came out in a high-pitched plea.

"Yes. Yes, I'm still going. But my uncle just broke his hip, and—"

"Oh, thank God. For a minute I thought you were changing your mind. I don't think I could bear it if you did."

Could she be any more dramatic? Lara thought irritably, but then scolded herself. The woman's husband had been horribly murdered. She had a right to act out.

Lara would go to the service and get it over with. Instead of picking up her shoes, she'd head straight to the hospital where Uncle Amico had been taken. She'd ask the bridal salon to ship her shoes to her—no biggie there.

Once Chancer's funeral was over, Bakewell would be out of her life forever.

* * * *

Lara felt like an interloper. She had no right to be sitting next to Karen, as if she belonged with the family. Even Gary Becker had stared questioningly at her. Didn't he realize she was there only at his daughter's request? Hadn't Karen told him anything?

An elderly couple sat on the other side of Lara. The woman, who was well into her seventies, had deep-set brown eyes and a face leathery from overexposure to the sun. An old-fashioned black chapel veil sat atop her thinning white hair. Her husband—Chancer's stepdad, Lara learned—sat beside his wife in a wheelchair. One side of his face drooped, and his entire body sagged to the left. His expression was sadly vacant. If they were curious as to who Lara was, they never asked.

The parlor itself was ornately appointed, plush blue carpeting stretching the length of the humongous room. Beige, velvet-covered chairs sat in neat rows for the mourners. Near the entrance, a guest book was propped on a mahogany platform. Chancer's closed coffin was surrounded by a sea of colorful flower arrangements. A massive, heart-shaped wreath made from white roses was propped on an easel behind the coffin. A banner stretching across its center bore the message *Beloved Husband*.

At one point, Becker drifted off to chat with some of the mourners who were milling about in the outer reception area. *So-called mourners*, Lara corrected herself. Who knew what most of these people were really thinking? Becker's face was etched with hard lines, his eyes bleary. His fingers twitched, and Lara suspected he was itching for a cigarette.

Lara's heartbeat spiked when Megan Haskell ambled in. Garbed totally in black, right down to her long wool coat and stylish beret, she was flanked by a woman Lara had never seen before. Slender, with ocean-blue eyes, the woman looked so strikingly like Megan that Lara knew it had to be her mom.

Megan signed the guest book, and her companion followed suit. Megan's aunt and uncle came in right behind them. Sally Emerson's face registered shock when she spotted Lara sitting beside Karen. Lara offered her a weak nod, but Sally's expression remained frozen.

After kneeling briefly at the coffin, Megan crossed herself and went over to Karen. Her gaze snagged Lara's and she took in a sharp breath. After quietly offering her condolences to the widow, she moved over to Lara. "What are you doing here?" she hissed in Lara's ear.

"Karen asked me to sit with her," Lara murmured, not that it was any of Megan's business.

Megan glared at her for a long moment, then grabbed her companion's hand and pulled her toward a row of chairs near the back.

"We meet again," Sally Emerson said quietly, her eyes as cold as glaciers.

Lara rose off her chair so they could speak more privately. "Mrs. Emerson, I'm here at Karen's request, and I'll be leaving right after the service. Is that Megan's mom who's with her?"

Sally nodded, and her gaze softened. "*Finally*, the woman had the gumption to leave her husband. She and Megan are going to get an apartment together."

Art Emerson came up behind his wife and touched her arm lightly. He nodded at Lara. "Let's go, hon. Meggie's saving seats for us."

Sally opened her mouth as if she had more to say, but then she clamped it shut. They strode off, leaving Lara wondering.

Visitors began arriving in clusters. Lara suspected that many of them were fellow members of the Bar. Three smartly dressed women clutching designer purses came in together. After signing the guest book and performing the obligatory kneel at the coffin, each of them offered Karen a half-hearted condolence and a squeeze from a bejeweled hand.

"Those women," Karen murmured to Lara after the three had swept past, "used to be my good friends. Now they treat me like I have typhoid."

Organ music began drifting softly from the overhead speakers. Lara glanced at her watch—it was ten to eleven. A balding man wearing liturgical vestments strode in carrying a prayer book. He took a seat in the front row and opened his book.

"Karen, why don't I move over there and sit with the other mourners," Lara whispered. "These chairs are for the family, plus your dad's here, and—"

"No, *please*." Karen grabbed Lara's hand and gripped it tightly, her eyes brimming with tears. "I'd really like you to stay." Her tone was pleading.

Lara knew, right then, that she was toast. As bad as she felt for Karen, she shouldn't have agreed to this. It would be a miracle if she could extricate herself from Karen's clutches after the service was over.

But she would. She had to.

Besides, she had a perfectly valid reason—she needed to be at the hospital with Gideon and Uncle Amico.

It was three minutes before eleven when a familiar figure entered the parlor. Lara brightened at the sight of Felicia Tristany—she was a breath of fresh air in a room heavy with gloom. Attired in a forest-green wool pantsuit, a white flower pinned to her lapel, Felicia scribbled hurriedly in the guest book. Without stopping at the coffin, she made a beeline for Karen. The two hugged tightly, while Lara tried not to stare.

"It will all be okay," Felicia murmured to Karen, "Everything will be okay."

Karen nodded, and a smile cracked her lips. "I know it will. Thank you, Felicia. You're a wonderful and dear friend."

Felicia's pink-tinted lips curved into a tiny smile as she moved over to Lara. In the next instant, Gary Becker appeared behind Felicia. He touched her shoulder, and she took Lara's hand firmly in her own. "There are two chairs free," she whispered. "Let's nab them."

Lara felt herself dragged by the hand and propelled toward a seat in the fourth row. In the same instant, Becker claimed Lara's chair next to his daughter, leaving the faint scent of cigarette smoke trailing in his wake. The whole thing happened so quickly Lara knew it had to have been choreographed. Karen looked bereft, but she took her father's hand and leaned into his shoulder.

What just happened? Lara asked herself. Either Felicia had sensed Lara's angst and decided to rescue her, or Gary Becker had found Lara's presence intrusive and arranged with Felicia to oust her from her chair.

Either way, Lara was grateful for the intervention.

"You naughty girl," Felicia scolded quietly as they sat down, a twinkle in her faded blue eyes. "You never told me you rescue cats. I found out yesterday from Tina. She told me all about you."

Despite the circumstances, Lara couldn't help smiling. She shrugged. "I guess it never came up."

Felicia patted Lara's hand, her brow creased with concern. "After the service, I'd like you to come home with me. Don't worry, I live close by. There's a stray cat behind my house that I've been feeding for weeks, but I simply can't bear to see him suffer in the cold any longer. I haven't been able to entice him inside, but this morning he was so cold and hungry that I managed to lure him into Lily's carrier with some tuna."

Lara squeezed the elderly woman's hand. "Felicia, I'm sorry, but I can't. My uncle Amico"—not really a fib—"broke his hip this morning and I have to get to the hospital."

Felicia's thin face fell. She looked heartsick. "Oh dear, I'm sorry to hear that."

"Have you called Animal Control?" Lara asked.

She shook her head. "Bakewell's AC officer is only part-time, and right now she's on maternity leave. The police won't do anything. I already spoke to them. They told me to contact a shelter."

Lara felt for Felicia—and for the kitty she'd rescued—but right now her hands were tied.

She took a moment to think about it.

She'd already decided not to stop at the bridal salon. The shoes could easily be shipped to her. Since Felicia lived close by, Lara could retrieve the cat, transfer him to her own carrier, and bring him to Amy's clinic for evaluation. After that she'd find out which hospital Uncle Amico had been taken to and meet Gideon there. After all, wasn't rescuing and caring for cats what High Cliff was about? How could she refuse to help this caring woman?

"Felicia, I'll make a call after the service, but I can't make any promises until I do," Lara whispered, as silence fell over the room.

The balding man with the prayer book rose from his chair, stood before the casket, and asked everyone to join him in a prayer.

For the next ten minutes, he sang Wayne Chancer's praises. Some of it sounded false to Lara, but the man was probably doing his best given Chancer's dubious past. Gary Becker scowled and twitched and sucked on cough drops during the entire eulogy, while his daughter clutched his hand and stared into her lap.

When the service was over, Lara breathed a sigh of relief. People began filing out. A low chatter, mingled with light laughter, sifted through the throng.

Before entering the funeral parlor, Lara had muted the sound on her phone. She quickly checked for messages. As she suspected, there'd been a text from Gideon.

> *Call me when you're leaving Bakewell. Soon,*
> *I hope! I'm heading back to the office. Uncle*
> *Amico is stable; hip not broken. No surgery*
> *scheduled. Love you.*

Lara sighed with relief, then turned to her companion. "Excuse me, Felicia, but I have to call my boyfriend about…my uncle."

Felicia nodded. "Of course, dear. I'll wait for you in the lobby."

In the short time since the service had ended, both Karen and her dad seemed to have disappeared. Lara skimmed her gaze around for any sign of them but came up empty. Had the funeral director escorted them out through a back door to avoid potential reporters?

She remained seated and called Gideon.

"Hi, honey," he said. "Thank God, Uncle Amico's hip isn't broken—it's only sprained. The ER doctor called it a first-degree hip sprain, which is a minor ligament tear. He should heal in a few weeks—maybe longer because of his age—but they're going to keep him there overnight. There's not much they can do other than ice it and give him painkillers."

"Oh boy, that's such a relief. How did he sprain it?"

Gideon gave a soft chuckle. "Evidently, his new female friend persuaded him to join a yoga class. During one of the moves, he twisted around too quickly and hurt his hip. I suspect he was trying to impress her with his athletic prowess."

"Poor Uncle Amico. At least he's being cared for. So, you're heading back to work now?"

"Yeah, the orthopedic doc said Uncle's going to be out of it most of the day from the painkillers. He suggested I come back this evening to visit him. You'll come with me, right?"

"You know I will. Call me once you know the timing, okay?"

"I will. Lara," he said warily, "how did everything go today?"

"Pretty well. I'm getting ready to leave now. I'll tell you all about it when I see you. I never did spot Cutler. Maybe it's his day off."

"Unlikely," Gideon muttered. "Anyway, let me know once you're home so I can start breathing normally again."

Lara smiled. "I will, I promise."

After they disconnected, Lara wondered if she should have mentioned her cat rescue mission. Well, too late now. Besides, it shouldn't take very long.

She glanced at her phone. It was almost noon. Once she picked up Felicia's rescue kitty, she planned to call Amy from her cell and let her know she was bringing in a cat for evaluation. If all went well, the cat would be joining them at the shelter within a day or two. Three new felines in as many days. The shelter was bustling!

Felicia was waiting in the lobby for her, huddled in one of the chairs lined up against the wall. Her face looked pinched as she checked her watch. There was no sign of Karen or her dad, which Lara still thought was odd.

Either way, it was over. Lara was done with Bakewell. What was that expression Tina Tanaka had used? *Mata ne. See you later.*

"There you are!" Felicia said when she spotted Lara. "I thought you'd gone off without saying goodbye."

Lara gritted her teeth and smiled. "I'm still here. Why don't I follow you to your house and pick up the cat? I have a carrier I can transfer him to."

Felicia nodded. "That will work perfectly." She slipped her arm through Lara's. "Come on. We'll be at my place in no time."

Outside, the sky was overcast, clustered with gray clouds that stirred up a chill wind. They were heading out to the parking lot behind the building when Lara spied a familiar face. From the driver's seat of an older green sedan, Tina Tanaka watched them.

Wait a minute. Hadn't Tina said she was working today?

Lara waved to her, but the young woman only stared at her in return. She probably should have gone over and asked Tina to have the wedding shoes shipped to her, but she didn't want to waste any more time. A quick phone call later would work just as well.

Once inside the Saturn, Lara locked her doors. She started her engine and followed Felicia out of the parking lot, onto the main drag.

Lara shot a glance at her rearview mirror. She saw Tina peel out of the lot and drive in the opposite direction.

Chapter 34

Felicia's bungalow-style home was in a quiet neighborhood of older homes on a charming residential street. The house itself, painted white with black shutters, sat on a patch of lawn that was probably quite lush during the warmer months. Alongside the house, remnants of flower beds huddled beneath frozen patches of snow.

Lara followed Felicia's aging VW along a driveway that wrapped around to the back entrance. Leaving her cell phone on the front seat, she got out of her car and glanced around.

The backyard extended toward a dense stretch of forest, thick with mature maples and oaks. During the warmer months it probably teemed with wildlife. Lara could easily imagine the kindly Felicia feeding squirrels and birds out there, leaving little tidbits to supplement their diets.

Lara grabbed her carrier from the back seat of the Saturn and followed Felicia toward a rear entryway.

"Be careful, it's a bit icy in spots," Felicia cautioned. She unlocked the back door and held it open for Lara, then locked it behind her. Lara found herself in a small entryway used primarily for coats and boots. A pair of plaid rubber boots rested on the floor, along with a plastic bucket filled with gardening tools and a set of pink flowered gloves. On one wall, a snow shovel hung from an iron hook.

"Come on in, Lara. The cat is in the kitchen. I closed Lily in my bedroom so she wouldn't get nervous with a strange animal in the house. Can you stay for a cup of tea?"

"I'd love to, Felicia, but I really can't stay. The uncle I told you about— he's in the hospital. His hip isn't broken—only sprained—but I still need to head home."

Felicia nodded distractedly. "I completely understand. Maybe another time."

"The other thing is," Lara said, "your poor kitty is probably terrified being trapped in Lily's carrier all this time. I think it's best if I take him right to our vet for evaluation."

"Of course. You're right," Felicia agreed.

Lara followed her into a cheery kitchen with lacy white curtains and old-fashioned linoleum counters. The walls were painted celery green, and the appliances were chocolate brown—a color that was popular decades earlier. On the floor next to the oven was a pink pet carrier. From inside the carrier, a wide-eyed gray cat with a white face and chest gazed up at Lara with suspicious eyes. From his size, Lara guessed he was barely a year old, if that.

"Hey, sweetie," Lara cooed to the kitty. "Where did you come from?" She turned to Felicia. "Have you given him anything to eat?"

"Only a bit of tuna. I wasn't sure what to do." Felicia wrung her hands.

Lara crouched down and unzipped the door to her own carrier, which was lined with clean towels. Then, very carefully, she unzipped Lily's carrier and reached in for the cat. With a sudden hiss and a swipe of forepaws, the cat wrangled past her and dashed out of the kitchen into the adjoining room.

"Oh!" Felicia cried. "He went in the dining room!"

Lara grabbed her carrier and hurried after him.

The dining room was small, graced with a long rectangular table, a corner hutch, and a sideboard cluttered with fussy knickknacks that had to be a nightmare to dust. Amid the various curios on the sideboard was a large, gold-framed photo. Lara stared at it, and the face of a little boy stared back at her. Dark blond, maybe six years old, he had adorable brown eyes, freckles, and a gap-toothed smile. A memory tickled her brain, but it zoomed out of reach before she could snag it.

The table was covered with a white cloth that looked more like a sheet than a tablecloth. Atop the table were a dozen or so leaves, maybe eight inches long, that were laid out flat, their edges dry and curled. Next to the leaves were glass jars labeled with the names of various herbs and spices—cardamom, cloves, lavender. A cardboard box about the size of a dictionary rested on the edge of the table. Was it at this table where Felicia blended her wonderful teas?

The cat had taken refuge beneath the hutch. Slowly, Lara set down her carrier and lowered herself to her knees. She spoke soothingly to him, hoping she could entice him into her arms, but the cat didn't budge. After several tries, she turned to Felicia. "Can you get me a bit more of that tuna?"

For a second or two, Felicia froze, then, "Tuna? Oh yes, of course." She turned and went into the kitchen.

Moments later, Lara heard the metallic sound of a pop-top being torn from a can. Felicia returned with a small paper bowl containing a few shreds of tuna.

Lara placed some of the tuna in the palm of her hand and held it out to the kitty. He sniffed the air, then began inching toward her. Then—yes, finally!—he gobbled it from her hand, licking his lips when he was through.

"Good job," Felicia murmured.

Lara opened her carrier and set down the tuna at the back. The cat moved toward it, and Lara gave him an encouraging nudge. The cat scooted inside, and she quickly closed the door, zipping him in.

"You did it," Felicia said, lightly clapping her hands.

Lara rose off the floor and smiled. "Wasn't so hard, really. A hungry kitty can usually be enticed with tuna. Thanks for trapping him, Felicia. If no one comes forward to claim him, we'll be sure he gets a good home." She lifted the carrier, and as she started toward the kitchen, the corner of the carrier caught the edge of the box on the table. The box toppled to the floor, scaring the cat, who yowled from his temporary prison.

"It's okay, sweetie, just an accident," Lara cooed to him. "Sorry, Felicia, I'll clean up all this stuff."

The box had spilled its contents. Felicia had already dropped to her hands and knees and was scrambling to retrieve it all. Her face was flushed bright red, and her eyes flashed with anger. Lara set down the carrier and bent to help her, until she realized what she was looking at.

Cigars.

Some intact, some half-rolled, others sliced down the center.

Other objects had also tumbled out—a spray bottle, an odd-shaped mold, metal cutting tools Lara had never seen before.

Ohmygod, ohmygod…

Felicia slammed the box shut and glared at Lara. "Mercy, but you're clumsy. Don't you ever watch where you're going?"

Lara stared at her, almost in disbelief, but then her gaze drifted to the table. The leaves—what did they remind her of? "Felicia, do any of these leaves come from lily of the valley?"

Slowly, her knees creaking, Felicia rose to her full height and plunked the box on the table, leaving the cover open. "Good guess. You're very observant, aren't you? It's a beautiful flower—my favorite, in fact. They don't blossom for long, maybe three or four weeks out of the year, but when they do, they're spectacular."

Lily. Of course. She probably named her dog after them.

Oh God. Lily of the valley were deadly—not only to cats and dogs, but to humans. They were the same flowers Amy had torn out of her flower beds after her dog had gotten sick.

Lara stared at Felicia, and in the next horrifying instant, light dawned. She tried to rearrange her expression into one of bland innocence, but it was too late.

Felicia gave up a regretful smile. "Oh, Lara, I can tell from your face that you've already figured it out. Too bad," she whispered, under her breath.

"Figured what out?" Lara asked, lifting the carrier again.

"Please. I'm not a fool."

No, you're not a fool. You're a murderer.

But why? Had she done it for Karen, so that they could become business partners? Or to release Karen from her marriage to a philandering oaf? Maybe both.

"I know how to Google people, too, you know," Felicia continued, moving toward the sideboard. She reached into the box that held the cigar makings and pulled out a gleaming knife. "I read all about you and your famous crime-solving escapades."

"Felicia, most of those articles were written by our town reporter. He's always exaggerating stories to make the paper look interesting."

Felicia waved the knife at her, not buying a word. "If you'll stop playing games with me, I'll tell you how I did it." She looked away, her gaze growing distant. "You deserve that much."

Lara remained silent. Where was her cell phone?

Oh no, it was in the car, on the front seat.

"Truthfully," Felicia said, growing animated now, "I've been dying to share it with someone because…well, honestly, it was just so inventive. Karen told me that her husband went outside every evening to smoke one of his disgusting cigars. So, I bought some, and I experimented. I even watched instructional videos on cigar making. I spent weeks learning to roll cigars—how's that for dedication?" Her brow creased, and her eyes took on a demented sheen.

A lump of fear gathered momentum in Lara's throat. She forced it back, willing herself to breathe.

"The cigar that killed Wayne?" Felicia went on. "It was wrapped in lily of the valley leaves, masked by tobacco leaves," Felicia went on. "I also blended the tobacco with crushed leaves from the plant—belt and suspenders, if you will." Her eyes glittered. "Wasn't that clever?"

"Very clever," Lara said quietly. Still clutching the carrier, she inched slowly backward, toward the doorway to the kitchen. "But who delivered them? How did you pull that off?"

"I paid a local teenager fifty dollars. He left them on the Chancers' doorstep early that morning, before dawn. The kid had no idea who lived there. The package was beautifully wrapped, little hearts all over the paper, with a card that said, 'from a special friend on your birthday.' I'm sure the blowhard thought it was from one of his sleazy girlfriends. Or ex-girlfriends."

Inside the carrier, the trapped kitty had gone quiet. *Thank heaven.* But Lara had to get herself, and the cat, out of there.

Then she remembered—Felicia had a landline. Lara had spotted it on the wall in the kitchen. She needed to get to it, *fast*, and call nine-one-one. Even if she said nothing, the dispatcher would send an officer to check it out.

"I guess now Karen can buy in to the gourmet shop," Lara said. "Worked out well for her, didn't it?"

Felicia shook her head. "Don't be stupid. This had nothing to do with Karen." She lifted the framed photo from the sideboard and held it up. "Do you see this child?"

Lara nodded.

Felicia's eyes misted. "This boy was my entire world, Lara, the light of my life. He was kind and funny and talented—the most wonderful boy a mother could ask for." Still clutching the knife, Felicia hugged the photo close to her chest. Her mouth twisted, and her eyes glistened with rage. "Until one day three punks decided to have a little fun and throw a rock off a bridge. One of their lawyers called it 'a childish prank that took an unfortunate fatal turn.' How's that for lawyer-speak?" she spat out. "That rock went through the car passing below and *crushed this beautiful boy!*"

Lara's heart jackknifed in her chest. She was talking about Jarrod Dandreau.

"I'm so sorry, Felicia. I didn't know."

Felicia turned and lovingly set the photo back down, running her finger along the top. "I've waited a long time, but I'm finally getting justice. Two down, only one to go."

"Two...down?" Lara almost choked on the words.

"The first one was easy. Despite what his *mommy dearest* claimed, he was a druggie, always looking for a fix."

The first one...Richard Mulhaney?

"Well, I gave him a fix—laced with a good dose of chlordane. Can you believe I kept some of that stuff? It's outlawed now, but back in the day I used it to kill those horrid earwigs." Felicia clasped her hands with glee. "Oh, you should have seen his expression when he opened the door that day and saw me standing there. Sheer panic, at first. Then I smiled and assured him I only wanted to talk. He made the mistake of turning his back on me after he waved me into his hallway. I shoved that needle in his arm so fast he didn't know what hit him." She laughed, a grating sound that chilled Lara's blood. "The chlordane was symbolic more than anything. To me he was lower than an insect. He fell to the floor, and while he screamed in pain, I shoved another needle in his arm—a whopping dose of fentanyl. That did the trick. Once he was out, I made sure his fingerprints were on the second hypodermic needle. I took the one with the chlordane with me and got rid of it."

In Lara's head, a memory clicked into place. She thought back to her exchange with Megan a few days earlier, when Megan admitted having eavesdropped on Wayne's cryptic phone call not long before she was fired. She'd overheard him mutter the word "overdose," but he'd also scrawled it on a yellow pad—O period, D period, as if to emphasize it. Megan had found the pad on his desk after he'd stormed out of the office.

Felicia sighed and turned to the sideboard, then opened the top drawer. "I know the police are close to figuring it out, but that's okay. I expected that. I just need to get the ringleader. After that I'm done. Lily and I will both be gone."

The ringleader. "Chad Walford?"

Her hand in the drawer, Felicia whirled on Lara. "How...did you know that?"

Lara didn't respond, because another thought struck her. Why hadn't Felicia checked on her beloved dog? Hadn't she claimed Lily suffered from anxiety whenever they were separated?

Terrified of the answer, Lara asked gently, "Felicia, where's Lily?"

Felicia smiled and shook her head. "You needn't worry about her. She's sound asleep, and I do mean sound. After today we'll both be in a better place. We'll both be with Jarrod."

Lara's heart clutched. "Oh my God. Felicia, you didn't—"

In a flash, Felicia's hand flew out of the drawer. The knife gone, she pointed a small handgun at Lara. "You don't stop, do you? You couldn't leave well enough alone, could you? I'm sorry I ever trapped that cat now. I wanted it to be my final good deed—rescuing a homeless creature before he succumbed to exposure. But you—you're like a terrier. You had to keep digging…"

Slowly, Lara set down the carrier. *I can get through this. I've been through worse.* Heart slamming her ribs, she said, "Please, Felicia, show me where Lily is."

Felicia shook her head. "She's at peace, Lara. Leave it alone."

Lara swallowed. "Did you give her an overdose, too?"

Wait a minute. Overdose…

O period, D period. If the letters stood for 'overdose,' why the periods? Because they didn't stand for overdose.

They stood for Olive Dandreau.

Felicia Tristany was Olive Dandreau.

The woman identified in the article about the rock-throwing incident as Jarrod Dandreau's mother.

* * * *

"How are you planning to kill Chad, Olive?"

Olive's eyes shimmered with hatred. "I have something special planned for him. I found him on Facebook—oh, how proud of himself he is! After he got out of prison, he found religion. Isn't that convenient? Now he shoves it down everyone's throat like some prairie preacher. Like that makes up for killing my child." Tears streamed down her cheeks. "Jarrod was like the lily of the valley, Lara. His life blossomed for only a short time before it was snuffed out. It's my job to see that he gets justice."

Lara felt beads of sweat popping out on her forehead. Was the house that warm, or was she perspiring from sheer terror? "Wh–what are you going to do?"

"Walford bragged on Facebook about how he switched booze for tea, and how it saved his life. But that gave me the idea. I created a phony Facebook page, using my engagement photo for my profile pic. You might not believe it, Lara, but at one time I was quite beautiful. My sister Felicia was so jealous of me. She dumped her husband and stole mine. He even moved to Ohio to be with her, but by that time I didn't care. I had my son—my wonderful boy. I was almost forty when he was born—I'd tried for so long to get pregnant. He was my world, Lara. My *life*." She gave out a harsh sob. The gun wobbled in her hand.

In a split-second decision Lara started toward her, but Olive was too fast. She aimed the gun at Lara's chest. "Sit," she ordered. "Since you've forced my hand, the least you can do is listen."

Panic rising in her throat, Lara lowered herself onto the dining room's only chair. She pictured Olive sitting at this very spot, concocting her deadly poisons…

"My ex died first—heart attack—then Felicia from pancreatic cancer. Her pitiful belongings were shipped to me from Ohio, including all her IDs. That's when I saw how Olive could disappear and reinvent herself as Felicia."

"How did you happen to live so close to Chancer?"

"That was by design, my dear. He wasn't hard to find. When I saw that the gift shop in town was closing, I took over the lease and opened my gourmet shop. You can imagine my delight when Karen Chancer asked to sell her fruit bits there. I knew, then, that it was my destiny—that this was all meant to be."

"Was it you who left the note, Olive? The one that said, 'I know who you are'?"

Olive smirked. "I'd stopped at Karen's that morning to pick up some of her jars for the shop. On my way out, I tucked it under a shrub. It was probably risky on my part, but it sickened me that his juvenile records were sealed so no one would ever know what he did. Not that it mattered, but I thought the police might find the note once the area became a crime scene. Sure enough…"

She thought of everything.

"Olive, please let me check on Lily," Lara begged.

"Shut up. I haven't finished telling you about Chad. I friended him on Facebook—we're practically best buds now. Of course, he thinks I look like my profile pic. We messaged each other, chatted endlessly about our favorite teas. I told him about the gourmet shop in my town, how they blended custom teas to suit the occasion. Tomorrow he'll be receiving a package from me—a very special birthday gift. He'll be thrilled when he sees my custom blend—strawberry tea with a hint of currant. He won't know, of course, that it's laced with a shocking dose of lily of the valley." Her eyes glazed over. "It won't take very long. One or two sips, and he'll be joining the other two in hell. I only wish I could be there to witness it."

Desperate, Lara glanced over at the photo of Jarrod. "Olive, you said Jarrod was a wonderful, kind boy. If that's true, he wouldn't want you to do this. He'd tell you to stop, right now, before someone else dies—"

Olive shook her head, and then a sudden thump from the sideboard made them both jump. A Ragdoll cat that only Lara could see had knocked over Jarrod's photo. In the next instant the picture toppled to the floor, shattering the glass.

"No!" Olive cried, tossing the gun aside. Her face contorted, and she dropped to her knees, clutching the broken picture to her chest. Her body racked with sobs as she called out Jarrod's name, over and over. A jagged shard of glass sliced her hand, and a stream of blood trickled toward her wrist.

Blood on her hands...

Lara didn't hesitate. In two strides she reached the gun and scooped it off the floor. With her free hand she grabbed the pet carrier and raced outside to her car. After setting the carrier on the back seat, she locked the gun in the trunk and retrieved her cell phone. She punched in nine-one-one and gave the dispatcher as much information as she could. Then she ran back inside the house.

Chapter 35

Lara raced through the house, checking every room, but the downstairs was empty. When she reached the top of the stairs, she found the door on the left locked. She rattled the doorknob.

No response. Not a sound.

From outside came the wail of a siren, and then the sound of car doors slamming. After a few moments, voices drifted from downstairs. "Up here!" Lara called.

Footsteps clomped up the stairs. "Are you the person who called nine-one-one?" said a tall uniformed officer with curly black hair and a striking, angular face. His nameplate read "Elliott Jackson."

"I am. This door is locked, and I'm worried that Olive might have harmed herself—and her dog."

He unclipped the radio transmitter from his belt and spoke in a crisp, urgent voice, while his partner, a petite woman with wispy blond hair and dark brown eyes said, "Who's Olive? I thought Felicia Tristany lived here."

"She does. Please, we need to get in there."

"Ambulance is on the way," Jackson said.

"She had a gun," Lara said, "but when she dropped it, I grabbed it. It's locked in my trunk."

"Good. Let's hope that's the only weapon she owns."

Without missing a beat, the female officer stood back about a yard, lifted her right foot, and kicked the door hard with the sole of her boot. The door cracked but held firm. On the second try it crashed open. "You stay out here," she ordered Lara.

Guns drawn, the officers rushed into the room. Hovering in the doorway, Lara saw Olive lying on her bed, her eyes closed, her skin the color of flour.

Lily lay resting on her chest, still as a stuffed toy. On the table beside the bed was a bottle of prescription pills and some loose pink tablets.

"Denise, take the dog," Jackson told his partner.

The woman lifted Lily off Olive's chest and set her gently on the floor. While her partner performed CPR on Olive, the officer—Denise—massaged Lily's head and chest. Lara couldn't stand it any longer. She rushed into the room to help.

"I think she's breathing," Denise whispered to Lara.

Tears filling her eyes, Lara nodded. *Please let her be okay.* "What about Olive?"

"Also breathing, but very shallow," Jackson said grimly. "And you were told to stay out of this room."

Everything happened quickly after that. The ambulance arrived, and Olive was lifted onto a stretcher and whisked out the door. One of the EMTs took the pills off the bedside table and placed them in a plastic bag.

Lily hadn't stirred, but her body was warm, and she was still breathing.

"Please—I need to take the dog to a vet," Lara begged. "And I have a rescue cat in the car. He can't stay out there in the cold much longer."

Jackson blew out a sigh, his face looking strained from anxiety. "I'm sorry, miss, but you'll have to wait downstairs for one of the detectives. Can't let you go just yet."

"But—"

"I'll take them," someone said quietly from the doorway. "I'll take them both."

Lara turned toward the source of the voice and took in a sharp breath.

The person standing in the doorway was Tina Tanaka.

* * * *

By the time Lara was permitted to leave the Bakewell police station, it was after four o'clock. The sky was nearly dark, the cold was biting, and her spirits were at an all-time low. One bright spot: The officer named Denise had graciously driven the Saturn to the parking lot behind the station, so at least Lara still had wheels.

She had to get home.

She had to check on Lily—and on the cat.

Before they'd begun questioning her, they'd allowed her to call Gideon to let him know what had happened. He'd listened silently as she'd given him a summary. When she was through and he didn't respond, she said, "Gideon, are you still there?"

His response had been almost inaudible. "I'm glad you're all right, Lara. I'll let Fran know you're okay," he'd said before disconnecting.

Buttoning her coat against the chill, Lara hurried out to her car. She was grateful to see that the parking lot was well-lit.

A sedan with its engine running sat next to the Saturn, a figure hunkered in the driver's seat. Lara hurriedly unlocked her own door. She started to slip inside her car when someone emerged suddenly beside her. She gasped, and in the next moment Tina Tanaka was encasing her in a hug.

"My God, for a minute you scared me," Lara said.

"Sorry," Tina said sheepishly.

Lara smiled at her. "Thank you for coming to my rescue today. But... how—?"

Tina shook her head. "I can't explain it, except to say that I woke up this morning with the craziest feeling. The pressure on my shoulder was like, nuts, you know?" She widened her eyes meaningfully. "It kept up, even at work, so I asked Valeria if I could have the rest of the day off."

"What made you drive to the funeral parlor?"

Tina shrugged. "Again, I'm not sure. Intuition? I'm also kind of nosy. But I got a weird vibe when I saw you follow Felicia out of the parking lot. By then, the pressure on my shoulder was killing me."

Lara swallowed. "Jade?"

Tina nodded. "I think so."

"Is it gone now?"

Tina smiled. "Totally."

Lara told her about Blue knocking Jarrod's picture off the sideboard.

"Why am I not surprised?" Tina said.

"Tina, how did you ever get past all the police at Felicia's house?" Lara asked. "I was surprised they let you go upstairs."

"I told them Officer Jackson had requested my presence." Tina quirked a smile. "Elliott and I...well, let's just say we're good friends. By the way, Lily is going to be okay. She'd been given several Benadryl—way too much for a dog her size. The vet's going to keep her until she's fully recovered. After that, she'll need a new home."

"Thank God. What about...Felicia?" Lara said, unsure how much Tina knew.

"I haven't heard. No one's keeping me in the loop." Tina shook her head. "All this time, none of us suspected."

"I know. She seemed like such a sweet lady." *She was a sweet lady.* "Tina, can I ask where the cat is?"

Tina chuckled. "I knew you'd get to that. He's at the vet, too, getting checked out. He wasn't chipped, and he needs to be neutered, but the vet said he's otherwise in sound health."

"Do you know when I can pick him up?"

"You're not going to pick him up." Tina let out a breath. "Lara, unless you have a strong objection, I'd like to take him home with me. I've already named him Shamrock because he's my lucky charm. We bonded almost immediately when they opened the carrier at the vet's office. In fact, the vet thought he was my cat."

Laughing, Lara reached over and hugged her. "Then I guess he is. Hey, I have to get home, but thank you for everything. Keep in touch, okay?"

"I will. By the way, your carrier is on your back seat, along with those gorgeous shoes you ordered. Have a great time at the wedding. And, Lara," she added quietly, "this...*thing* you and I share, with the cats? Just remember, we're not crazy. We proved that today, didn't we?"

Choked up now, Lara couldn't speak. She nodded and hopped into her car. She wanted to go home.

* * * *

Gideon's car was in the driveway.

Swallowing hard, Lara shut off her engine, her heart lodged in her throat. She murmured a silent prayer as she climbed the porch steps. The moment she stepped inside her aunt's warm kitchen, she was pulled into a hug that would put a grizzly bear to shame.

"Thank God," Gideon murmured, kissing her hair over and over.

He finally released her to Aunt Fran, who also wrapped her in a hug, tears shimmering in her lovely green eyes. "Oh, Lara, we were so worried."

Released from her aunt's grip, Lara sat in a kitchen chair. Her legs felt shaky.

Munster and Panda padded into the kitchen, both angling for position on Lara's lap. It was a welcome sight, reminding her that she was home, and she was safe.

"How's Uncle Amico?" Lara asked Gideon, rubbing Munster's head.

"He's doing fine, but he's worried about you. We'll see him tomorrow at the facility, if you're up to it."

"Of course, I am," Lara said. "Maybe I can bake him something—"

"I'll do the baking," her aunt lectured. "You need to take it easy for a few days."

Lara smiled and squeezed her aunt's hand. "I'll take you up on that."

Over tea and sandwiches, Lara told them everything, even the part about Blue knocking over Jarrod's photo. It was the one detail she'd withheld from the police.

Reliving it made it all the more real, and her head began to throb. Aunt Fran gave her two ibuprofen. Lara gulped them back with water.

Gideon's face was still pale. He fortified himself with a sip of Aunt Fran's strong tea. "Lara, if you hadn't gone over to Felicia's—Olive's—after the service, Chad Walford would've ended up as her third victim. I have no doubt you saved his life."

Lara shook her head. "We don't know that for sure."

"I do," Aunt Fran said.

"I think Olive knew the police were getting close," Lara said. "All she had left to do was to poison Chad Walford. After that she was ready to do away with herself, and Lily."

That day, in the gourmet shop, when Blue cozied up to Lily—she was instinctively trying to shield her, to protect her...

"In a way, my heart breaks for Olive," Aunt Fran said. "She wasn't in her right mind. She'd never gotten past her grief. At some point, revenge became a powerful motivator—it kept her going. We've seen it before, haven't we?"

Lara nodded, remembering. "I'm just glad it's over."

After they cleaned up the dishes together, Lara pulled Gideon into her studio and closed the door. "Gideon, I know you're disappointed in me. I promised you nothing would happen to me, and I broke that promise."

"Oh God, Lara." He pulled her close, so close that she felt the beating of his heart. "You didn't disappoint me. You *never* disappoint me." He ran his fingers lightly over her cheek. "I get it now, I honestly do. In the future, no matter what you choose to do, I'll be there to support you all the way. I would've been there today, except that Uncle—" He broke off and shook his head.

"Except," Lara said quietly, almost to herself, "that Olive had rescued a cat and she needed my help. She called it her final good deed."

Lara had hit on something—she was sure of it. She mulled everything over in her mind.

Karen asking her to the service...

Olive trapping the cat...

Tina knowing instinctively that Lara would need help...

What happened today was supposed to happen, exactly the way it went down.

For a long time, they held each other in silence, Lara's arms wrapped tightly around Gideon's waist. He finally broke the spell. "I want you to get some rest, now. We'll both feel better tomorrow, and we'll go see Uncle." He smiled. "As soon as I get home, I'm going to indulge in something a little stronger than your aunt's tea."

Lara laughed. "Go ahead. You deserve it. Aunt Fran and I might just do the same."

"I love you, Lara."

Lara started to respond, but his deep kiss swept it all away.

Chapter 36

"Do you, Sheryl Ann Bowker, take this man, David Jeffrey Gregson, to be your lawfully wedded husband…" Pastor Folger's voice, well-modulated from years of practice, filled the coffee shop.

Lara's eyes blurred, and she blinked back tears. They were happy tears—the best kind—but she'd promised herself she wouldn't smudge her makeup, especially the teal eyeliner Sherry had persuaded her to buy.

On the back wall hung a swag made of red roses wrapped loosely around a swath of ivory-colored tulle. In the far corner, a table draped with a white linen cloth boasted a three-tiered wedding cake. Instead of a bride/groom figurine, a cluster of roses crafted from cranberry-red frosting graced the top of the cake. Individual sugary roses meandered down along the side, wrapping around to the silver tray at the bottom.

Sherry looked radiant in a floor-length, pale blue gown that skimmed her curves as it fell from an empire waist to a scalloped hem. The cap sleeves and the yoke were semi-sheer, embroidered with floral appliques. Her raven-colored hair was pulled back and held in place by a cluster of tiny, white silk roses. Three short spikes of jet-black hair jutted from the roses. It was her hairstylist's nod to Sherry's original look—the one David fell in love with.

The ceremony over, rings exchanged, the pastor closed his prayer book, then turned to the justice of the peace. She beamed and they clasped hands—they'd worked well together, alternating the reading of the passages Sherry and David had chosen themselves.

Pastor Folger turned to the bride and groom and said, "You may now seal this blessed union with a kiss."

And they did.

The guests yelled and clapped, while Daisy and Loretta—the mothers of the married couple—cried and cheered together.

Gideon slipped his arm around Lara's waist and pulled her close. "I've never seen either of them so happy."

"I haven't either," Lara said, dabbing at her eyes with a tissue. "You said you had news. Can you tell me real quick before the celebration starts?"

Gideon cupped her elbow and guided her to one side. "Had a long chat with the Bakewell police chief this morning. Olive's been released from the hospital, but she's being transferred to another unit where they can evaluate her further."

Lara knew what that meant. They needed to determine if she was competent to stand trial. "I still get sick every time I think of those tea bags she shipped to Chad Walford."

Gideon nodded. "They were delivered on his birthday to his Rhode Island home, just as Olive planned, but he'd already been warned by the police not to open the package. The tea bags have been analyzed. There was enough lily of the valley in them to kill five people. If he'd shared them with anyone, they'd have been poisoned, as well. Once the leaves are steeped in water, they make for a deadly potion."

Lara shivered. "What about that phone call to Chancer that Megan spied on? Was that Chad?"

"It was. He found out Mulhaney's mother was raising a ruckus over her son's cause of death. She was demanding his body be exhumed and reexamined. Chad figured something was up. Last he knew, Mulhaney was clean—he'd totally kicked his drug habit. He called Chancer to warn him to be careful. He couldn't prove it, but he suspected Olive might have had something to do with Mulhaney's death."

"And all the time she was right there in Bakewell," Lara mused, "running a gourmet shop and plotting to get rid of them both. What I don't get is how Olive disappeared so thoroughly and reappeared as her sister. These days, isn't that nearly impossible?"

Gideon blew out a breath. "After her sister's death, she quit her nursing job with only a day's notice, sold her house and her car, and closed out her bank accounts. After that, she pretty much fell off the radar. No one was really looking for her. They think she lived on her cash for a while, until she found out Chancer had moved to Bakewell. She lucked out when the gift shop closed, and she was able to take over their lease. Her business was doing well, too," he said ruefully. "Too bad she was so bent on revenge."

"It was like a perfect storm of everything falling into place for her, wasn't it?" Lara said.

"You could put it that way. Hey, I almost forgot. You know why you never saw Cutler at the memorial service?"

Lara smiled. "I can't even guess."

"Poor guy had the flu, big-time, couldn't even get out of bed."

Again, the perfect storm of everything falling into place. If Lara hadn't gone to Olive's that day to rescue the cat...

She shuddered. She didn't even want to think about it.

"I'm glad Karen took Lily in. I talked to her yesterday. She's been in touch with the lawyer who's handling Olive's affairs. They're still working out the details, but Karen is hoping to buy out Olive's assets and take over the operation of the Peach Crate. Though she's still in shock about Felicia—Olive, that is."

"I'll bet. You texted me this morning that you had some news, too."

Lara nodded. "Nothing earth-shattering, just that Megan and her mom found a nice apartment near the Emersons."

Lara had spoken to Megan a few days earlier and was surprised at how happy she sounded. Megan was still looking for a job, but in the meantime her mom was paying the rent on their new place. After leaving her bully of a husband, Megan's mom was determined to reconnect with her daughter and help her all she could. And with the Emersons living close by, they were truly a family now.

"I'm really happy for her, Gideon. She sounded like a new person, ready to take on the world and make her place in it. Oh, and she and her mom have applied to adopt Panda. Aunt Fran and I are going to approve it as soon as we recover from the wedding festivities." *Especially since a certain Ragdoll cat has already given her blessing.*

Gideon pulled Lara close. "I'm so lucky to have you in my life."

"Hey, you two. What gives?" Sherry stalked toward them and threw her arms around Lara.

"Oh, Sher, you look"—Lara swallowed back tears—"so beautiful. And so happy."

"Yeah, well, this isn't my usual getup, but I guess it works for today, right? And I am happy, more than I ever thought possible." She beamed at David, and he kissed her soundly.

They all laughed, and Gideon hugged the bride, and then David hugged Lara. It was a hug-fest all around.

Aunt Fran came over with her arm linked through the chief's. She looked almost like a bride herself, her handsome suitor at her side.

Kayla joined them. She'd decided to attend solo, despite Sherry having invited her to bring along a friend. She looked stunning in a knee-length, royal-blue chiffon dress with a swirly hem. "Hey, you guys, they're passing out champagne." She lifted her bubbly-filled flute. "This stuff is good!"

Servers had been hired to serve champagne and to set out Daisy's fabulous array of goodies. They were also going to perform post-wedding cleanup so that Daisy could reopen the coffee shop in the morning.

Lara and Gideon joined Daisy and Loretta at the bride and groom's table.

Champagne flowed, and food was piled on plates. After everyone had eaten their fill, Sherry and David materialized with a large basket stacked with delicate, die-cut boxes. They strolled among the tables, handing out the favors. The guests marveled at the oversized fortune cookie they found nesting inside each of their boxes. Each cookie had been hand-dipped in white chocolate, and then again in red sugar hearts.

"Mine says I'm going to meet a mysterious stranger!" Lara heard Kayla giggle.

Lara smiled to herself—she couldn't help it. The coffee shop—the same place where Sherry first met David, where their love sprouted and blossomed—rang with the sounds of joy and laughter. She was glad Sherry and David had insisted on having the wedding there. They'd known it was where they needed to be on the day they exchanged their vows.

Her mind skimmed over the events of the past few weeks. Despite all the challenges, and the worries, so many things had fallen into place.

Jeannie Jennings had picked up Sienna, who was loving her permanent digs with her new bestie, Bunny. Aunt Fran had joined an active online writing community and was making new friends every day. Holly and Noella had taken a keen interest in Twinkles, who'd been enticed off Aunt Fran's bed long enough to play with their new catnip mouse.

A warm wave of sheer happiness washed over Lara. Maybe it was the champagne, or maybe it was the company. Probably a little bit of both.

The bride moved toward Lara and Gideon, a wicked gleam in her eye. "I saved you two for last," she told them, handing them their favor boxes.

Gideon cracked open his cookie. His face flushed a deep red, and he winked at Lara.

"What does it say?" Lara prodded.

"Uh, tell you later. Open yours."

"Hmmm." Lara snapped open her cookie and pulled out the fortune. Smiling, she showed it to him, and he pulled her into a bone-crushing hug.

You're next, cat lady!

Keep reading for a special excerpt of CLAWS OF ACTION, a Cat Lady Mystery by Linda Reilly!

Purr-suing a killer…

The only thing that could make the High Cliff Shelter for Cats even cozier is a reading room where kids can snuggle up with a furry feline and a book. But as Lara and Aunt Fran prepare for the reading nook's official opening, the health inspector in their New Hampshire town, Evonda Fray, decrees that the shelter qualifies as a "cat café," thanks to the free snacks it serves to visitors—and that it must be shut down.

When Evonda's body is found in her car clutching a copy of the cease-and-desist order, suspicion naturally falls on Lara and Aunt Fran. But there's a whole litter of potential culprits, including a tenant in one of Evonda's buildings who'd been ordered to give up his rescue cat, a disgruntled daughter-in-law, and more. Now Lara—with some help from her aunt and her spirit cat, Blue—has to pin the tail on the right suspect…

Look for CLAWS OF ACTION on sale now!

Chapter 1

Lara Caphart could hardly believe it. The official reading room of the High Cliff Shelter for Cats was completed.

She swung the new storm door back and forth, then pushed it closed. It clicked into place with a soft snap. "Perfect," she proclaimed. "I know it sounds silly, but I am so thrilled with this door!"

One chunky hand resting on his hip, Charlie Backstrom—the contractor who'd built the cat shelter's addition—stood back and inspected his work. "Looks good," he agreed. "Now, remember, when the cold weather gets here, you gotta lower the screen and—"

"You're repeating yourself, honey," Nina Backstrom said, slipping her arm through her husband's. "You've shown Lara three times now how to lower the screen and pull up the glass pane."

"Hey, that's okay," Lara said lightly. "It never hurts to get a refresher, right?"

Charlie, handsome in a rugged sort of way, with melt-in-your-mouth brown eyes, smiled at his wife and kissed her cheek. He winked at Lara. "Wives. What would we do without them?"

Nina feigned a scowl. "Oh, I'm guessing you'd be living on frozen dinners and cardboard pizza and watching sports on TV every night."

"Instead of those scintillating mysteries you're always trying to get me to watch?" He quirked a smile at her. They both looked at Lara.

Lara held up both hands. "Don't look at me. I'm not getting in the middle of that one."

Charlie and Nina, who were both around thirty, were one of the sweetest couples Lara had ever met. They teased each other a lot, but the banter was always good-natured—at least it seemed to be. Perpetually outfitted in a gray work shirt and blue knee-length cargo shorts, Charlie was a total contrast to his petite wife. Today Nina wore a stylish, pale-pink jersey top over white cotton shorts, a flowered bathing suit peeking out over the jersey's neckline. Beneath her strawberry-blond bob was a sharp head for numbers. She acted as financial guru—and organizational genius—for the business, while Charlie performed the labor and hired the subs. He walked with a slight limp, which he jokingly referred to as an old football injury.

"So, what do you think?" Nina said. "Are we done?"

Lara looked all around the new room and felt her smile widening. "Yes, I think we are. It's been a long haul, but now that I see the finished product, it was all worth it."

On Saturday, she and her aunt were having a grand opening for a few close friends. The following day would be the first official "read to a cat" day in the new room.

The idea for the addition had sprung from a little girl who'd tried to sneak into the shelter one day, book in hand, determined to read to a cat. After a bit of research, Lara had discovered that several other shelters in New Hampshire had "read to a cat" days.

With the help of their part-time shelter assistant, Kayla Ramirez, Lara had set up a similar program. It gained popularity more quickly than they'd anticipated, but they had only one problem: space. Aunt Fran's Folk Victorian home was the entire shelter, the small back porch having been transformed into the "meet-and-greet" room. In that room, cats and prospective adopters made permanent matches, some of which seemed almost magical.

Earlier in the year, Lara and her aunt had made the decision to add the room to the rear of the house, adjacent to the back porch. A local architect designed the plans, and Lara hired Charlie Backstrom to oversee the project. He used subcontractors when needed but did most of the work himself. A master carpenter, he'd built custom shelves with adjustable tiers for the children's books.

He'd pulled off a near miracle, completing the project by the date specified in the contract. Over the course of the construction, which had dragged on for nearly four months, one thing after another went wrong. A pipe burst in the new bathroom, the floor tiles had been damaged in shipping, and a large shrub in Aunt Fran's yard had to be uprooted because the building specs hadn't accounted for it.

To save money and to speed things up, Lara had done a lot of the painting herself. She'd even finished the bathroom ceiling—no easy task. Despite the problems, Charlie's work was impeccable. He performed every task to perfection, even if he had to do it over three times.

Lara was anxious for Aunt Fran to return from her lunch date with Jerry Whitley, Whisker Jog's chief of police. Lara wanted to surprise her aunt with the custom-made door. When the oversized box had arrived two days earlier, she'd rested it against the wall and warned her aunt not to open it or try to peek.

"Lara," Nina asked, "where on earth did you ever find a storm door with a cat on it?"

The new storm door, made from sturdy aluminum, bore the shape of a cat in the center. It was a splurge, but Lara couldn't resist spending a bit extra for it. She knew Aunt Fran would love it. Thanks to a few hefty donations from generous sponsors, the cost hadn't broken the budget.

"I scoured the internet and found a manufacturer that made custom designs," Lara explained. "Luckily, they were able to make a cat."

"Do you mind giving me the company's name?" Nina asked. "I'd like to check them out and refer our customers there, if that's okay."

"Sure," Lara said, and gave her the name. "It'll come right up if you Google it," she added.

Nina pulled her phone out of her pocket. "I'll add it to my notes. Thanks, Lara." She tapped her phone a few times, then slipped it back into her pocket and rubbed her hands together. "Now, before Charlie and I head out to White Lake for an afternoon swim, may I take advantage of your hospitality and play with a few of the cats?" She wiggled her fingers. "I need a cat fix."

Charlie rolled his eyes. "Here we go."

"Oh, be good." Nina swatted his arm lightly with her fingertips.

Charlie stayed behind to fiddle further with the door as Lara led Nina through the kitchen toward the large parlor. On the way, she noticed the red message light blinking on the shelter's landline.

Nina followed her gaze. "Do you need to check that?"

"No, I'll check it later." She held out a hand toward the large parlor, where a carpeted cat tree rested in front of the picture window. Nina went ahead of her into the room.

Orca and Pearl, their newest arrivals, had planted themselves on separate levels of the cat tree. The two were siblings, each with forepaws the size of catchers' mitts. Orca was long-haired and black, with four white feet, while Pearl was silky soft and pure gray. Lara called them "double trouble" because of their feline antics. What one didn't think of, the other did. Orca had been known to distract Lara by kneading her shoulder and purring in her ear, while his sneaky sister batted all the trinkets and lip-gloss tubes off her bureau. Lara now kept her possessions tucked safely away in drawers, out of reach of their huge paws.

From his perch, Orca leaned over the edge and batted at Pearl with one gigantic paw. Pearl swiped at him with her own paw as if he were a furry toy.

"Oh my gosh, those two are so cute. And those paws—they're so big!" Nina cooed.

"They're polydactyl cats," Lara explained. "Instead of five toes on each forepaw, they have six."

Nina gazed at them, her pale-green eyes lighting up. "Do you think the gray one will let me hold him?"

"That's Pearl, and she's a girl," Lara said. "I'm sure she will. She's very lovable."

Nina stooped and held out her hands to the gray kitty. Pearl leaned into her, and Nina swept her into her arms. Pearl purred into her ear, and a wistful look crossed Nina's face. "Oh, you're so sweet. I sure wish I could take you home."

"Charlie's not big on cats, is he?" Lara asked her. She'd sensed that when he was working on the addition. Even Munster's attempts at bonding with the contractor had been soundly, if gently, rebuffed.

Nina shook her head. "Don't remind me."

She hugged Pearl for a while, then sighed and released her to the floor. Snowball padded over and brushed against Nina's arm. Nina laughed and tickled the white fur between the kitty's ears. She straightened. "I'd better be going. I'm sure Charlie's getting—"

The jingle of the front doorbell interrupted her.

Lara shrugged and looked at Nina. "Will you excuse me a minute? I have no idea who that is. We're not expecting anyone."

Nina stepped away to one side. Lara opened the door to find a scowling, fiftysomething woman standing on the top step.

"Hello. May I help you?"

The woman, tall with stringy blond waves that brushed her shoulders, held up a clipboard thick with papers. She wore the expression of someone who'd just stepped in a wad of bubble gum and couldn't get it off her shoe—or, in this case, her bright red sneaker. Around her neck she sported a chain from which a large pendant dangled, a blackbird with a jeweled eye perched on a golden branch.

"Are you Miss Caphart or Mrs. Clarkson?" she said brusquely.

The woman's tone was so rude that for a moment, Lara had to stop and think. "I'm Lara Caphart. What can I do for you?"

"I'm Evonda Fray. I'm the health inspector."

Lara hoped her face didn't register the shock she felt. "Um, health inspector?"

The woman heaved a sigh, as if she were tired of explaining herself to dolts. "Yes, health inspector. Surely you've heard of them. They protect the public from unclean environments?"

A wave of ire rose in Lara's chest. Was she implying that the shelter wasn't clean? And why was she here in the first place?

Lara took in a calming breath. She tried to think why a health inspector would show up, unannounced, at the shelter, but nothing came to mind. Had Aunt Fran made an appointment with the woman and forgotten to tell Lara? Not likely. Aunt Fran was too efficient to let something like that slip.

"I'm sorry," Lara said, attempting to soften her tone. "I...we weren't expecting you. Did you make an appointment with my aunt?"

Evonda Fray barked out a laugh. "Health inspectors don't make appointments, Miss Caphart. You ought to know that."

Maybe she should have, but she didn't. Even in her days working part-time in a Boston bakery, she couldn't recall a health inspector making a surprise visit.

Lara suddenly remembered that Nina was there. "Ms. Fray, you'll have to excuse me for a moment. I have guests, and I need to explain the interruption."

"It's *Mrs.* Fray," she snapped. "I'd appreciate you addressing me properly."

Oh, if only, Lara thought.

She nodded and turned toward Nina, but she had already ducked out. Lara strode off and went back to the new reading room. Charlie and Nina were still there, whispering in low tones. It looked as if they were preparing to leave.

"Nina, Charlie...I'm so sorry about the interruption. The health inspector showed up without warning."

Charlie absently picked a piece of lint off the arm of Nina's pink jersey. "Health inspector? Whoa. Major bummer," Charlie said. He waved a hand around the room, then his face relaxed. "Hey, look, I wouldn't worry. This whole place is spotless. You guys keep it so clean..."

"I know. We do. But—"

Nina reached over and hugged Lara. "We'll get out of your way. You've got enough to deal with right now. And give Fran our regards, okay?"

Lara swallowed. "I will," she said glumly.

"We drove Nina's car today," Charlie said, "but I'll come back tomorrow with my truck and get rid of that big box the screen door came in. I leaned it against the back of the house, so it won't be in your way. Oh, and one more thing. I noticed that the storm door has a slight gap at the bottom. When I come back, I'll add some weather stripping."

"Thanks, Charlie. That would be great. We have a permit for the recycling station, but that humongous box will never fit in the Saturn. You're both coming to the open house on Saturday, right?"

"We wouldn't miss it," Nina assured her.

With her aunt away and the Backstroms leaving, Lara didn't look forward to being alone with General Evonda. Gideon had planned to stop over with BLT wraps from the coffee shop when he got a break, but he must have gotten tied up at the office.

She almost begged Charlie and Nina to stay, but then thought better of it. They'd driven Nina's car here instead of Charlie's truck so they could head directly to White Lake after the door was installed. They deserved a break and were looking forward to an afternoon of relaxation.

Besides, she and Aunt Fran had nothing to hide. She could handle Inspector Red Sneakers.

She'd dealt with worse.

Much worse.

Author photo credit: Photo by Harper Point Photography

Raised in a sleepy town in the Berkshires, **Linda Reilly** has spent the bulk of her career in the field of real estate closings and title examination. It wasn't until 1995 that her first short mystery, "Out of Luck," was accepted for publication by *Woman's World Magazine*. Since then she's had more than forty short stories published, including a sprinkling of romances. She is also the author of *Some Enchanted Murder* and the Deep Fried Mystery series, featuring fry cook Talia Marby. Linda lives in New Hampshire with her husband, who affectionately calls her "Noseinabook." Visit her on the web at lindasreilly.com.

The meow of death...

Whisker Jog, New Hampshire, is a long way from Hollywood, but it's the place legendary actress Deanna Daltry wants to call home. Taking up residence in a stone mansion off Cemetery Hill, the retired, yet still glamorous, septuagenarian has adopted two kittens from Lara Caphart's High Cliff Shelter for Cats. With help from her Aunt Fran, Lara makes sure the kitties settle in safely with their new celebrity mom.

But not everyone in town is a fan of the fading star. Deanna was in Whisker Jog when she was younger, earning a reputation for pussyfooting around, and someone is using that knowledge against her. After being frightened by some nasty pranks, Deanna finds herself the prime murder suspect when the body of a local teacher is found on her property. Now, it's up to Lara, Aunt Fran, and the blue-eyed Ragdoll mystery cat Lara recently encountered to collar a killer before another victim is pounced upon...

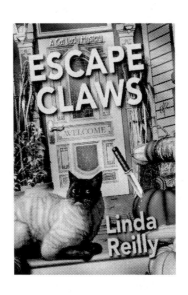

Here, killer, killer, killer…

For the first time in sixteen years, Lara Caphart has returned to her hometown of Whisker Jog, New Hampshire. She wants to reconnect with her estranged Aunt Fran, who's having some difficulty looking after herself—and her eleven cats. Taking care of a clowder of kitties is easy, but keeping Fran from being harassed by local bully Theo Barnes is hard. The wealthy builder has his sights set on Fran's property, and is determined to make her an offer she doesn't dare refuse.

Then Lara spots a blue-eyed Ragdoll cat that she swears is the reincarnation of her beloved Blue, her childhood pet. Pursuing the feline to the edge of Fran's yard, she stumbles upon the body of Theo Barnes, clearly a victim of foul play. To get her and Fran off the suspect list, Lara finds herself following the cat's clues in search of a killer. Is Blue's ghost really trying to help her solve a murder, or has Lara inhaled too much catnip?

Printed in the United States
by Baker & Taylor Publisher Services